You Can't Go Home Again

Liars and Vampires, Book 3

Robert J. Crane
With Lauren Harper

You Can't Go Home Again
Liars and Vampires, Book 3
Robert J. Crane
with Lauren Harper
Copyright © 2018 Ostiagard Press
All Rights Reserved.

1st Edition

Chapter 1

I was being hunted by a vampire.

It probably looked strange to passersby seeing a seventeen-year-old girl running down a sidewalk, stumbling past deserted side streets and alleyways. It was just now getting dark, but since this was Tampa, Florida, that didn't mean it was getting any cooler. All of the streetlights overhead flickered into life, creating pools of light on the street below, bathing everything else in darkness.

The brighter the light, the darker the shadows.

I chanced a glance over my shoulder. The long, dark street behind me, tinged with the faint scent of saltwater carried in from the Bay, was deserted, but I knew better. I wasn't alone.

My chest hurt, my breath coming in heaving gasps, the warm air providing little relief to my overheated, exhausted body. Sweat trickled steadily down my back, making my blouse cling to me as I pumped my arms, trying to push myself to run even faster.

The city buildings were packed tightly together, giving my super-powered assailant way too many places to hide. Every sound, every movement I caught out of the corner of my eyes made my heart constrict painfully.

I had been running in a straight line for too long. That was strategically as good as suicide. The next opening I saw to the right, between a donut shop and an antique store, was just wide enough for me to squeeze through.

The narrow gap was full of trash, which crinkled and

snapped beneath my feet. A fresh flood of fear pumped through my veins like acid. If my pursuer had by some miracle lost me for a second, he would know where I was for sure now.

And look how easy I made it for him! Trapped and unable to move much faster than a turtle through molasses, I squeezed along. I hoped that this narrow passage would throw him off for even just a second. Every advantage helped.

The back of my shirt kept catching on the bricks behind me as I pushed myself along as quickly as I could. Bursting free, I reached the other side of the alley, peered around the corner. There was what looked like another alley, filled with back entrances used for deliveries to the businesses on the main road.

Silence. The quiet in the alley was eerie. A look over my shoulder revealed no evidence of my vampire follower. But then, vampires had a nasty habit of showing up when I least expected them.

Left or right? I couldn't stop here; I only had a fraction of a second to decide.

A car horn blared into the night a few streets over, and with a jolt of my heart, I threw myself across the alley and into another tight gap on the other side.

There were too many open spaces, too many nooks and crannies, too many shadows. As I pounded against the pavement, running in the night, I looked desperately for an escape.

Wood. Where could I find wood? Something, anything that I could use as a weapon.

I broke free of the small cutover between roads into yet another alley, dark and shadowed. Not good.

I needed light. I needed to see. Ahead, there were street lamps, lit against the dusky night. I ran, trying to keep from gasping. Trying to hold it all together.

Breaking out of the shadows, I found myself back on a main street, the lights shining brightly against the darkening sky.

I had to hide. He was still behind me. A shoe scuffed on

pavement, back the way I'd come.

I took off. Now a siren howled into the night, in the distance. Not nearly close enough.

Déjà vu washed over me in its eerie way.

I'd fled like this before. Under a darkening sky, the cool air growing warm and stifling, I'd hurtled along deserted streets countless times, evading a vampire foe dead set on catching me. Sooner or later, I was going to get caught.

Another side street. Distance. I needed distance.

My palms were slick as I caught myself on the concrete wall, the stone rough as I wheeled myself around the corner. My chest heaved, my breathing was raspy. I didn't know how much longer I could go. My cardio game was weak. Apparently I needed to start marathon training if I was going to keep this up.

The buildings around were closing in around me. Claustrophobic, confused—in my panic downtown had become a maze. Footfalls echoed on concrete. Mine alone? Or was he right behind me?

A long line of dumpsters spewed their putrid, rotting smell into the tight space, making me sputter and gag as I dashed past it.

Focus, Cassie. Keep an eye on the goal. Avoid the vampire, avoid death.

Who was I kidding? He was toying with me.

I gritted my teeth.

Finding people wouldn't help me. He'd kill me anyway. Daylight was nine hours away, maybe ten. I had no idea where I would find enough fire to protect me.

It came back down to wood. And I was without a stake.

I skidded into another side street, another wild dart to throw him off my tail—then gasped with excitement. Wooden pallets! Sidelining for now the question of whether or not this was theft, I lurched forward, hands out—

With effortless silence and unnatural speed, a dark, hooded figure slipped into the space between me and my prize.

My feet nearly slipped out from underneath me as I flailed my arms, trying to gain my balance. A strangled scream burst from me, just half a second. Then I clamped down on it.

Already turning, I forked away, chest heaving—*Damn it, damn it, damn it!* I'd been so close. Down another side street, an alley between two shops, one boarded up and long closed.

A chain-link fence blocked my way.

Climb. Unless you want to—

No need to finish that thought. I knew what awaited if I didn't evade the vampire. Pointed teeth and defeat.

I raced to it. Grasping the cold metal, I dragged myself higher. But the footholds were too small, and my feet flailed. Cold metal bit into my fingers as I fought for height.

I was just about to the top when I saw the same hooded, black shape standing just on the other side of the fence.

I gasped, and my fingers slipped.

I slammed into the dirty ground below, a spasm of pain running through my back, the force of impact knocking the wind from my lungs.

Rolling over onto my side, I grasped my aching ribs, sputtering, trying in vain to draw in a breath. I could taste blood in my mouth from my split lip.

"End of the line, Cassie," the voice said, a deep laugh behind the words.

He leapt into the air and cleared the fence easily, landing lightly without a sound in front of me.

It was too late. I had lost.

He had me.

Chapter 2

I grasped at the ground, fingers sliding on the loose dirt and gravel beneath the tips, scrambling to get away, trying anything to prevent him from getting to me.

He snatched at the back of my shirt, his grip like iron, unyielding and powerful.

A low laugh came from below his hood as I tried to pull away from him.

I reached in my jeans pocket for a small, glass vial. Biting down on the tiny stopper, I yanked it open. Cold, clear water sloshed onto my hand before I tossed it over my shoulder.

A loud hissing came, along with a snarl of anger, but his grip on me released, and I fell to the ground as he leapt away from me.

Without turning to look, I ran back down the alley toward the street.

He was there in front of me again, black cloak flaring in the night wind, barring my escape.

"I don't think so ..." His voice was a low growl of malice. I guess the holy water had made this personal.

He lunged for me again, lightning fast. I jumped aside, anticipating his strike. That was the best you could hope for with a vampire. They were so quick, unless you knew which direction they were going to go, there was no avoiding their attack.

Beside me, snaking up the side of the building, was an old, rusty fire escape. I grabbed onto the metal ladder, paint flaking off under my fingers, and started up it.

But he was right behind me.

He latched onto my ankle. I kicked out, my foot colliding with the side of his head with a satisfying thud. It was maybe not enough to hurt him—vampires were rock solid, like living statues—but it caught him off guard: he released me, and I pushed myself higher.

I had made it up to the next level when he jumped into the air and met me there, on the fire escape.

"That was a pretty dumb move, girl," the shadowed face laughed. "Trapped yourself again."

"Not so much," I replied, and I snatched a small, wooden planter box from the windowsill leading into the building. I smashed it against the wall, creating a jagged knife of sorts.

I held it out in front of me.

The vampire hesitated for only a moment before he swiped to knock it out of my hand.

But I was already tearing it through the air. It made contact with his arm, slashing through the black fabric, leaving a shallow but long slash.

He grabbed onto his arm, hissing in pain, the acrid stench of black vampire blood filling the air.

I turned and slid back down the ladder to the ground, preparing for the next assault.

Which came almost immediately. He was there, now growling with every step.

I moved into a fighting stance. *Don't lock your knees. Listen. Don't turn away from your opponent. Remember he's faster and stronger than you.*

Don't get cocky.

He dashed for me once more, and I dodged, knocking his injured arm out of the way. It was like hitting an iron pipe swung at your face: I couldn't stop it; all I could do was redirect it slightly.

That done, I ducked underneath his extended arm and started for the street again. If I could somehow slash his arm again, incapacitate him long enough to prevent him from following—

"All right, Cassie, that's enough."

I stopped. The growl was gone. The voice was familiar again.

"What, we're done already?" I asked, turning to face the hooded vampire. I tossed the broken wooden planter to the ground near a dumpster.

The vampire stood straight, lowering his hood.

Mill.

He glowered at me, his dark, thick eyebrows furrowing together. He pulled his gloves off in a huff, stuffing them into his pockets.

I walked back down the alley toward him slowly so my heart could have a chance to calm down.

Wincing as he pulled at his sleeves, he glared at me again. Black blood ran down his forearm. "Was that really necessary?"

"If this was real, definitely." I looked at the pale skin, tinged inky by his blood. Kinda gross.

He ripped his shirt above where I had cut him and attempted to staunch the wound with the fabric. "You're getting better," he said. "But you were still way too reckless."

"Reckless?" I asked. "I was running almost the entire time. How was I reckless?"

"The narrow alley, the fence, the fire escape?" Mill replied. Using his teeth to grip one end, he moved to tie his makeshift bandage in place, but I rolled my eyes and stepped over, finishing off the knot for him. Way more artfully and with fewer teeth.

"Thanks," he said. His glare did not soften. "I'm serious. You should have focused on distance, not clever maneuvers."

"You're a vampire. Superhuman strength and speed, remember? How could I have possibly gotten away from you?" I asked. "You can smell me from a mile off."

"Maybe cut back on the perfume, then, for the sake of other vampires," he said.

I took a step back. "You don't like my Viva La Juicy?"

"I like it fine," Mill said, and I caught a hint of discomfort, like he'd accidentally stepped in something uncomfortable and wished he could retreat. "I said 'for the sake of other vampires.'"

7

"Mmm hmm," I said, not really buying it. "Regardless … you were right on top of me the entire time. Perfume or no, you can smell a human from a mile off—"

"Not so," he said. "Our sense aren't that finely tuned. But when we do get a good whiff … it is possible to track a distinct human for at least some distance. Which is why you have to use your surroundings to your advantage. We've discussed this at least a dozen times. Don't make it easier for the vampire."

"That's exactly what I was doing, though, using my surroundings." I waved at the dumpsters. "See? Trying to cover my scent."

"Didn't work," Mill said.

"Oh yeah?" I set my feet, crossed my arms in front of me. "Then how would you recommend I do it?"

His response was lost on me as my phone vibrated in my pocket. I pulled it out to check. "Whoa, never mind, hold the critique," I said. "It's ten to eight. I have to get home, like, now."

"I know," Mill sighed. "That's why I called off the exercise."

"Then why didn't you say that?"

"I was just about to—you know what? Never mind."

It was my turn to glower.

"You are getting better, Cassie," Mill said, his gruff voice a little gentler. "You executed the defensive position well. And even though I'm not exactly happy with it, I am impressed with your improvisation with the wooden planter. That was clever."

A roll of thunder sounded overhead. No rain yet, and when it came it would be hot and stifling. But it might dispel some of the clammy humidity in the air, making our next session less grueling. "Well, thanks. I'm getting good at finding makeshift stakes."

"And that's why I insisted that you go into this fight without them tonight," Mill went on. "Better to learn how to deal without them instead of relying on them too heavily." His long brow arched. "But still, carry them whenever possible. There's no point in having to hunt one down if you don't have to."

"Makes sense." I paused. "Also … were you making a pun with 'point'?"

His eyes flickered, and there was no amusement there. Guess it wasn't intentional. "Come on, let's get you to the car," he said. "Don't need your mom murdering you after I almost did."

"You so didn't," I said. "I would have gotten away."

"Yeah, okay," he said, ruffling my auburn hair like I was some sort of kid.

We stepped out of the alley and back onto the main road, the lamp posts sparkling merrily. Cars rumbled by, their headlights like stars against the blackening night, the smell of exhaust heavy in the sticky air.

"I still don't think I could take a vamp head on," I said, shoving my hands deep into my pockets, "but I do feel more confident that I could hold one at bay."

"Maybe," Mill said slowly. "I don't think that you're quite ready to tackle another Roxy situation again, though. Not any time soon."

"That's for sure," I said, goose bumps rushing over my skin as I thought back to that night with horror mingled with fury.

A sleek, black Mercedes town car was idling beside the sidewalk a little ways down the road. It was parked outside of a pizza parlor, and the smell of garlic made my stomach flip over hungrily.

"Oh my gosh, that smells so good …" I grabbed my stomach. "I haven't eaten since lunch."

"I'd buy you a slice, but you need to get home," Mill said.

Another sensation took the place of the hunger. Butterflies. My cheeks flushed. "Maybe some other time?"

"I'd like that," he said.

"Even with the garlic?" I teased, stepping up beside the limo. Vampires and garlic.

"Garlic doesn't bother me." He smacked his lips. "I mean, it does some damage to your breath, but otherwise, it's fine."

I started to ask whose breath he was worried about, but the car door opened, and a tall man with startlingly green eyes

9

stepped out, peering over the top of the Mercedes at me.

"Miss Cassandra," he said in his jovial voice. "Wonderful to see you."

"You too, Lockwood," I said, grinning at him.

"Shall I get you back to your house before your mother has another meltdown?"

I groaned. "And I was only ten minutes late that time ..."

"There is no wisdom in seeking fights you don't have to." Lockwood tipped his chauffeur's hat to Mill. "All is well, sir?"

"It's getting there," he said, glancing down at me. "She's coming along."

I smiled in spite of the flash of annoyance within.

Mill opened the back door as Lockwood got back inside.

"I'm sorry things are tough at home still," Mill said after he closed the door behind me. He leaned in through the open window, arms resting on the sill.

"Yep," I said. "It sucks."

"They'll get better. Your mom and dad will come to trust you again."

I sighed heavily, falling back against the seat. "I kinda doubt it. This wasn't exactly my first time getting caught lying. There's a history. Probably way too much to forget at this point."

"Nonsense," Mill replied. "Parents are very forgiving people. It just may take some time."

I really didn't think he knew what he was talking about, but I smiled up at him anyways and nodded. "Sure." Why argue?

Mill stood up straight and thumped his hand on top of the limo, signaling Lockwood that I was ready. "I'll see you later, okay?"

"Definitely," I said.

Lockwood pulled the car away from the curb and slid smoothly into the street, speeding away from Mill and the quiet, dark side of the city of Tampa.

I swallowed hard as I glanced up at the rearview mirror. Mill waited on the sidewalk, arm still bandaged with torn sleeve, his sandy hair melting into the shadows beneath the darkening sky.

I looked away. Those butterflies were back. Just anxiety to prove myself. Yeah. I wanted nothing more than to impress Mill. I wanted him to see that I was getting better, that I was learning. I wanted him to know that I was doing all I could. Nothing more than that.

But he had offered to take me out for dinner … hadn't he? In a weird way.

I sighed, looking up at the rearview mirror again, unable to stop myself. Mill was gone. The night had swallowed him up like the dark creature he was.

Chapter 3

"You better let me off on the corner here, Lockwood," I said, dread washing over me as I approached my street. "Mom thinks I was at Xandra's, studying. She might question the car."

"I still think telling your parents the truth is the best policy, Cassandra," Lockwood said, but he obliged, pulling over.

I normally hated hearing my full name, but Lockwood had sole permission to use it.

"You keep saying that," I said. "But you don't know them. I've been trying to leave them out of all of this since Byron. They still don't know about him being a vampire."

"Are you certain they would not believe you?" His bright green eyes watched me for an answer, filled with concern.

"One hundred percent," I said.

The car came to a stop. I reached for the backpack I had tossed onto the seat beside me when he had picked me up earlier that afternoon.

"I appreciate your desire for me to have a solid, honest relationship with my parents," I said. "There are a lot of times … a lot of things … I wish I could tell them. But it's safer if they aren't involved. You know?"

"I suppose," he replied, though his disagreement was made plain in his voice. "Have a good night, Cassandra. Shall I pick you up the same time next week?"

"I look forward to it," I said, and clambered out of the back of the car.

I swung my backpack over my shoulder and waved as Lockwood pulled away.

The enticing aroma of smoky meat hung in the air. One of our neighbors was grilling. I could hear the excited shrieks of children playing on a squeaky trampoline from a nearby backyard. A siren wailed somewhere in the distance. Plenty of those, now that summer loomed, the sound another harbinger of still hotter days ahead.

I squared my shoulders as I set off toward home.

The door to the garage was unlocked, and I stepped inside hesitantly. Dad's car was inside, and Mom's car was parked right beside it.

Great. They were both home.

My heart thumped against my ribs as I put my hand on the knob. It should not be this terrifying to walk into my own house.

"I'm home," I said, pulling my backpack off of my shoulder.

"Hi, honey," Dad said. He was standing in the kitchen, at the stove, stirring something that stank to high heaven of garlic with a wooden spoon. Mill would have cringed at the damage my breath was about to take. Or something. "You're just in time for dinner."

"Yes," came another voice, this one a lot cooler. "*Just* in time."

"Hey, Mom," I said, closing the door to the garage, and stepping fully inside.

"Cutting it a little close, aren't we?" Mom asked, checking her watch with a glance. She had the air of a warden dealing with her least favorite prisoner. Or a mother, burned many, many times and in many unfortunate ways by a lying daughter.

"I'm sorry," I replied automatically. She really had no reason to be upset. I was home before my eight-thirty curfew. "We got caught up in the middle of our chemistry workbook."

Mom held out her hand to me just as I knew she would, and so I pulled out my chemistry book from my backpack and handed it over to her.

She flipped it open and started thumbing through the pages.

I wasn't worried. I had done all of my problems on the way to train with Mill that afternoon. They were finished, if a bit sloppily done.

"And your history test today?" she asked, handing me back the book without a word about it.

I returned it to my bag. "I got a ninety-four."

Her eyes flashed. "I thought you said you would ace that one?"

"Sweetheart," Dad said from the stove. "That's still a really good grade."

Mom chewed on her lip but turned away. "All right. Can you please set the table for dinner?"

"Gladly," I said, dropping my bag near the door—not only because I was starving, but because it gave brief respite from her laser-focused probing lawyer stare.

Even though it had been a few weeks since the little escapade that had taken me all the way to Miami for a vampire club/murder night, Mom had barely let me out of her sight. And if she wasn't satisfied with what I was doing every second of the day, she made no bones about telling me what she thought.

I tried to engage Dad in talking about his day as I set the table, but my head wasn't really in it. I was too busy trying to ignore Mom's glares of suspicion.

It wasn't as if I had been trying to screw up the fragile trust I had built with them after the whole Byron fiasco. I really had wanted to mend things with them. And it felt like we were actually getting somewhere. I was being good, doing all of my work, and staying out of trouble.

Then Roxy and her little gang had showed up and ruined everything.

Mom had nearly skinned me alive when I got home that morning. I had expected it. But how could I tell her how glad I was to still be living, that they should maybe be grateful they still had a live daughter after all that? I'd had to lie again—a lame excuse about saying at Xandra's, my ripped and torn and bloody clothing explained with a story about a fall out of a tree house. A nasty one—I'd broken my finger, and a handful of ribs too. Mom was suspicious, of course—but she stifled it just long enough to get me to hospital and patched up.

I was grounded for a month, a sentence I was still serving. No television, no Netflix, no nothing. I was only allowed to have my phone when I wasn't at the house. And I was required to do any and every chore Mom came up with, regardless of child labor laws.

Dad's phone rang on the counter.

"Hey, honey, could you come answer that for me?" he asked from above two butterflied chicken breasts.

"Sure," I replied, laying the last fork down on the little table.

I smiled when I saw the contact.

"Hey, it's Uncle Mike," I said.

Mom, who was sitting on the couch, wheeled around. "My brother Mike?"

"Hello? Uncle Mike?" I asked. Couldn't control the smile that spread across my face at the sound of a familiar—and friendly—voice.

"Hey, kiddo!" he said, clearly pleased. "How are ya?"

"Doing fine," I said, taking a seat at the island counter. "How are you doing?"

"Oh, I'm just fine, kiddo," he said. "The farm is keeping me real busy. You know how it is."

"And how's Fancy?" I asked.

"She's a spitfire, that horse," Uncle Mike replied. "Misses you something awful, though."

I smiled.

"So how is my favorite niece liking Florida?" he asked.

"I'm liking it okay, I guess," I said, tracing my finger along a particularly dark vein in the milky marble countertop. Somehow it reminded me of Mill's skin and the wound I had given him earlier … A quiver ran across me.

"Just okay? But you've got all those beaches and restaurants and palm trees."

"Yeah, but none of that is any fun when you have to go to school."

Uncle Mike chortled. "It's good for you to go to school. Makes ya smart. Provides a future that doesn't involve shoveling horse manure like your dumb uncle."

It sure would ... if I managed to survive all these vampire encounters.

"I don't have any dumb uncles," I said. "But I'm sure you didn't call to talk to me, huh?"

"Hey now, I love talking to you!" he said, then laughed. "But yeah. I'd like to chat with your mom, kiddo. Thanks."

I handed the phone to Mom, who gave me a skeptical look. "What?" I asked.

She didn't say anything, just took the phone and answered with a big smile that didn't quite reach her eyes. "Hey, Mike. How are you?"

I stepped back to the island and resumed my seat.

"We're fine, fine," Mom answered Mike. I went back to tracing my finger along the marble veins.

The sound of the chicken hitting the hot pan filled the air, sizzling and spitting. The dull thud of Dad's knife on the cutting board followed it as he diced up some onions.

"Yeah, work is fine. Just finished a big case ... yeah, I know."

I sighed. Hearing Uncle Mike's voice made me homesick. It had been a long time since I had thought of New York so fondly, but hearing him and thinking about his horse—one that I had grown to love—made my heart ache for home.

"Really? In Onondoga Springs?"

My ears perked up.

"What happened exactly?" my mom asked. She was wearing her concerned face. Which was different from her angry-and-concerned face, something I'd seen a great deal of lately. Dad glanced over his shoulder, his spatula hovering over the skillet.

"That's crazy," she said, voice falling to a hushed tone. "Was anything stolen?"

I started to relax, at least a little.

"Wait, what?" Mom asked. She stood, mouth hanging open. She started to pace the living room, bare feet padding across the fluffy rug.

"You're joking … someone actually burned it down? Intentionally?" Mom stopped walking, her eyes not focused on anything particular, just staring into space. "Did they have security cameras?" A pause. "Well, what did they look like?"

I frowned, listening to the one side of the conversation, trying to make sense of what I was hearing.

"What do you mean, 'Eurotrash'?"

Dad threw some more olive oil into the pan. The glug muted the sizzle briefly, then it rose to temperature, starting it up again. The smell would have been mouth-watering, but my interest in dinner had been replaced by the one-sided conversation I was listening to as intently as I could manage with sizzling pans blotting out Uncle Mike's responses.

"Odd," Mom commented. "So, these pale, weird foreign people just show up out of nowhere? And they're the ones responsible for this crime wave?"

Pale? Weird?

Oh. Oh no.

"It's such a small town. How can the police not be all over them?" My mom was huffing outrage. "I mean, this is ridiculous. There's never been this kind of—we grew up there, for crying out loud, never saw anything like that … It's making me sorry we didn't sell the house before we left." She sniffed, shaking her head. "Pale foreigners. That's all they have to go on …?"

My fingers tightened on the marble counter. Breath hitching, I bit my lip, staring into the middle distance. My mind made the leaps.

Pale.

Strangers.

Crime.

This was worse, way worse than I could have thought.

There were vampires in my hometown.

Chapter 4

Breathe, Cassie, breathe. I must be jumping to conclusions. Maybe they actually *were* just Eurotrash foreigners without any respect for property.

But Mom definitely said pale. And weird.

And vampires are always pale and weird. I knew this from unfortunate experience.

I chewed on my fingernails, trying to decide what to do.

I had to find out what was going on. But in order to do that, I was going to have to make a call.

Just to be sure. I had to know. I had to make sure.

Vampires in my little hometown would not be good. Not only would no one ever believe that vampires were real there, but it would be super easy for people to start disappearing.

But why were vampires showing up *there*, of all places? And why now? There was absolutely nothing special about Onondoga Springs, New York—no monuments, no beautiful state parks, no tourist centers. Just a lot of hills, trees, and cows.

Then it hit me.

They were there looking for me.

But that was insanity, right?

Dad's back was still turned as he finished making dinner.

"I'll be back in a few," I told him, snatching my phone off the counter while Mom was facing away.

"Okay, but dinner's in ten," he called after me.

I hurried up to my room, slamming the door behind me. I collapsed onto my bed with trembling fingers.

Scrolling through my contacts, I was surprised at the sheer amount of them I'd added since moving to Florida. Only four months ago, I was a total stranger here. Now I had friends—and enemies. Vampire enemies, too—not the usual fare for a seventeen-year-old girl outside of friggin' *Twilight*. I found the name I was looking for. I clicked it, and then clicked video call.

It was better to do it face to face. And it would be nice to see a familiar face from home.

The girl who answered the phone had a thin face, dark hair, and dark eyes. Her hair was tied in a long braid that hung over her shoulder. I was glad to see that some things never changed.

"Hey, Jacquelyn!" I said happily, waving at her, hoping my smile was convincing enough.

"Cassie," she replied dryly, chewing on a piece of gum like she always used to. "What a surprise to hear from you."

I faltered, and then laughed, even though I knew it sounded hollow and insincere. "Hey, yeah, I'm really sorry about that. Life has been totally insane since I started school. I've had to deal with annoying teachers, tons of homework, and I joined math league down here. And let me tell you, the schools down here are so—"

"Save it, Cassie," Jacquelyn said, rolling her eyes. "I only answered because I wanted to hear what giant lie you had to tell me this time."

"Ah … no lie," I said hastily. "Seriously."

"Really?" Jacquelyn stared at me over the video connection. "So why are you calling now? Why not … months ago?"

"I've been grounded almost constantly since I got here." An excuse—only it wasn't, I realized with a sinking feeling. I really had been grounded pretty much round the clock since moving—and especially since this vampire business started. "My parents are like Captain and Sergeant Punishment."

Jacquelyn raised an eyebrow. "Knowing you, you probably deserve it."

I pursed my lips, the words stinging. "Okay, I guess I earned that," I said, hoping to pacify her. "Look, I did have a reason for calling you."

"An ulterior motive?" She put her hand up to her cheek. "What, you didn't want to just catch up with your former bestie?" Her eyes flashed dangerously.

I exhaled heavily. "Jackie, you have to know that I've missed you. Just because I moved, it doesn't mean that I stopped thinking of you as my friend."

Jacquelyn, who was lying on her bed, adjusted her arms and didn't answer.

"Have you been okay?" I tried again.

Jacquelyn rolled her eyes, but she didn't hang up on me, so I took that as progress.

"I've been fine," she said. I could see she was having an internal debate with herself, the corner of her mouth twitching. "Gary Haze asked me out last week."

Low blow, Jackie, low blow.

"Did he now?"

"Oh, that's right," she said. "Didn't you have a crush on him since … what … second grade?"

I forced a smile. I did not want to play her little game.

Sure, I had liked Gary Haze for pretty much forever. Sure, I had hoped that he was going to ask me to Homecoming my sophomore year. It wasn't like I had dreamed of going on an actual date with him, or him asking me to be his girlfriend.

But I had bigger fish to fry right now.

Only … it hurt. And whether I masked it or not, that was what Jackie had been aiming for.

"I'm happy for you," I lied. She grinned, though it was more of a sneer, really. A victorious, smug sneer—she had hit her mark, and she knew it.

"Anyway, look, I have a question for you," I said, not wanting to give her another opportunity to upset me. "I was just talking to my uncle. He was mentioning all of these weird things happening."

"You're going to have to be a little more specific," Jacquelyn said.

"Crimes," I said, trying to not let my thoughts get ahead of themselves. "Theft. Arson. Stuff like that."

She gave me a quizzical look.

"It just sounds … out of the ordinary for home," I said. "I know there's always been minor stuff. But I just wanted to know if it's gotten worse. If people have noticed."

"This is what you call me about after months of no contact?" she asked, but I knew her well enough to recognize the edge in her voice.

"Something is going on, isn't it?" I asked.

Jacquelyn licked her lips. She looked down. "Yeah. Some stuff has been happening."

A thrill of terror filled me, and I homed in on her, turning up the call volume to make sure I didn't miss anything that she said.

"A couple of weeks ago, there were reports of a break-in at the bank in town. In the middle of the night. And they managed to steal not money, but documents. Banking records. It was all over the news." She frowned. "Then a few days later, there was a report of Kabold's bar getting set on fire."

Her face darkened. "A couple of people who were there that night were killed."

The skin on the back of my neck stood up. "It's hard to believe that anything that level of awful could happen in Onondoga Springs."

"Yeah, I know," Jacquelyn replied, her air of arrogance gone for the moment. "What's really weird is that the victims were all found in the woods, not the bar – and killed the same way."

"How did it happen?" I asked, really not wanting to know the answer—and acutely aware that I could probably take a really good guess.

"The police won't release the information to the public," she said, shrugging.

"Who was it that was killed?"

"That's the other odd thing," she said. "There's no connection between them. They aren't related, they are all different ages, men and women." She paused. "People at school think it's a serial killer."

How screwed up was the world that I now lived in that I seriously wished it *was* a serial killer doing this?

"That's pretty scary," I said before I could stop myself.

"I'm sure they'll catch whoever it is soon," Jacquelyn said dismissively.

Silence again.

Jacquelyn kept glancing away from the camera.

"Look, Cassie, let's not try and pretend that everything's good between us, okay? You have your life, I have mine. I think we've been fine without each other, you know?" She couldn't look at the camera as she said it.

"Yeah," I said.

She forced a sympathetic smirk. "Bye, Cassie."

And she clicked off the call before I had even said goodbye.

I lay back on my bed, my stomach clenching in a way that had become all too familiar.

Things had been too quiet. Life had been too easy. I had been waiting for something like this to happen ever since that night with Roxy and her crew.

But I'd expected it *here*. In Tampa.

Not back home.

It was vampires. It had to be. And the reason why the police weren't telling anyone about how the people had died was because they had been drained of all their blood. That sort of information was the stuff of nightmares, and not suitable for the six o'clock news.

I felt sick. It couldn't be a coincidence that it was happening in *my* hometown. Too much had happened, and I had pissed off too many vampires to not recognize the signs.

"Well, this is bad," I muttered to the ceiling.

I knew I had better get my phone back to its designated jail cell before Mom realized what was going on.

But before I went back downstairs, I made sure to type out a text—

I need help. Meet me here at midnight—and sent it off to both Mill and Iona.

Chapter 5

I feigned exhaustion around eleven while watching a movie with Mom and Dad, and retired to my room. I had no interest in hanging around them when I knew Mill and Iona were coming. I also knew that Mom would check on me at least once before she went to bed, and sure enough, fifteen minutes to midnight, she stuck her head through my door.

I was prepared. I was lying in bed, my blankets pulled up to my shoulders, reading one of my favorite books by the light of a small LED cat nightlight that she had gotten me for Christmas the year before.

"Still awake?"

I didn't look at her. "Just finishing this chapter."

"All right." But she didn't leave. "It's sort of strange, all of that stuff happening back home, isn't it?"

I looked over the top of my book at her. She wasn't looking at me; she was staring into the distance, like when she was talking to Uncle Mike. Arms folded, she chewed her bottom lip.

She was really worried about it. Mom might've gone a little hardline lately in her approach to me, but I still wanted to make her feel better.

But how could I? After all of the lies that I had told her, saying that everything was going to be all right seemed … cruel. Because it really wasn't okay. Something was going on in the vampire community up there—something that could very well have started right here. With me.

I also couldn't tell her that I spoke with Jacquelyn. Aside from murdering me for taking my phone when I wasn't allowed to have it, she'd ask way too many questions about our little talk. I didn't need that, and I didn't want it, especially when I was already sad about my frayed relationship with Jacquelyn.

"So, they have no idea what's causing ... it?" I asked.

"Uncle Mike's friend is a police officer," Mom said. "Says it's the most bizarre string of occurrences the town has ever seen. And I can't say I remember anything like this ... ever."

She seemed to come to her senses, forcing the worry off of her face, replacing it with a small smile. "I'm sure it'll be fine."

"Sure," I said. She believed it about as much as I did.

"See you in the morning, kiddo."

I tried to stifle a yawn, real this time. "Yeah."

"Love you," Mom said.

"Love you, too."

And she closed the door.

I tossed the covers back with a whoosh and stood, still fully dressed.

I looked out the window onto the small outcropping of roof beneath the windowsill, and saw Iona's silvery blonde hair before she could rap on the glass with a perfectly filed fingernail. I slid open the window—which I had taken to greasing with WD-40 to keep it from squeaking—and slipped out.

Iona stood off to the side, the wind catching her long, perfectly straight tresses, sending them swirling around her face. She looked like a supermodel in her white silk blouse that tied up the back and her skin-tight black denim pants with tears in the thighs.

Mill lingered on the opposite side of the roof from her, dressed in all black and his leather jacket, glowering at Iona.

"What's she doing here?" he asked.

A breeze wafted the scent of his cologne at me, a subtle but oh so heady mix of leather and bergamot.

"I could ask the same thing of you," Iona said, jutting her chin in his direction. Her expression was perfectly forbidding, cold and pointed.

I glanced between the two of them and realized that while I had been relying on them both for my survival, I didn't know how much they knew about each another.

I also realized that I was playing with fire. I had never considered if they would get along. Just because they'd both helped me with Roxy didn't mean that they would choose to do so again—together.

"Look, whatever this is between you two, I need you to put it aside for a second and listen to me," I said. "My mom got a call from my uncle back in my hometown in New York. There's been weird stuff happening. Crimes. And they've found bodies."

"You suspect vampires," Mill said. He slid his hands in his pocket.

"I do," I said, and explained what Uncle Mike had said about them being pale and foreign.

"Foreign is interesting," Iona said. "What did he mean?"

"You've got to understand that the town I'm from is really small," I said. "Anyone who isn't from there is 'foreign.'"

"Must have been a shock moving to Tampa," Mill said wryly.

I ignored him.

"I'm guessing that it's also got to do with how they dress. He called them 'Eurotrash.'"

"Ah," Iona said. Apparently she got it.

"Well dressed, snobbish," Mill said. "Act like they're better than anyone else. Sounds familiar."

I pinched the bridge of my nose. "Roxy and her gang are dead. Are you telling me that most vamps are like her group?"

"No," Mill said, trading a knowing look with Iona. "But a lot of vampires do have money, since they have centuries to accumulate it."

"And, as you know, most vampires are not in the same camp as we are, believing that we should embrace our humanity instead of fight against it," Iona said. "People are cattle to them. You don't trouble yourself worrying if a cow doesn't like your attitude."

"I understand all of that," I said, and then a lump formed in my throat. "But why are they showing up in my hometown? And now?"

Mill looked down at his boots.

Iona stared at me, unblinking. "You called us here to run your theory by us? You already know it's no coincidence."

"That was my guess," I said. "Draven's hunting me. Based on where I told him I was from."

Mill looked back up at me, concern evident even when half his face was lost in shadow.

"Remember?" I nodded at Mill. "He asked me at the party."

"He did, but you weren't very specific," Mill said.

Iona looked skeptical. "Draven has connections literally everywhere. And we still don't know how much he actually knows about Cassie."

"Not very much," Mill said.

"From what my source tells me, he's still looking for 'Elizabeth,' not Cassie. So he hasn't discovered your real name yet," Iona said.

"Then how did he find the right town?" I asked. "I mean, it has to be him; why else would vampires all of the sudden start causing havoc right there? Of all the small towns in New York State?"

"Murders, arson ... it's as if they mean to draw attention," Mill said. "Stir the pot enough to get you to notice."

"Okay, so what?" Iona said. "Draven sends hunters to your hometown to shake things up, and you want to ... what? Feed yourself to them? Make it easier for Draven to find you?"

"I agree," Mill said. "This is a trap, Cassie. It has 'dangerous' written all over it."

"What am I supposed to do?" I asked. "Let them destroy my town?"

Iona scoffed. "Why not? It doesn't affect you."

"The hell it doesn't," I said. "What if they find my uncle? My mom's sisters, my cousins?"

Iona sighed, shaking her head. Mill just furrowed his brow.

"I get that the decision would be easy for you both," I said,

"But I can't just turn my back."

"You'd be playing right into his hands, Cassie," Iona said, hair blowing over her eyes.

"Cassie," Mill said, far more gently, "This is like a chess game, with players who are of a higher power than you can imagine. So please …"

I glared at him.

"I understand. Truly, I do. Trust me. But you're going to have to hope he gives up and moves on. And he will—eventually."

I glanced out over the backyard. It was easy to feel safe halfway across the country. Easy to feel empowered with my resume of vampire slayings behind me. But those meant nothing. I had been lucky. I should have been killed. Or turned. It was only because of these two that I hadn't.

So why was I so willing to ignore the advice of my vampire mentors when I knew that they were right?

"Fine," I said, feeling like I was choking, and I caught the look of relief from Mill, and triumph from Iona. "You win. I'll stay out of it."

For now, I didn't add … to anyone but myself.

Chapter 6

I had fitful dreams after Mill and Iona left, disappearing into the night. Their warning stayed with me. But I didn't know if it was possible to think objectively about this. It was one thing to get involved with the vampires in Tampa. It was an entirely different story to open myself up to those in a different state.

In one dream I was racing through a dense forest, with nothing to light my way except the moon. Everything was eerily silent; I couldn't even hear the sound of my own footsteps as my feet pounded against the hardened dirt. It was as if I was watching it all through someone else's eyes.

There was no end to the woods. No wind rushed past me as I ran, no bite of cold or burn of heat. It was a void, pressing in on me from all sides.

Mill appeared from behind a tree, trying to bar my way. He was all shadows and darkness, his eyes the only brightness about him. I turned away and kept running.

Iona stepped out from behind another tree, her hair like liquid moonlight spilling over her shoulders. Still I did not stop.

The first sound reached me. It was a distant ringing, almost like a bell. It echoed all around, filling me as it swelled to a crescendo.

I gasped, sputtering, my hair in my mouth.

The ringing continued, broken by several seconds of silence in between chimes, echoing the thundering of my heartbeat.

I opened my eyes. It was dark, and I was lying in bed.

The ringing was not from my phone, I realized, but my mom's, muted through the walls and doors.

Squinting, I checked the time on my clock. Three thirty.

I heard Mom open their bedroom door and step out into the hall to avoid waking Dad. So much for that, though. If the phone's ring had woken me, it definitely would have woken him.

"Hello?" Her voice croaked with tiredness.

I lay as still as I could. I wanted to be able to hear whatever she was going to say.

"What?" Mom said, her voice suddenly more awake.

I closed my eyes, gripping my blankets tight. Not good news.

"What happened?" she asked.

My mind started to race. Who could it be? Was it Grandpa Paul? Great Aunt Edna? Was it Kyle, who was serving in the military in Iraq?

"Okay," Mom said, putting on her lawyer voice. She was shutting the emotion out.

It was really bad, whatever it was.

"He's in the hospital?"

I heard my heart pounding in my ears, could feel my pulse thudding against my neck as I stared up at the ceiling.

"Is he stable?"

A moment of tension.

"That's good," she said.

Faint relief came over me at that. At least someone wasn't dead.

"I can call Kathleen," Mom said. "Yeah, I'll call her right now." She said a short goodbye. Then there was quiet, for a long time. I waited, my breath held, staring up to the ceiling with unseeing eyes in the night. My heart thudded. If not for the vampires I kept crossing paths with, I'd have cursed its betrayal, threatening to drown out Mom's whispered words when they came.

Finally, someone answered.

"Hi, Kathleen? I'm sorry to bother you this early, but I just wanted you to know that Mike was in an accident."

No.

My heart sank. I closed my eyes, bidding back tears. I'd spoken to him just a few hours ago.

"He's okay, in the hospital in stable condition." Another pause as Kathleen asked the question I, too, wanted answered: *What happened?*

"Becky said that he was in town with some of his friends on his way to play poker when he was attacked by someone out on the street. One of his buddies found him and rushed him to the hospital. He didn't lose too much blood, but ..." Mom took a shaky breath.

"He was just telling me earlier tonight that there have been all of these strange new people in town, and he thinks they're the ones causing all of these problems in town. There have even been a couple of murders. Becky was terrified that this was another attempt."

My poor Aunt Becky. She was having to deal with way more than she should ever have to, watching her brother go through something like this.

"No, he didn't get a good look at his attacker. He wished he had. He wants to press charges." Mom let out a small laugh. "He can't be too hurt if he's that angry, you know?"

Hand clenched into a tight fist, I punched the mattress.

Enough was enough. I couldn't sit back and let more people get hurt. My fears were rightly placed.

If Draven was trying to sniff me out, then he was going to face the full wrath that was Cassie Howell.

I was going to New York.

Chapter 7

Mom was in court all day, and Dad had a twelve-hour shift. Good: it allowed me to use my brand-new Florida's driver's license and drive the car to school long enough to be counted for home room. Then I headed out through a side door before first period.

Xandra caught me before I slipped away.

I gave her a brief run-down. That was all I had time for though. The rest, I promised to tell her later, as I tried to extricate myself from her presence.

"No way," she said. "You aren't seriously going to go all the way to New York?" She stared, incredulous. I shrugged, turned—

"Cassie, you're crazy!" she called after me. But she didn't try to stop me, instead finishing, "Call me later!"

I made a mental note to thank her for being the best bestie I could've hoped for, then I ducked out of the doors into the bright Florida sunshine, threw my sunglasses on my face, and jumped in the car.

I was glad that I remembered the way to Mill's condo. It was about twenty minutes from my school, but I knew that I had to get there as soon as I could; the sun had been up for a few hours, and Mill was surely going to be heading to bed soon.

I jumped out of the car, handing the keys to the valet at the door, and ran to the elevator. I arrived at his door, banged on it. Mill opened it maybe ten seconds later.

The inside was dark, all the drapes pulled shut, veiling the apartment from sunlight. It was the sort of place a rich, insomniac hermit gamer might live, cocooned in darkness and glued to a television screen.

"Cassie, what are you doing here?" he asked, his thick eyebrows knitting together and his forehead wrinkling with concern.

"I need to talk to you. Now."

I pushed past him into his condo, looking around. It looked different in the day. I still thought it captured his personality so well. Simple, clean, nothing too fancy. Everything was sleek, masculine, well taken care of.

I glanced over my shoulder at him. He followed me slowly into the living room, watching me cautiously.

I realized with a flash of embarrassment that this was the first time we had ever really been alone together.

"So, is your girlfriend here?" I asked, looking around, shoving my hands into the pockets of my jeans.

"No," Mill said. "She's visiting some friends in Tallahassee."

"Ah," I said. My stomach tightened uncomfortably.

"Is this about our conversation from last night?" he asked.

I looked up into his face and nodded. "I'm going to New York." I didn't expect a particularly positive reaction—and my expectations were met.

"You can't be serious," Mill said.

"Mill, they attacked my uncle—my family."

His jaw fell. "What happened?"

I repeated to him what my mom had talked about with my aunt, and about everything she had told me that morning before she had left for work.

"She was really shaken up, my aunt—Mom and Uncle Mike's sister," I said.

"That's understandable," Mill replied slowly. "But that doesn't mean that you need to race up there."

"Mill, all of this is my fault," I said. "Draven's after me. That makes me responsible for the deaths of those people."

My bottom lip was starting to tremble, but I pressed on.

"Do you have any idea how that makes me feel? Knowing that their blood is on my hands? Real people, who had futures that were ripped away from them because some teenage girl pissed off a vampire Lord in Florida. And now my uncle …" I furiously wiped the tear that had leaked from the corner of my eye. "He's lucky he isn't dead, you know? I don't know what I would have done if I was going to have to fly north for a funeral that was entirely my fault."

Mill's face hadn't changed as I freaked out. He just listened patiently, watching me.

"This is a terrible idea," he said when I had nothing left to say. "It's obviously a trap."

"I know," I said, letting my hands fall to my sides.

"I'm not going to change your mind, though," Mill said. Not a question. He sighed heavily. "I understand. It's your family. You don't want it to get any worse."

"Right."

He glanced around. "All right," he said. "I am saying it now. This is a bad idea. So …" He looked at me with a narrowed, surprisingly piercing gaze. "I'll make the arrangements. We leave tonight."

"Wait … what?" I asked.

"What, you thought I was going to let you go alone?" He reached into his pocket and pulled out his cell phone. "Yeah. Right. Which airport is closest to your hometown?"

"Syracuse," I said, my throat tight and dry. "Syracuse is the closest."

"All right," Mill replied.

I only half-listened as Mill made the necessary calls. My mind was whirling, a fog of chaotic thoughts and fears. Now it had become even more concrete, and I had no choice but to wait for Mill to be able to act with me.

I couldn't believe I was doing this—or that Mill was, once again, willingly throwing himself into Lord Draven's firing line for me. I owed so much to him already, and the list was lengthening by the day.

I almost wanted to tell him to stay home, not to come; he'd done enough already.

But I was too cowardly for that. I'd had too many lucky kills and escapes. Mill, meanwhile, knew what he was doing.

I needed him if I was going to have any hope of stopping

Lord Draven's minions.

I set my jaw.

I was going to stop it, come hell or high water.

Draven would not frighten me away.

Chapter 8

"You better get on back to school," Mill said, pulling his phone from his pocket. "I'll call Lockwood to take you."

"I drove here," I said.

Mill arched an eyebrow. "You have your license?"

"I'm not a kid, Mill." My cheeks burned. Never mind I'd just gotten the Florida one.

"I never said you were," he said. "It's just something I didn't know about you." He considered something for a minute. "I'd feel better if you let Lockwood take you. He can keep an eye on you for the rest of the day."

"I don't need a babysitter."

"Who said anything about a babysitter?" Mill asked. "You're capable of dealing with more now than you could before. But why do you think I'm not letting you go to New York alone?"

"Fine," I said, more harshly than I should have. "I'll let Lockwood take me. Here." I tossed my keys onto the long table against the wall. They landed right beside the keys to Mill's Mustang.

"Is something wrong?" Mill asked, peering around to try and look me in the eye.

I turned away toward the door. "I'm fine."

Mill hesitated, but eventually lifted his phone to his ear. "Lockwood? Could you take Cassie to school?"

I stared around Mill's apartment, shame preventing me from looking up at him.

So, that was what he really thought about me? That I was just some kid? That I needed to be babysat?

I chewed on the inside of my lip, breathing heavily through my nose.

"He'll be downstairs waiting for you," Mill said, laying his phone down beside my keys. "He's coming down the street now. I'll get your car home for you. And if I can find a flight, Lockwood will be ready to bring you here, or the airport, immediately."

I deflated a little. He hadn't even reacted when I'd thrown my keys ... like a child.

"Thanks," I said.

"Hey," Mill said, grabbing my shoulder before I started toward the door.

I felt a rush of heat in my face as his cool fingers touched my shoulder, but I reluctantly met his gaze.

His eyes, a deep, dark blue with flecks of grey, were looking intently at me—only at me—like I was the only thing in the world.

"We're going to fix this. And we're going to protect your family. All right?"

I swallowed nervously. "Yeah ..."

Mill clapped me on the shoulder and then gestured to the door. "Better get back to class before anyone misses you."

My heart clenched, but I forced a smile. It sucked to be simultaneously in his debt while realizing he thought of me as just a kid. Damn. I forced a smile that was faker than a starlet's chest. "See you later. Keep me updated."

The door behind me closed with a click, and I exhaled slowly. That probably could have gone worse, but maybe not by much.

How had he dissipated my anger so easily? No one disarmed me like that. And yet Mill ...

I stepped into the elevator, glad that it was empty, and sagged against the back wall when the doors slid closed.

Whoever had been in here before me had been wearing too much cologne, which sort of brought me to my senses. I had never really had a real boyfriend before, and it was obvious that I had literally no idea about anything in the romantic department.

I shook my head. Romance? Mill? No.

Besides, he had a girlfriend. My nose wrinkled and my chest tightened. He was nice to me, but it didn't really mean anything.

And it wasn't like I wanted it to, anyway.

School. Right. I should probably get there.

Lockwood was waiting for me just outside the condo's front doors, leaning against the limo. I had ridden in it so often by this point that I felt more comfortable in it than my own car. Mom and Dad's car smelled like the scented plug-ins Mom bought to cover the odor of stale take-out. Lockwood's limo smelled like immaculately kept leather and cedarwood … what Mill's shirt had smelled like that time he had let me borrow one.

"Good morning, Lady Cassandra," Lockwood said, his bright green eyes twinkling.

I smiled. Lockwood had knack for making me feel better, even when I didn't really want to. "Lady again, huh?" I asked.

He bowed, grinning. "Off to school?"

"Yes."

He pulled the door to the back seat open for me.

"I can open the door myself, you know," I told him, not unkindly.

"You are a very capable lady indeed," he said, but didn't let go of the door. He stood there patiently, waiting for me to slide inside.

I sighed but got in.

He closed the door behind me and returned to the front of the car.

As he moved the car away from the curb, my phone sang in my pocket.

It was Iona.

How are you doing today?

Figuring the conversation would be too difficult via text, I called her.

She answered after one ring. "Hello?"

"This would be easier to just tell you," I began, and

37

launched into the plan that Mill and I had concocted.

There was a great sigh on the other end of the line—a very typical Iona reaction, bringing me to two for two in the expectations/reality game this morning.

"I'm not surprised," she said. "I assumed that you'd do something like this."

"Am I getting to be that predictable?"

"You were always that predictable."

Irritation flared again at that. But I tamped it down—having two fights before ten a.m. didn't bode well.

"So what's the plan?" Iona asked. "You're going to go to New York and … what? Place you neck in front of a vampire's teeth?"

I hesitated.

"You really don't have anything in mind other than 'show up, find vampires,' do you?" She sighed again. "You actually have to do something once you run across them, you know. They're not just going to see you and run."

"Give me a break," I said. "I just decided even to go this morning."

I could just see her rolling her eyes.

"Teenagers. Always so impulsive."

"Why is everyone having a go at my age today?" I asked.

"Because we're old, and you're doing something crazy," Iona said, and let that hang for a moment. "So, New York. I suppose you're taking that Cro-Magnon idiot with you, since you can't drive all the way there or afford a plane ticket?"

Everyone was just determined to piss me off today, it seemed. "Yes, *Mill* is coming," I said.

"At least he isn't as dumb as he looks," she said. I frowned, more annoyed by that than I had any right to be.

"All right," Iona said. "You convinced me. I'm going with you."

"What?" I asked. Obviously I hadn't heard her right. "Convinced you how?" I hadn't made any argument for her coming that I remembered. Not even a, "Hey, Iona, whatcha doing tonight? And for the next several days? Want to visit scenic upstate New York, famed for its farms and now its vampires?"

"I'm coming along," she said. "I can't trust that goon as far as I can throw him. Mark my words: you need competent help."

I wanted to argue, I really did—but Iona was right, just like Mill, and I knew it. I had been bailed out by both of them during my long night with Roxy and her cohorts. So I just pursed my lips and stayed silent, torn between regretting telling either of them when I should've just gone, and aware that putting my neck on the line, quite literally, to prove a point was grade-A stupid.

"Let him know that he has to buy another ticket," Iona went on.

Um. "I'm not sure he's going to be all that crazy about you coming with us ..."

"To hell with what Forehead wants." Her voice got harder. "Do you want me to come?"

My palms grew sweaty. I wiped my free hand on my jeans. "You guys were weird around each other the other night. The idea of us all going on a little trip together doesn't exactly sound ... stress-free."

"Do you want to be comfortable, or do you want to be safe?" Iona asked.

"That's not much of a question."

"Great, then let him know."

We were just pulling into the parking lot now. Entirely deserted, because it was the middle of third period.

"Okay. I gotta go," I said. "School."

"This would be so much easier if you were older," Iona said.

"See you later," I said before hanging up.

"Do try and avoid throwing your neck in front of any vampire teeth today, will you?" Iona said as I started to push the END CALL button. "It'd be shame to deprive those New York vampires of their long-awaited meal—"

I ground my teeth as the call clicked off.

She was right, of course, at least about one thing.

This would be so much easier if I were an adult.

Chapter 9

After bidding Lockwood goodbye, I ducked back inside the school building and down the hall toward my locker without getting spotted by a teacher. Sneakiness wasn't quite the same as lying, but I was good at both by this point. After the visit to Mill's apartment, and the ride in Lockwood's town car, walking into school was even less appealing than usual. The over-sanitized smell of it was a distant cry from Mill's addictive leather and bergamot scent, and the air, having leaked in from outside, was sticky and humid.

Yay for Florida ...

Part of me was thrilled at the prospect of going back north. I'd have the chance to see the town I had grown up in, the place that I still thought of as home. I missed the trees, the mountains, the winding rivers, the clear lakes. I missed the cool evenings, the fireflies, the smell of the pine trees and freshly tilled dirt from nearby farms.

It was just a shame I was going home under these circumstances.

I grabbed my chemistry book from my locker and walked through the halls and up the stairs. Twenty minutes of class to go—too long to dawdle in the halls, unfortunately.

Mrs. Tozer was writing frantically on the board when I stepped inside the classroom, and I wished I could disappear into the wall as every eye in the room turned to me.

Xandra's gaze was particularly intense. I could see a million questions on her face.

"Miss Howell," said Mrs. Tozer in her nasal voice. "Nice of you to join us."

I flashed a smile at her. "Sorry. My stomach was really upset all morning. I've been in the bathroom since first period."

Xandra rolled her eyes. Lame lie—and damned embarrassing, come to think of it.

Mrs. Tozer didn't seem pleased either. "Really? Why didn't you to go the nurse?"

Oh, damn it. The initial lie was bad enough. But to double down on it …?

Her gaze was unrelenting though, so after a long, painful pause, I finally said, "Well, it was … you know …" The class stared. Titters and chortles broke the quiet.

My cheeks burned bright pink. Mrs. Tozer pursed her lips. "Stay home next time, if you feel that sick." And she turned back to the board and went on as if I hadn't interrupted.

I slid into the seat and took a steadying breath.

A few other students glanced over their shoulders at me before returning to their notes. Xandra stared at me, eyes practically popping out of her head. She wanted answers.

This was not the time or place. But I was a student, and I knew how to game it. Pointedly avoiding her gaze, I flipped open my textbook and notebook—then used them to block Mrs. Tozer's view as I unlocked my phone in my lap.

Xandra beat me to the punch.

What the heck? she sent me.

I had to go see Mill, I replied.

Why couldn't it wait until later?

Because I have to go back to New York.

What? Why?

I looked across the room at her. She stared at me in confusion, her eyebrows knitted together in one tight line.

Vampires in hometown, I answered, shorthanding furiously but trying to make my text understandable. **Draven sent minions. Figured out where I was from. My uncle was attacked last night. Going up to sort things out.**

I pretended to listen for a few minutes as Mrs. Tozer discussed phosphates … then, the moment her back was turned, I looked down to—four brand new texts from Xandra, all waiting accusingly.

Wait, what?

U going alone?

What r u going to do when u get there?

What if Draven finds you?

The last was the one I focused in on most. Because I had thought about it, at least in the moments of downtime when I couldn't shy away from it. I didn't have an answer though … so all I could do was turn toward Xandra and lift my shoulders in a small shrug.

Her face softened a little, but she looked more determined than not. She went back to her phone.

This is insane.

I paused, chewing on the inside of my lip. She was right, of course. I knew it. But I needed to do this, no matter how crazy or dangerous it might be. People were in danger because of me. I had to stop anyone else from being hurt.

My phone lit up again. **I'm worried for u. What if Draven's vampires are like ultra assassins?**

What if something happens? To you?

Oh, thank goodness. She hadn't gone with "2 u." I wasn't a huge fan of English class, and I could handle some of the abbreviated text shorthand, but too much and I started to gag.

Mrs. Tozer was yelling. I looked up in surprise, hoping it wasn't directed at me or Xandra. We hadn't been caught; a guy in the front row had drawn her ire.

Careful to keep my phone out of sight, I sent Xandra a reply.

I appreciate your concern. But this is going to keep happening until I step out of the shadows. People are going to keep getting hurt.

I watched as she read the message and then shifted uncomfortably in her seat.

She sent two words back.

You're crazy.

I gritted my teeth.

People keep saying that.

Well, people are right. And the longer you push this, the bigger chance there is of someone, or YOU, getting hurt.

What would have happened to Laura if I hadn't gotten involved? She could have been killed. Or worse!

Xandra's reply was short, concise, and I read it with all the venom I'm sure she intended: **Stay out of the vampire world, Cassie.**

I shot daggers across the room at her. She was making a solid effort not to look at me, but I hoped she felt my gaze boring through her.

She was my friend. Why couldn't she understand this? She more than anyone should have been able to see that I needed help and support right now, not opposition.

I rattled off another reply, fingers dancing quickly across the screen. **My Uncle Mike was hurt. Because of me. He has no idea, and probably never will. I am the only one who can stop this. I'm not letting this happen to anyone else. This is bigger than me. Much bigger.**

The lump in my throat was painful.

Besides, I'm not going alone. I have two vamps coming with me. We'll sort this all out and be back in no time.

Xandra's reply was prompt: **Let me guess. Little Miss Sunshine and the handsome Neanderthal?**

I made to text her a nasty reply when another text came in.

What about your parents? You letting them know you're going?

There was a burning in my chest at the thought, and a weight like lead landed in my stomach.

No.

Her reply was swift and to the point. **I'm not covering for you this time. You're on your own.**

My jaw clenched. I was going to need dental work before this day was done, I swear.

Xandra sent one last message—**I am not supporting your suicide mission.**—and then she stuffed her phone in her pocket, crossed her arms, and scowled at the back of Mrs. Tozer's frizzy head, refusing to meet my eye. I slid mine away too, quietly seething at her.

Suicide mission? Did she really have that little faith in me?

Again, a little voice reminded me: I'd had so much help in getting to this point, been saved at the last minute several times. My margin of victory kept narrowing. Eventually, the luck propelling me forward would run out.

Maybe Xandra was right. Maybe this was the end of the line for me.

The idea alone was sobering enough. Was going to New York really the only thing that I could do?

I couldn't see another way out of this, aside from approaching Draven directly. And I definitely would not survive that.

My hands clenched into fists under my desk.

I was going to die either way, right? Might as well be fighting instead of hiding like a caught rabbit.

And why was everyone so against me all of the sudden?

My phone buzzed with a message, and I glanced at Xandra, wondering if she had decided to send along something else nasty.

But it wasn't her. It was Mill.

No night flights to Syracuse.

Lockwood can drive us. We will travel through the night, arriving sometime late tomorrow afternoon. He'll pick you up after school and bring you to my place. You will have to, I repeat HAVE TO, shut your phone off as soon as you leave so as to avoid being tracked by your parents and the police when they go nuts and report you missing.

I felt sick. They had already reported me missing once since moving down here. And they knew that I had somehow been mixed up with kidnappers. This was going to absolutely kill my mother.

My heart beat painfully against my ribs.

There was no other option.

I had made my choice. I had dug my grave.

Now it was time to lie in it.

Chapter 10

Lockwood was waiting for me in the parking lot after school let out, just like Mill said he would be.

I watched Xandra walk down the sidewalk toward home, just like every other day, her blue hair swirling in the salty air breeze. She hadn't spoken to me the rest of the day, but I did catch her staring at me from time to time. I knew she wanted me to change my mind, and pretty much ninety percent of me wanted to change it too.

But I couldn't. I knew I couldn't.

I looked down at my phone, knowing that in fifteen minutes Mom would be calling to ask how my day was and make sure that I got home all right. She would probably ask me if I could pull something out of the freezer for dinner, or ask if I wanted to get take out instead.

I gripped the phone tighter and my eyes burned with tears.

I could still back out. I didn't have to do this.

No. Not happening.

Before I shut it down, I needed to let Iona know what was happening. **Mill said there weren't any flights during the night that were right, so Lockwood is driving us. Where should we pick you up after sundown?**

She got back to me quickly, fortunately, specifying a corner. I didn't know where it was exactly, but this was what GPS was for.

Thanks, I answered. **I'll have him text you when we are on our way. I have to go silent now. Shutting my phone**

off. See you then.

Now was the time to shut out the rest of the world while I did what I had to do.

My fingers shook as I pushed the power button on my phone, hoping against all hope that Mom wouldn't text or call me before I shut it off.

If she did, I knew I'd crack. I'd stay. I'd go on with my life.

My phone asked if I really wanted to power it off.

I hesitated only for a second before confirming. It shut off.

I shoved it in my pocket and walked across the lot, digging my fingernails into my palms until it hurt to keep myself from breaking down crying.

Focus on the pain, not on the inevitable breakdown.

I got in the back of the car and slammed the door shut behind me.

Lockwood didn't say anything. He just looked at me in the rearview mirror, his bright green eyes curious. Sunlight filtered through, washing out his features.

I avoided looking at him as I pushed my phone deep into the bottom of my backpack. Maybe it wouldn't suck so much if I couldn't actually see it.

I was grateful that Lockwood was quiet the entire way to Mill's place, which felt like the longest trip in the entire world when my head was racing like it was. Sundown was still long hours away, and getting later by the day as spring ramped up toward summer.

Funny to think that, six months ago, I'd have drunk in a day like this one. Blue, clear skies, a blazing hot afternoon to enjoy ... I might've been like any of the people we passed by, going about their business in an unchanged world. A couple on a rumbling motorcycle, speeding by; kids playing football in the street, running out of the way before the town car passed, then back in behind us as their game resumed; a pair of joggers going at a leisurely pace, chatting amiably ...

Everything was normal for these people. They didn't have to worry about vampires or being hunted or their entire lives being turned upside down.

A jealously that I had never known flared inside of me. What I wouldn't give—what I wouldn't do ... if I could just have a normal life like any of those people.

"I hope you know that I think you are very brave, Miss Cassandra." Lockwood's words broke my reverie.

I glanced up to see him gazing at me with his usual twinkle in the rearview mirror.

"Brave?" I asked. "Guess you don't really know me all that well."

"Perhaps I don't," he said with an easy grin. He tipped his hat toward me. "But from what I have seen, you're much braver than you give yourself credit for."

I looked away, back out the window.

He really didn't know me at all.

"The way that you handled that vampire, for instance … Roxy, was it? Nasty business. But you held your own."

I didn't reply. He must have not seen the same fight that I did.

"And Mr. Mill is extremely proud of you," he went on, checking over his shoulder for oncoming traffic. "He says that you have great potential. He's glad that you're taking your training so seriously."

"He said that?" I asked.

Lockwood nodded. "More than once, in fact."

I crossed my arms. "I figured he thought I was nothing more than a kid," I said.

"'Kid'?" Lockwood asked as we came to a stop at a stoplight. "I think not. Besides, he isn't much older than you are."

"I don't know that."

Lockwood chuckled, glanced in the rearview mirror. "He claims to be twenty-two in the human world."

I pursed my lips. "Well, good. In five years, I can start calling *him* kid."

"Did something happen, Miss Cassandra? I am sensing a great deal of animosity toward Mr. Mill."

"It's nothing," I lied.

I really didn't want to have to explain to Lockwood all of these … feelings that I was dealing with about Mill.

Especially since I didn't understand them anyways.

"Hey, Lockwood?"

"Yes, my lady?"

I smiled reluctantly. "Thank you for all of the help you've given me. All of this driving me around."

"I am pleased to be of service."

I knocked on Mill's door only ten minutes later.

He answered the door less than a second later.

"Waiting for me with bated breath?" I asked. I brushed past him, getting a whiff of his cologne. Bergamot.

I hated that I enjoyed the smell so much.

"I move fast. Remember?"

I did a quick scan of the room. Everything was in its place. Immaculate. Minimalist. Tasteful.

No girlfriend.

"Where's Kate?" I asked.

His eyes narrowed. He ran a hand through his sandy hair. "Burr in your saddle?"

"Most people don't use saddles or horses in this day and age," I snapped, unsure why I was being so nasty to him.

"She's not here," he said. He kept an even tone. "You have some ... problem with her?"

"I heard the way she talked about humans." I clicked my tongue. "Most of my people would have a problem with Kate, because would have a problem with all of us."

He shrugged. "She is who she is. Just not sure why you're so sore about it. Rather suddenly."

I stared at him. "I just don't know what you see in someone who's so ... hateful."

He made a face, and when he spoke, it was low. "Are we really going to have this fight again? Right now? When we should be planning our strategy for New York?"

"I—" I snapped my mouth shut. My argument dissolved like a balloon being punctured. "Yeah. You're right."

Mill gave me a look, as if uncertain whether or not I had been defused, then motioned toward the couch. "Go sit. I'll make you something to eat while we talk."

"You have food here? Actual, non O-neg type food?"

He paused on the way to the kitchen. "Since we started training, I thought it would be best if I kept a little food around for you."

My heart squirmed in a way that I didn't like.

He stopped at big, stainless steel fridge, hand hovering at the pull. "So ... what do you like? Pizza? Waffles? Ice cream?"

Wait, he had all that? "Um ... I don't know," I said.

Mill watched me patiently.

A thought struck me that made me both sad and curious.

"What's the one food that you miss the most since being turned?"

"I ..." he started, taken off guard, and then smirked. "You know, I haven't thought about that in a long time."

He glanced at the fridge.

"Chocolate cake," he finally decided, forehead loosening now that he'd warred it out in his mind and come up with that. "It just tastes like ash when I eat it now."

Quiet. Mill seemed to recede, a gulf forming between us— one that, I noted with sadness, I would never be able to cross.

"I'll, uh ... I'll have the ice cream," I said at last. Probably least wise, but damn if it didn't sound the best to me.

Sunset came after a wait that seemed minutes shy of forever. I kept a close eye on the drapes, lest the Florida sunshine slide across the floor and sear Mill, who was waiting patiently on the couch.

"It's down," I said, watching it slip below the horizon.

Mill stood, checking his watch. "Right on time." He picked up two bags next to the couch and tossed one to me.

I caught it. "What's this?" It was a black gym bag.

"Clothes," he said. "For you."

I looked at it with suspicion. He didn't elaborate, so I unzipped it. Toiletries lay across the top—a red toothbrush with the faded blue bristle strip that indicated heavy use, a tube of my brand of toothpaste, carelessly squeezed down to almost halfway, a blue packet of dental floss.

I frowned. "Figures the vampire would focus on dental hygiene." I looked closer. "Wait a minute," I said, rummaging past it for the clothes. There was a black halter top that I'd worn last week, a pair of jeans from two days ago and—my unmentionables at the bottom of the bag—

I looked up at Mill, mouth hanging open. "These are *my* clothes."

Mill was utterly unruffled. "I assumed you would need them."

"How did you get *my* clothes?"

He shrugged. "I dressed in a motorcycle suit and visited your house." He must have seen my eyes get plate-like in their wideness. "You invited me in before, remember?"

I couldn't form words. Not any of them. My jaw just moved up and down. Finally, I stuttered out a weak, "When?"

"Once when we were training," he said with a light shrug. "We were talking about that Net-flux thing with the internet and you said, 'You should come over and we'll watch *Parks and Rec* on my dad's bigscreen'."

I vaguely recalled that, maybe. An offhand comment about getting together to watch a TV show at my house counted as an invite? Yikes. Then again, Byron had taken my opening a freaking window as an invitation to come in.

All thoughts of vampires invading my house paled in comparison to the issue of the now. "But—these are my clothes! My—my—my—" And I waved the bag helplessly.

"Ohhh," he said, finally getting it. "I didn't touch anything or, uh … rummage your, uhm … garments. I just … emptied a laundry basket into the bag."

If he'd had blood flow to … anywhere … he might have been blushing.

"Lockwood is waiting for us," he said, practically rushing for the door at vampire speed.

I stared at the bag of my clothes, then looked at Mill, who would not meet my eyes. I had a feeling he had not gathered my stuff from a laundry basket … but I decided to leave it alone.

For now.

Lockwood was waiting in the parking garage below with the silver Mercedes town car that Mill sometimes called for. He took the corner Iona had given me and we were off, cruising through the dusky streets of Tampa under the purpling skies. Mill didn't say anything, and neither did I. It was better this way.

Iona was a bundle of sarcasm when we arrived at the street corner where she asked us to meet her. Apparently she wasn't keen on the idea of Mill knowing where she lived, because there were no houses around. Unless she lived in the back of a convenience store, we were at least a short distance from her place of residence. I would have guessed quite a ways, based on the icy look she gave Mill when she opened the door.

"Hello," she said, slipping into the back seat with me. Mill was shotgun with Lockwood up front and barely turned his head to acknowledge her.

"How long of a drive is this?" I asked Lockwood as Iona stared out the window.

"Just under twenty hours," he said. Rather cheerfully.

I looked at Iona, already lapsed into silence. Then at Mill, doing his own 'look out the window brooding' routine. Two vamps, lots of feels, no buffer.

Why couldn't Lockwood have taken the limo for this? Gas mileage, I assumed. Anonymity, for another. A limo would stick out in Onondaga Springs like...well, vampire violence, probably. Still...

"Great ..." I said. Lockwood pulled away from the curb, and we were off.

It was odd knowing I was going back home. Going back to a past that I thought I had left behind forever. My two worlds, Tampa and New York, had become strangely entangled, even at this distance. Now I was crossing the gap between them, and it felt ... weird. Kinda nerve-racking.

But it had to be done. I was the only one who could do it. Step back from the new one into the old, taking everything I'd learned—and a couple moody vampires—in Tampa and bringing it back to fix a problem I'd caused in New York.

My life was bleeding over from one place to the next.

Heh. Vampires. Bleeding.

I stared out my own window as the streets of Tampa blurred together under the growing darkness. They really were bleeding together. Soon I wasn't sure I'd be able to separate one world from the other.

Chapter 11

For the first hour or so, I was content to just stare out the window at the landscape rushing past. Nothing looked much different as we traveled north. It was still like a jungle, with a lot of stretches of wild forests broken by grassy fields.

As we got closer to the Florida-Georgia line, though, I was starting to see that an entire day in the car might actually drive me crazy.

"Hey, Mill?" I asked. I was leaning against the window, my sweaty forehead pressed against the cool glass. "Can you maybe turn that music down? It's giving me a headache. I mean, I know that most people can handle some big band swing, but three hours of it …?"

He looked sheepishly over his shoulder. "Sorry. Any requests?"

"Maybe something a bit more modern?"

Iona snorted.

A flare of frustration bubbled up in me. "You're in a pleasant mood this evening."

She didn't reply. She just looked back down at her book.

"How can you even read that?" I asked. Aside from the occasional street light or car passing by, the inside of the car was entirely dark.

She still didn't look up.

"You don't need light or something?"

But Iona was determined to ignore me. Which was just *excellent*—like dealing with Xandra all over again.

"Vampire eyes are different," Mill said, shooting a glare over his shoulder in Iona's direction. "They're more adapted for the dark."

I smirked. "So you're like cats?"

Mill shrugged. "As good a comparison as any."

Lockwood slowed to get off at the next exit. The bright lights of fast food restaurants and gas stations lit up the street, like an oasis in the dark.

"Where are we?" I asked, stretching my legs out. Sitting for so long in one position made my muscles tight and sore.

"We are just about to cross into South Carolina," Lockwood replied.

He turned into one of the gas stations. Once we'd stopped, he stepped smoothly out of the car as if nothing bothered him.

I wondered, not for the first time, if Lockwood was a human. He wasn't a vampire, because I'd seen him in daylight, but … there was something not quite normal about him.

"Are you hungry?" Mill asked, turning around in his seat to look at me. I shrugged. "I don't know." Then, more confidently: "Not really. I don't need anything."

Mill didn't seem convinced. "Look, if you want something, I can run in and get it for you."

I shook my head. "No, I'm fine."

"Not even some water?"

"I'm fine, Mill!" I said, maybe more sharply than I should have. What was with this constantly treating me like a freaking baby? Not trusting me to fight alone was one thing, but totally undermining my decision-making, asking me three times as though I might not actually know the state of my hunger and thirst—that really pissed me off. I glared at Iona for no reason other than that she was next to me. Before I could stop myself, I spat, "Are you going to be a recluse this entire drive?"

Iona shut her book with a loud snap. "Why are you so worked up?"

I blinked at her. "Is it just me, or am I the only one who remembers what we're going to New York to do?"

Mill and Iona exchanged glances.

I groaned. "I'm going to get out and stretch my legs, seeing as I'm the only one who needs to do *that*."

I slammed the door behind me and started off toward the convenience store, hoping I could work out some of my obvious touchiness. Not likely, given how determined the people in my life were to drive me crazy today.

The sight of the colorful bags of chips and candy bars made my stomach rumble painfully. That ice cream that I had eaten at Mill's felt like days ago.

I pulled my wallet out of my pocket and frowned. I only had a couple of dollars.

Okay. Maybe some of the people in my life had a point.

Maybe I really hadn't thought this through.

I wandered down the drinks aisle. The chilled air from the cooler would've been wonderful during the day. But the night was cool, and all it succeeded in doing was raising goose bumps on my arms. I considered the offerings, overpriced like all gas stations' stock, and twirled my keys, when—

A thought struck me.

Our house. My parents' house. They hadn't sold it yet. It was just sitting there, empty.

I wasn't sure why I'd thought of it. A base of operations, maybe, while we figured this out?

While *I* figured this out. Because I'd been sitting on this thing for close to twenty hours now, and I still had absolutely no idea how I was going to fix this mess.

Suddenly I wished I was back home in Tampa. This whole thing was so impulsive, so ridiculous.

I sighed. Xandra was right. This was crazy. In the end I settled on buying nothing at all—best to stretch these last few dollars as far as possible, I guessed, since I also had no idea how long exactly this would take. (Come to think of it, the sheer lack of information I had was spectacular, given that I was running headlong into another battle.) So I wandered outside again.

Lockwood had already refilled the car, paid, and gotten back in. He waited, hands resting on the steering wheel.

He gave me a smile and a wave as I approached.

When I slid in, he said, "Here you are, Miss Cassandra."

Mill passed a plastic bag back to me, and I found it was full of snacks, drinks, and a face mask.

"Thank you," I said. "I'll ... pay you back as soon as I can."

Lockwood shook his head. "Nonsense. You need the food. To keep up your spirits."

"Yeah, but I was just thinking ... this is a really expensive trip," I said as we got back out onto the road. "I was so worried about my uncle and everything, I just—"

"Cassie," Mill said quietly, "do you remember what I said about vampires? About how we never really have to worry about money again after a certain point?"

I flushed. "Yeah, but this whole thing was my idea, wasn't it? We're going up there because I wanted to."

"And we weren't going to let you go alone," Mill said.

"But the money—"

"Is not an issue," Mill said. "Look, Cassie, this is not entirely about you. Yes, Draven is looking for you, but Iona and I are accomplices in this. And I don't know if she would agree, but Draven could do with being taken down a notch. I, for one, do not like the idea of vampires running around like these are. Too many vampires kill recklessly. They think it's fun." His face contorted. "It disgusts me."

Iona hadn't turned a page in her book for a few minutes. Listening.

"I don't understand how they could have forgotten their humanity so quickly," Mill went on. "I understand that some vampires felt mistreated as humans, and so when they turn, they get drunk on their immortality. Wreak havoc on those who had made their life so terrible. But those who weren't ..." He trailed off, gazing out of the windshield. "How can they forget what it's like to fear? To know that death was coming? How can they forget what it's like to live?"

Iona huffed. She rolled her shoulders, but still didn't look up at us.

"I just hope that you don't take it for granted how hard we're trying to ensure that you have a good, long life to live,"

Mill said quietly. "A life that doesn't end in being forcibly turned into a … monster."

I looked down at the bag in my hands and suddenly understood the true length that the people in this car were going for me. It wasn't just on a whim that they decided to help me.

It was to save me.

Who knew; if I were to be turned, it could start a snowball effect where all of those in my life could be affected as well. And it was possible to think that—given how much of a pain I'd been in his immortal ass—with me out of the way, all of Tampa could fall peacefully into Draven's hands. They wouldn't even know.

That was probably a little presumptuous. But the point remained—Mill and Iona had their own vendettas with Draven.

It was like the build up to a war. The tension was thick enough to cut with a knife, and with the swing of a pendulum, the tides could change.

I intended to change them in my favor.

I grabbed the bag of cheesy puffs from inside the bag and pulled it open with a small pop. The fake cheese smell was almost overpowering, but I was grateful—for it, and the yogurt I ate with a plastic spoon next, and a blue drink with packaging boasting about electrolytes.

"You should get some sleep," Mill said when I'd finished. "It might be one of the last nights you can actually get any rest."

Morbid, but I appreciated that he didn't mince words.

"I usually don't sleep very well in cars," I said.

Lockwood glanced in the rearview mirror. "I also purchased a small box of non-habit-forming sleeping pills. Just in case you needed them."

"All right," I said slowly, digging through the bag for the small plastic bottle. "I guess it can't hurt …"

After taking one, too afraid I wouldn't wake up with the full dosage, I pulled a sleep mask down over my eyes, rested my head back against the seat, and allowed the constant hum of the car to lull me into a dreamless sleep.

Chapter 12

I was rudely awakened a few hours later. I had a nice kink in the back of my neck from lying with my head against the window, along with a crease across the front my neck where the seatbelt had dug into it.

Mill was trying to speak softly, but Iona was doing nothing to keep her voice down.

"We don't exactly have a choice," Mill was whispering.

"I am not going to crawl in there with *you*."

I groaned. My neck was going to snap, I just knew it. I rubbed it as I unstuck my crusty eyes and blinked blurrily at them.

"What's going on?" I mumbled. My mouth was sandpaper dry.

"Sorry, Cassie," Mill said. "Someone doesn't seem to think that the fact dawn is coming is important."

"It's fine," Iona said. "Just give me a blanket."

"And if it slips?"

"You're acting like I've never done this before," she snapped, her arms and legs crossed as if she were in a straitjacket.

"I'm just trying to protect you," Mill said.

"I'm a big girl." She glared icy daggers. "I don't need protecting."

"What's going on?" I asked again. We weren't moving anymore.

"Wait, are we in New York?" I asked, staring wide-eyed out

57

the window.

"We're in North Carolina," Mill said. "But the sun's going to be up soon and we need to make sure we're out of it."

We were sitting in a dark, deserted rest area. I could hear cars and semi-trucks driving by on the highway in the distance. One of the large lights overhead in the parking lot was flickering.

True enough, dawn loomed: the sky was lightening, the horizon a frail pink. Before long that would brighten into a yellow band—and then the sun would be up.

If it touched Mill's or Iona's skin, they would turn to dust—an agonizing death, if Roxy's demise had been anything to go by. "What about the tinted windows?" I asked. "Won't they help?"

Mill nodded. "For a few miles, sure. But we still have a good ten hours to go on our drive. The midday sun is going to be a straight shot to hell for us."

"So what are you going to do?" I asked.

"I'm not doing it," Iona said.

Mill was doing a great job restraining himself, but the look in his eyes could have melted steel.

"Get in the trunk," he said. "The sooner, the better for your health, since the sun is quickly approaching."

"How …" I asked. "How are you both going to fit in there?"

"Exactly my point," Iona said.

"You know, for a guest in my car, you are being unnecessarily difficult right now. This whole trip, in fact, *you* have been difficult," Mill said. "I'm starting to suspect you might just be a difficult person in general."

Iona glared icy fire right back. "I didn't come on this trip to be stuck in a dark trunk with you for ten hours."

"If I may …" Lockwood cut in pleasantly, smiling at the two of them. "The trunk has ample space. If it would make you more comfortable, I can provide you with a blanket to hang between yourselves so you have some more privacy."

Iona snarled in a way that reminded me way too much of Roxy, threw open the car door, and slammed it behind her.

Next second, the trunk opened.

A slight dip indicated that she was climbing inside, her thin, light frame barely able to shift the car.

"Sorry that we woke you up," Mill said. "If you need anything, just bang on the back of the seat. Or call me from Lockwood's phone."

"Okay," I said as I watched him get out of the car.

The silence that fell after he closed the door seemed to press in on me from all sides.

It was worse still after the less-subtle dip of the car as he clambered into the back ... and then reached up to swing the trunk door closed with a resounding *THUMP*.

I suddenly felt strangely alone—and vulnerable. Which was crazy, as they were both less than a couple of feet away ... but the daylight rendered them unable to help, if everything hit the fan—and I liked Mill's company. There was something relaxing about him. He made me feel at ease, even when neither of us were speaking. Heck, even when we were arguing.

His absence was like a hole.

"Miss Cassandra," Lockwood said after he turned on the ignition of the car. "I packed you some activities to keep your mind occupied during this part of the trip." He passed a backpack to me.

Inside I found a few books, a book of crosswords, and a fully charged tablet.

"A crossword puzzle book?" I asked, flipping through the thick, slightly rough pages.

"I thought a little challenge might help bring you out of your slump," Lockwood said.

"This is really sweet," I said. "Thank you ... for looking out for me."

"That is my job," he said, his reflection smiling at me.

I watched the sky until the moment that the sunlight broke over the horizon, washing the land in glorious, golden light. It was so beautiful—and almost heartbreaking, knowing that this simple, awe-inspiring sight forced Mill and Iona to cram themselves in the trunk in fear of it. We were still driving—*Lockwood* was still driving. Definitely not a vampire, this proved it yet again, now that Iona and Mill had been forced to cower in the trunk. But Lockwood soldiered on, even though we'd been driving all night.

"Aren't you exhausted?" I asked.

He shook his head. "Not at all." I settled into a book Lockwood had packed—a children's story, with almost crude illustrations, and a darkly humorous rhyming story. Not necessarily my first pick ... but it rekindled something childlike in me, turning it over in my hands and then flicking through. I needed something like that right now—someplace to regress, at least for a while.

"How are you feeling, Miss Cassandra?" Lockwood asked after a few hours. It was the first he'd spoken, and the first time he'd broken a quiet, tuneful hum he'd kept up, and which somehow did not annoy me but rather helped keep the tension out of my neck.

"I'm fine," I said without looking up.

"Truly?" Lockwood asked. "I admire your bravery," he said. "These vampires...nasty business."

"Yeah..." I said.

"I am glad that Mr. Mill and Miss Iona are here with you."

"Me too."

"I know that they aren't quite seeing eye to eye yet," Lockwood said, "but I know that they will find something to agree on. You, for instance. If they can find one thing in common, they can find another. And then another. And ... given enough time, perhaps they'll even become friends."

I highly doubted this, but I appreciated his optimism nonetheless. "I hope you're right."

"Just a few more hours to go," he said, apparently moving on in the conversation.

My stomach somersaulted. Home. Rolling hills, trees—a landscape I'd missed intensely since moving to Florida. It would be a feeling like no other, seeing it again for the first time since moving.

But I was heading headlong into danger. And it was all my fault. It all stemmed from my terrible choices—and the consequences that had driven my family and me out of New York to begin with.

My past and my future. My childhood and my adolescence.

It was all coming to a head.

My two lives were converging, smashing into each other like a car accident—broken glass and crumpled metal frames included.

Chapter 13

New York State of mind … It was about an hour before reaching Onondoga Springs that I began to recognize the places we drove by. My old stomping grounds. There was the shopping mall I'd go to on the weekends with my friends. It looked really run down now compared to my Tampa neighborhood. And my favorite restaurant, *Vino Italiano*, was still there. The closer we got to town, the more I saw. The hill where Dad had slid off the road the winter I had turned ten, totaling his car. The candy shop that Mom used to take me to after a long grocery shop as a reward for my good behavior. The lone streetlight, which was located in the middle of the quiet main street, and didn't work half the time.

I always pictured a trip home as a much brighter, happier event, Mom and Dad with me, making plans to see as many people as possible in the short time we were there. Having dinner at Uncle Mike's house, seeing Aunt Becky and my cousins for lunch. Getting my favorite brown sugar coffee from my favorite coffee shop with my friends. Enjoying real buttery, spicy buffalo chicken wings. Relaxing. Having fun.

Not vampire hunting.

Not rolling back into town, cowering beneath the window, hoping that no one would be able to see me or recognize me. Not being exhausted, barely able to keep my eyes open.

Not having a trunk full of vampires who were certainly ornery after being crammed in there for hours on end.

"That's my old high school …" I said quietly, lifting my head to peer out of the window. I was surprised how much my heart hurt to see it.

School was in session, and my eyes stung as I recognized a few of the cars that were parked in the parking lot. The black Nissan Maxima with the dent in the driver's door belonged to my old crush, Gary Haze. The silver Toyota Corolla with the pink dice hanging from the mirror was Jacquelyn's.

"Is it?" Lockwood said gently. "It's a nice place. Small. Wonderful architecture."

Being here, seeing everything with my eyes instead of my memories, was a lot harder than I had expected.

"A lot nicer than the school I'm at now," I said.

I guess that wasn't entirely true. I did have Xandra. And Gregory and Laura weren't so bad.

But it wasn't the same. My life here in New York had been vampire-free. I had known safety.

These vampires had literally ruined my new life in Florida. If Byron had just left me alone, I wouldn't be involved in any of this. They wouldn't care about me, and I'd be blissfully unaware that they existed. Not riding in a car with two vampires rustling in the trunk behind me, occasionally cursing quietly through the leather seats. Yet because of Byron's sick interest in me, the vampire world had bled, not just into my new life, but into my old life too, tainting the perfect world of my past.

The injustice of it all disgusted me.

I wished I'd been able to make him suffer more before he died.

Even then, I doubted it would be enough.

"What is the address of your house, Miss Cassandra?" Lockwood asked. I'd spitballed the use of it as a base of operations as I devoured cheesy puffs—and, like Lockwood said, Mill and Iona found themselves in a rare agreement that it was worth utilizing.

"It's just up this road," I said, wincing as I stretched my back muscles and tried to relax.

I peered out of the windshield at the road that I had spent most of my life on. There were no cars, as usual, and the blacktop was littered with all the same pot holes I'd ever known.

"Take a left here," I said.

Lockwood complied.

And there it was. Even though I had seen it thousands of times, it still felt surreal to see it for the first time in almost four months.

A two-story white house with blue shutters, a large front porch, and a two-car garage. There were windows along every side, and a huge backyard with a swing hanging from an oak tree with thick, stretching branches.

Lockwood's voice interrupted my thoughts. "Would you like a minute?"

"Yeah …" I said, and I stepped out of the car.

The smell of farmland filled the air, along with the rich, earthy smell of the forest around the house. Wind rushed through the dense, tall branches, a sound more pleasing to me than wind chimes or seagulls on the beach.

The sun was not as bright here, either. The sunlight that danced through the dense trees was softer, more comforting. Leaves were still popping out on the branches, returning after a long winter's absence.

And the grass! The grass was a dark, rich green, almost blue. Soft to the touch. I had grown so used to the spiny yellow-green grass that hurt to walk on in Florida. How had I forgotten this color?

I grabbed my keys from my pocket and stepped up onto the front porch.

I'd be able to do this with my eyes closed. I'd even miss the squeaky board on the porch three steps before the door.

I slid the key home in the lock, turned it, and pushed the door open.

Silence.

This house had never been so quiet, so … lonely. There probably hadn't been anyone here since we'd left. Once my parents had decided to move, they'd wanted to be gone as soon as possible. So, deciding against waiting months for the house to sell, they'd just made it available as a rental. No one had taken that offer yet, either—something my mother liked to frequently remind me about.

That we didn't live here anymore because of me.

The sun behind me bathed the foyer's hardwood floor in watery light as I stepped inside. A thin layer of dust covered the small table beside the door where we all used to toss our keys when we got home. Mom hated it; called it a crap collector.

The stairs leading up were directly in front of me, but I stepped through to the living room just off the foyer.

It was eerie. It almost felt as if someone had passed away. Everything was so still. And the house didn't smell right. It was musty and smelled like furniture polish. It used to smell like Mom's favorite cinnamon candles and Dad's chocolate chip cookies.

I could see Dad sitting on our couch rooting for the Buffalo Bills every Sunday during football season, reassuring me every season that they would make their comeback the next year. It used to be my favorite way of avoiding my homework on Sunday afternoons.

I wandered through the living room into the small kitchen. I knew that Mom and Dad liked how large the kitchen was in Florida, but this had worked. The large window over the sink looked out into the backyard and surrounding forest. There wasn't an island, but Mom had picked out the bluish granite countertops herself after months of searching.

Dad had baked so many Thanksgiving turkeys in this kitchen. The small dent in the oven door where he had tripped trying to pull three pies out of the oven was still there. There was a distinct coffee ring on the corner of the sink where Mom would leave her coffee cup every morning.

How had my life changed so much? How had my parents, and I, changed so much?

I never thought I'd miss this place as much as I now realized I did. I longed for this place. For home.

Standing here, I realized … Florida just did not feel like home.

And I didn't think it ever would. Some part of me wanted to stay here forever. But this place had changed. It wasn't the house from my memories anymore. Sure, it looked the same, it had all the hallmarks … but this was a shell, with none of the life that I wanted nothing more than to get back to. And so I turned away, leaving my sadness behind me, wandering back outside feeling as though a bit of me had been cut out in my sleep, one that I couldn't feel exactly, but which I knew was gone.

I unlocked the garage doors from the keypad outside—the code was the same—and Lockwood pulled the boat-sized Mercedes into the garage. I closed the door, shutting out the sunlight so Mill and Iona could clamber out without being burned to a crisp.

I went back around to the front of the house to meet them inside when I heard someone call my name from the driveway—someone whose voice I had not heard in a very long time.

Wheeling around, I saw a slender, tan Native American girl with dark hair tied in two braids. She had a pretty face with dark eyes. Not a trace of makeup, but it wasn't as if she needed it.

"Genesee!"

The girl grinned at me, her teeth brilliantly white. "Haven't heard that name in a long time, from you or anyone else."

I nearly jumped off the porch and raced across the driveway to her, throwing my arms around her neck.

"Whoa!" Genesee said, startled by my extreme show of affection. "It's good to see you too, Cassie."

"I am so sorry that I haven't called," I said, pulling away from her, hoping she could see the truth on my face. No lie.

Genesee dismissed my words with a wave. "Don't be. Life must be insane for you since the move." Genesee looked past me to my house. "Saw someone pulling into your driveway. I didn't recognize the car. Figured it was either new tenants or burglars."

"Well, you're awfully brave, coming up here alone to confront burglars," I said.

She shrugged. The reaction was so familiar it made my heart hurt. "That never used to be a problem. But lately …" She trailed off, her pretty face tightening. "Crime has been crazy. Some people have died." She shook her head.

"I heard that there have been some weird people in town," I tested, watching her face.

"Exchange students from one of the SUNY schools is my guess," she said. "I don't know, though. It's just been weird the last few weeks. The whole town is uneasy."

She looked at something past me, and I turned to follow her gaze.

Lockwood was passing by the foyer, which could be seen through the open front door, hauling some suitcases into the living room.

I turned back to Genesee, one of her eyebrows arched. "So, what are you doing back here?" she asked. "And who is that?"

"He's a sort of family friend," I said. It wasn't a complete lie, but I still hated saying it. Gen was one of the last people I wanted to lie to. Our friendship was one of the few in my life that hadn't been torpedoed by my lying. "He helped to get me up here to see my uncle."

"Your uncle? What happened?"

"He was attacked the night before last," I said. "Mom's sister—you know Aunt Becky—thinks it's connected with the other stuff going on here."

Gen's eyes widened. "Is he okay?"

"He's stable," I said. "But I had to see him. He's one of the few people that didn't ... after ... we're really close. I had to come see him."

"Your parents didn't come with you?"

"No," I said, unable to meet her eye. "Not this time."

"Bummer," she said. "I know my mom would have loved to see them."

"They would have loved to see you, too," I said. That much was the truth.

"Well, I should let you get settled," Gen said. "When are you going to see your uncle?"

"As soon as everyone inside has had a chance to rest. Long drive, you know."

"Yeah." She smiled effortlessly at me. "Come and let me know how he's doing, okay?"

"Okay," I said.

She waved, and I watched her go, and a strange feeling came over me. Something connected to the one I'd felt in the house minutes ago—that this was not home anymore, but that neither was Florida. Seeing Gen just drove that strange sense of isolation, made it plainer. I walked back inside the house that was no longer my home, in this town where I no longer lived. And nothing about it felt remotely right.

Chapter 14

It was very odd to see Iona and Mill, aspects of my new, Florida life, walking through my childhood home. Pale as they were, they almost looked like ghosts, lonely and wandering as if they were trapped.

Well, they sort of *were* trapped until the sun went down.

I had pulled every drape closed, but the house was not nearly as fortified for blocking the light out as Mill's place was. Iona was particularly unhappy—possibly because I had relegated her to the basement until tonight.

"I'm sorry," I told her, standing at the bottom of the stairs. "What would you like me to do?"

Her jaw snapped shut and she stalked off.

It was a fully furnished place, where my dad had once kept a pool table as well as a series of arcade games. A makeshift bar top stood in one corner. I remembered the tiny dancing Santa that Mom would put there every Christmas.

Dad had taken the large flat screen television that he had kept down here for movie nights. He had tried hard for years to make it feel like a movie theater.

"It's the best place for you," I said.

Iona paced, steam practically rising off her shoulders. "First a trunk, now a basement. What am I, some sort vampire stereotype? Got a coffin for me to sleep in?"

"Get used to it," Mill said. "This probably is where we'll be sleeping."

"Great," Iona said. "Just what I wanted. A slumber party

with all my best friends."

The sun would dip below the horizon a little before eight that evening. Seeing Uncle Mike, in addition to being the nice thing for a niece to do, and assuaging my guilty conscience, was also the best—and only—place to get accurate information. If we could locate where he had been attacked, and how, it might help lead us to the vampires. And their lair.

"I just hope he isn't totally out of it, or we might have to fall back on Plan B," I said.

"Which is ... what exactly?" Iona asked.

"Probably setting a trap of some sort," I said.

With the vamps settled (as settled as they could be, anyway—Iona was still breathing fire), I offered Lockwood the guest room, against his protestations of sleeping on the couch. I found air mattresses in the linen closet for Iona and Mill.

And then, my breath catching in my throat, I made my way back to my old bedroom.

The room was a lot bigger than my new room in Florida. It was also a lot less cluttered than it ever used to be. The closet was totally empty, as was the dresser and the desk beneath the window. Mom had bought all of the furniture for this room at a garage sale, but it still felt like my room, even if everything in it was totally different—wasn't mine.

I sank down onto the bed, the mattress a little too firm for my liking.

Pulling my bag open for the first time since my little confrontation with Mill, I was pleasantly surprised to see that he had the measure of me better than I expected. He'd packed a variety of warm clothes. The jeans he'd picked were my favorites. A couple of sweatshirts. And...

The T-shirt that he had lent me.

My cheeks burned.

"Damn you, Mill." He hadn't emptied a laundry basket.

Still ... he'd done well.

Out the window, I could see the single street light that followed along the road through the trees, like a bright star in the night. How many nights had I stared at that solitary light, thinking about Gary Haze or the test I hadn't studied for?

Life had been so easy here.

I fought the urge to cry. I didn't understand these feelings—didn't want to, almost; just wanted to banish them away, and get on with this whole vampire thing.

"Hey, Cassie."

The voice roused me from a sleep I hadn't realized I'd slipped into.

It was dark. Mill stood in the doorway. He had changed into a black leather jacket, navy blue shirt, and dark jeans.

The look suited him. I had to force myself to look away so I didn't stare.

"Hi," I said. "Is the sun down?"

Mill nodded. "You ready to go? I don't imagine the hospital will take visitors for much longer."

"I can be," I said, the spike of adrenaline at the thought of talking to Uncle Mike banishing my fatigue. "Just let me change." I rose, going for my bag, still open at the edge of the bed. "I'll meet you guys at the car."

We were on the road again in less than five minutes.

Familiarity washed over me again—but it was a discombobulating sort. Things weren't quite right, somehow. The evening was as quiet as it had always been, the few cars on the road driving slowly, as though afraid a child might lurch out in front of them. The single chain coffee shop in the area was usually flooded with people, but although there was a line of vehicles around the building now, no one was actually inside.

So why, if things were more or less as I remembered them, did it seem ... wonky, somehow?

"Everything seems so ... dead," Iona remarked as we slowly passed by a small shop whose front windows had been smashed in. Caution tape crossed over the broken bits in a large, yellow X. "I mean, I've been through small town America, and it's not like it used to be, but this ..." She stared out the window, pale hair catching stray rays from every street lamp we passed. "This is dead."

I tried to swallow the lump that had appeared in my throat.

The hospital was nestled up on the hill just outside of town, not far from the high school. The parking lot was dimly lit, something which I hadn't remembered. All of the bright and fancy lights at Dad's new hospital in Tampa had made me realize just how small and insignificant this hospital was.

How did Dad work here for so long?

I stepped out into the cool night. Mill and Iona followed.

Iona flicked her silvery blonde hair over her shoulder and glared up at the building. "This place is a hospital?"

"Yeah. Only one for thirty miles," I said. "It sees a lot of traffic."

"Probably more lately," Mill said.

"I will be here when you need me," Lockwood said, then rolled the window up and drove off to find a parking spot.

"Shall we?" Mill said, gesturing toward the doors.

We took one step before I found myself standing behind Mill instead of in front of him, my hair whipping around my face as if a car had just sped by me.

It took me a second to get my bearings. Somehow, in the span of a fraction of a second, Mill had moved from behind me to in front of me.

"Wha ..." I started, but I fell silent as I heard the snarl of an unfamiliar voice in the night.

"Well, well. Lookee what we found. Vampires."

Vampires?

Three people stood in the shadows between us and the front doors. The dim lights made it hard to make out their faces. Their shapes were apparent though: two males and a female. The first, the one who had spoken, was built like a pro-wrestler—thick muscles with shoulders that looked like small boulders. The other male was slender and scrawny-looking. The woman had wildly curly hair, and was tall and wide-hipped.

"This your territory?" Mill asked.

"Not exactly," the other vampire said. "Here on orders."

"Doing what?" Mill asked.

"What's it to you?" the female said.

"Finishing off someone who shouldn't have lived," the first

said, ignoring the woman.

My heart sank to my feet.

Uncle Mike.

I latched onto the back of Mill's jacket, tugging.

He must have taken the hint.

"What? You get fledgling regret?" Mill asked. "Decide you didn't like her as much in the cold dark of the next midnight as you did the night before?"

Iona whipped her head around to show him a glare. "You're a jackass."

Mill's frowned. "I—we're not talking about me, okay? It happens with other vampires … I didn't …"

I looked between the two of them, hopelessly caught in the middle of a discussion I didn't fully understand, but got the edges of. "Uhm …?" I asked, pointing at the vamps in front of us.

The lead vampire across from us sank into a fighting position. "You're nosy. What business is this of yours?"

"We've been hearing that a lot of humans have been found drained around here," Mill said. "It's not exactly good for business."

Mr. Boulder Shoulders let out a little hiss. "To hell with your business. You have no idea what you're dealing with!"

And before he spoke another word, he threw himself across the distance between him and Mill.

I found myself flying through the air, landing on the pavement behind a car with a painful, sickening thud.

Chapter 15

Had ... had Mill *shoved* me?

I gritted my teeth, gravel biting into my palms as I attempted to push back to my feet. An ache throbbed around my ribs, only recently healed after my fight with Roxy. Not broken again, I thought—but damn, it smarted.

Snarls and growls rent the night, along with the sounds of punches meeting vampire flesh. It sounded more like stone smashing against stone.

My ears rang, and I reached up behind my head to check and make sure that I wasn't bleeding. My fingers came back dry, which was good. But the coppery taste in my mouth wasn't.

Great. Blood plus vampires always equaled good things.

I struggled to get my bearings, for the second time in barely as many minutes.

I had landed behind a car, somehow missing it entirely as I spun over its hood. I braced against it, rising, to see—

It was insane. Mill was going toe to toe with Boulder Shoulders, and Iona was after the girl. It was a whirlwind of hard punches and intense kicks, all faster than I could actually make out.

But where was the other one?

"Hello there, gorgeous. Why are you hiding all the way over here?"

With horror, I looked up to see the third vampire, the lanky one, fangs flashing in the pale light.

Adrenaline flushed through my veins, spiky and dark.

Just a few weeks ago, I would have reacted out of sheer panic. But after training with Mill, honing my instincts, I was ready. So when the vampire flung himself at me—

I ducked. My shoulder scraped against the green Toyota Corolla next to me, but I didn't stop.

He swung at me, but I expected that too. Spinning on my heel, I reached up into my hair and yanked out my trusty stake, smooth to the touch and filed to a sharp point, from my hair tie.

"You're a pretty little thing," the vampire said, grinning nastily at me.

"Tell me something I haven't already heard," I said. His eyes flashed with desire.

I backpedaled, putting extra room between us—and getting me away from the cars so I had more space to maneuver.

A gust of wind rushed through the parking lot, so strong it nearly knocked me off of my feet. I opened my bloody palms to steady myself, the world swaying around me.

The vampire in front of me hesitated. Eyes glazed over, he inhaled deeply. His gaze came back to me—hungry, intoxicated.

"I smell blood," he purred. "You're human." He stalked forward. The presence of the stakes in my hands held him back, just out of striking distance—but it didn't stop him from pushing closer, eyes drinking in the bead of blood that was growing in the corner of my mouth, threatened to spill over, trace a crimson line down my chin—

"You're not getting so much as a drop from me," I said.

"Oh, I'll drink more than my fill—"

Before he could say anymore, I reached into my pocket with my free hand, withdrew a vial of holy water—and threw it full force into his face. It exploded in a shower of glass, water exploding across his skin.

The effect was instant.

His scream tore through the night, pitched and unending. He clawed at his face, skin sizzling. I savored it for just a fraction of a second—and then leapt in, aiming with the stake for just under his breastbone.

It collided—met resistance—and then pierced.

Black, acrid, sour-smelling blood gouted out around my fingers as I plunged deeper, and the vampire's screams grew higher still, the keening wail of a banshee like none other as my stake penetrated the blackened, shriveled, unbeating glob that was his heart—

I wrenched the stake free and leapt backward.

His hands went to his chest, his fingers trembling as they scraped through the blood spurting from the wound as if trying to shove it all back inside.

His eyes snapped to mine, his anguished howl changed to rage.

But it was done. Black blood poured from his mouth, his ears, the corners of his eyes.

He made a last-ditch attempt to grab out at me, to take me down with him, but instead he fell to his knees with a thud, then rolled onto his side, already beginning to decay, becoming black and tarry as decomposition finally caught up with him.

Breathing hard and fast, I turned to see if Mill and Iona were all right.

Iona's opponent had a nasty gash across her cheek but still seemed to be holding her own.

Mill, however, had just latched onto his vampire's neck and proceeded to jump into the air, swing around him onto his back, and then snap it.

The vampire crumpled, and Mill proceeded to pull another glass vial from his own jacket, wrench the vampire's jaw back with a sickening snap, and shove the entire vial inside.

Flames erupted, consuming the vampire from the inside out. He screamed, a manic, pained, gargling cry—but it was already too late.

Mill wheeled around, eyes settling on the black puddle behind me.

"Did you do that?" he asked, gesturing to the growing smear of sludgy tar that had, less than thirty seconds ago, been my own attacker.

I nodded. "And before the two of you."

Iona must have heard that, because she lashed out with an almighty kick that sent the other woman vampire sailing through the air to land on the pavement with a sound of breaking rocks. With her inhuman speed, Iona was on her opponent in a second, driving in the stake while the woman was still on her back. She hit her three times—first through the leg, then through the abdomen, and then through the chest. So fast the woman didn't even get out a scream.

Mill and I just stared at her as she straightened up, her opponent dissolving into tar, blowing a few strands of her silvery blonde hair from her face.

"What? I had some anger I had to work through. Seemed like a good outlet."

Not for the first time, I was very glad that she was on our side.

Mill gave her a meaningful look before he rounded on me.

"I'm glad you were lucky this time—"

"Lucky?" I asked. "That was all skill."

"Regardless," he said. "You did well."

I smiled, swelling a bit. "Thank you."

"This time," he added.

"You just can't give me a compliment, can you?" I asked. "I did everything that you taught me. Used distraction like you said, then—"

"When you two are done bickering like an old married couple, we should probably make our way inside," Iona said with a flick of her hair. Her heeled boots clacked on the pavement as she started toward the doors.

Mill didn't move. "Did you use the holy water?"

"Of course," I said.

He sighed. "I've warned you before, but I'll say it again. You depend on holy water too much. You need to rely more on your own two hands, your feet, and what you are capable of with those, because at some point, the holy water is going to run out, and those are what you'll be left with."

I arched an eyebrow at him.

"Says the guy who uses it literally all the time."

"I don't need it, though. That's the point. If I didn't have it—"

"Are you two coming?" Iona called from across the parking lot.

77

I glared at him.

"Coming," I said, and I crossed across the pavement toward Iona, not looking over my shoulder at Mill.

Chapter 16

Before we even reached the doors, they were flung open. A harried nurse came running out, clutching a clipboard to her chest, her stethoscope bouncing. I didn't recognize her, but that didn't mean anything; the hospital was turning over staff constantly while Dad worked here. "What was all that screaming?"

I clenched my hands, which were covered in drying vampire blood, and hid them behind my back.

"Oh, I'm sorry," I started. "That was me. My boyfriend over there thinks it's funny to pick me up from behind and cart me around."

The nurse hesitated. "That sound ... was you?"

I flashed an abashed smile. "I have a kind of masculine scream. Especially when spooked. Arghhhhh," I said, trying to make it deep. Not my most convincing lie ever.

"Oh ... okay," the nurse said. She wasn't quite buying it, but it wasn't as though there was anything else going on out here. Anymore. "Well, next time, tell your boyfriend to have some more sense. That scream scared half of my patients."

Tell Mill to have more sense? With pleasure.

"I'm sorry," I said.

The nurse sighed, still bristling. "Are you here to see someone? Or are you just disrupting the sick and injured because there's nothing else to do around here?"

There really wasn't. "Here to visit," I said. "My uncle. Mike Anderson?"

"Follow me," the nurse said. "And no screaming, masculine or otherwise." She turned back toward the doors without looking back at us.

"Smooth," Iona said as she fell into step beside me.

I couldn't tell if she was being snarky or if she was impressed.

The warmth of the hospital washed over us as we stepped over the threshold. The sterile, chemical smell that all hospitals have pierced my nostrils and prickled my skin.

I hated hospitals.

"Does the whole having-to-be-invited thing apply to hospitals, too?" I asked out of the corner of my mouth as we followed the nurse toward the check-in desk.

Iona shook her head. "Public place. That's only private residences."

Mill appeared behind me. I flinched. They could move so fast.

"Okay, Mike Anderson?" the nurse said, taking off her stethoscope as she sat down in front of the computer. "Brought in yesterday? Some kind of accident?"

My stomach clenched. "That's right."

The keys clicked, and then she looked up at me. "Room 302. Third floor. Take the elevator down the hall." She pointed.

"Right," I said, and ambled away, down a corridor of cracked floor tiles and uncomfortable green furniture.

Mill stared at me as we stepped inside the faux wood paneled elevator. "Are you okay?"

"I'm fine," I said, shoving my hands in my pockets. For some reason, his compassion really annoyed me after our fight in the parking lot. I was too stubborn to take his pity.

Room 302 was a short ways down the hall from the elevator bank. The door was closed.

"We'll wait over here," Iona said, gesturing to a waiting room down the hall.

"Right," I said. Why was I saying that so much tonight?

Why did I feel so defeated?

"And you should probably wipe your hands down," Iona whispered, pointing me to an antibacterial gel dispenser on the wall. "He doesn't need any of...*that* near him." The black vampire blood practically oozed off my hands. Lucky the nurse hadn't seen it. Or had written it off as oil from a car I had been masculinely working on, maybe.

I nodded numbly.

A doctor walked past, his eyes glued to his clipboard. I hid my face, because I recognized him. Peterson. Another nurse sat behind the desk on the other side of the hall. What was her name? Julie something? My dad's old co-workers. I recognized their faces and needed to make sure they didn't see mine, in case they still had his number. The good news was that no one seemed to be fretting. No one seemed to be in mortal peril.

It gave me little peace.

Now that I was here, everything felt way too real. Uncle Mike actually had been hurt. It wasn't just some story I heard about over the phone. And I had traveled halfway across the country to see him.

With a brief, sad smile, Mill and Iona turned and left me standing there, apparently unaware of the emotional tide surging through me.

I scrubbed my hands with the antibacterial gel, some of the blood still caked beneath my nails, then knocked on the door.

"Come in," I heard Uncle Mike's voice call.

I pushed the door open and stepped inside. He was awake, lying back with a Sudoku book in his hands, pen poised. His dark hair had more flecks of grey in it since the last time I had seen him, I realized with a pang of sorrow. He was tall, like my mom, and built like a runner. His thin arms were patched with bandages, and a thick, white gauze pad was taped just above his left eye. His left hand was wrapped up tight, and I could tell from the way he sat that his ribs must have been hurt. He was focused entirely on his Sudoku puzzle.

"I'm not all that hungry tonight," he said, still not looking up. "Unless you have macaroni and cheese. Then I'm definitely hungry."

I didn't say anything. I was caught, stuck on the threshold.

Part of me wanted to just … watch for a while, take him in. He was older, banged up … but he was alive.

My heart panged. People my age shouldn't be thanking their lucky stars for that. He looked up—and his hazel eyes, like my own drew wide. The book and pencil fell into his lap. "Cassie?" he said, disbelief ringing clear.

I smiled and laughed, even though I really didn't feel like laughing. I shrugged my shoulders. "Yeah."

"What the …" he began, searching me up and down intently. "What are you doing here?"

I crossed to his bedside and sat down on the edge, peering into his face.

His face split into a smile as he wrapped his good hand around my shoulders and pulled me into a hug.

"I had to come see you," I said, extremely aware of every ounce of pressure I was putting onto him, not wanting to hurt him. I knew all too well what it felt like to have broken ribs. He winced a little as he readjusted himself on his bed, but his eyes were lit with happiness at the sight of me. Uncle Mike's eyes were always the thing I liked best about him. They were wide, happy, and attentive. His kindness was always there, no matter what.

"Can I help?" I asked, edging out of his embrace so as not to hurt him. "Fix your pillows? Get you some water?"

He grit his teeth, but smiled and shook his head. "No, no. I'm fine."

We sort of stared at each other for a few seconds, disbelief passing between us.

"What are you doing here?" he asked, wrapping his injured hand across his torso.

"I'm your only niece," I said.

"That's … not an answer," he said, studying me intently.

A great weight was starting to lift off of my shoulders. "It's good to see you're sitting up," I said. "I was worried that I might find you unconscious, all hooked up with tubes and stuff in here."

"Nah," Uncle Mike replied, dismissing my words with a wave. "I'm fine. I should have been sent home this morning."

The IV drip and the record of what painkillers he was on

hanging on the wall said otherwise.

"What happened?" I asked, unable to stop myself. I didn't want to totally blow my cover about what I was doing there, but I had to know. I needed to set the demons in my mind at rest. And anyway, he wouldn't expect little ol' me to have come this far to exact revenge. After all ... I was just a 'kid.'

A flash of dark terror twisted Uncle Mike's face, a horror like none other. Unconsciously, a hand went to his ribs as he relieved his attack, however briefly.

Then he shut it down.

"This isn't something I should worry you with," he said, forcing himself to sound as easygoing as he had just a moment ago. "Seriously, kiddo."

"I know that someone attacked you," I said. "Mom said as much. But who? Why?"

Uncle Mike pursed his lips. He considered me ... deciding if he could confide in me—whether I was old enough now to have the uncomfortable truth of the world laid bare.

"Well ..." he said finally, "I don't know who it was. Never saw their face. It happened fast."

"What did they want?"

"Probably my wallet," he said. "Not that I was carrying anything. I tried to tell them that. But it didn't matter. They just kept hitting me and—"

His smile turned forced and sad. It didn't reach his eyes.

"I told your mother all of this over the phone," he said.

His eyes narrowed and he looked at me as if seeing me for the first time.

"Speaking of your mom, kiddo, where is she? Parking the car?"

Now it was my turn to lie and cover the story. Easy as pie, right?

Actually ... no.

Because for this ... there was no easy lie. Almost any I could come up with would be seen through by Uncle Mike in seconds.

"Well, technically she's back at the house ..." I said slowly. "But not here in New York."

His eyes grew wide.

"Cass, you came all the way up here by yourself?"

"I had to see you, make sure that you were all right," I said.

"You could have *called*, Cassie," he said. "You didn't have to come all the way up here!"

I didn't respond. How could I tell him that this was so much more than what he could even begin to understand? Or, more importantly, believe?

"I mean, I'm flattered, don't get me wrong. But I don't need my niece to become a runaway just to make sure I'm okay."

"Come on, Uncle Mike," I said softly. "You know how important you are to me."

"I know, I know ..." he said. "But this seems impulsive ... even for you."

I swallowed, but tried to keep my face blank.

"I seriously did come here for you," I said. And it wasn't entirely a lie.

"Uh huh," he replied, in that jaded way that adults have. Judging my words. He knew my history.

I shrank back from him a little. He was too much like Mom. Too nosy.

And now he put his adult hat back on. "I'm very happy to see you, kiddo, but ... do you realize the situation that you've just put me in?"

My stomach sank. "Kinda ...?" Of course I did. I wasn't stupid.

"Your parents," Uncle Mike said, "they don't know you're here?"

I did my best to look blankly back, like a poker player holding her cards close to her chest. But Uncle Mike was too good at this. I couldn't bluff him into thinking I had four aces; he knew my hand was nothing but trash.

He sighed. "So ... I guess I'll have to lie about you being here when I talk to your mom."

My heart skipped. Was he seriously offering to cover for me? Knowing just how uptight Mom could get?

"Yeah, I guess ..." I said, almost not daring to hope.

Uncle Mike grinned. "It won't be the first time that I helped smooth something over with your mother. She likes to jump off the deep end."

I nodded, releasing the tense breath I'd held in my chest. "Yeah. She's wound a little tight."

"I wonder why, daughter running off across the country unsupervised." He shook his head and clapped me on the shoulder. "I appreciate your concern, Cassie. I really do. I'm going to be just fine."

"All right," I said.

He shifted—and winced. Those ribs hurt a whole lot more than he was letting on, I guessed.

"I should let you rest," I said, rising. "But I'll be back tomorrow to visit again?"

His brow arched. "Yeah? See you then, I guess."

"Maybe I'll bring you some coffee," I said.

"Appreciate the offer, kiddo, but I've gotta stay off caffeine until I'm off some of these other meds."

"Oh...well, I'll think of something," I said. I shoved my hands into my pockets. "Donuts, maybe. It was good to see you, Uncle Mike."

"It's been great to see you too," he said, the ever present kindness glowing in his gaze.

And with that, I turned and left the hospital room, feeling more guilty than I had ever felt in my life.

Chapter 17

As soon as I stepped out of Uncle Mike's hospital room, a nurse came bustling in with a tray stacked high with food.

"Hey, Mike. How you feeling?" she asked.

"Doing well. Just had a visitor," he said.

"Oh, yeah?"

She closed the door, and I heard no more.

I hovered nearby, not wanting to go find Iona and Mill yet. I needed to wrap my head around the reality of everything going on around me.

I could understand why Uncle Mike wouldn't want to tell me, a kid, about what had happened. But the haunted look on his face had told me enough. He'd seen something scary. Something he knew no one else would believe.

I knew those feels—because that was the exact way I'd felt when Byron had first appeared in my life.

Gritting my teeth, I turned and wandered back down the hall toward the waiting room.

Iona and Mill stood as I entered.

"Well?" Mill asked.

"He didn't tell me much," I said. "But he seems to be in good spirits. And I think he's going to make a full recovery."

"That must be a great relief to you," Iona said, though I could hear the icy edge to her words. Like she was forcing them out, or she and Mill had just had a huge fight. It was hard to get a read on why she sounded like a strangled cat.

"It is," I said.

"I understand that all of this is a little overwhelming right now," Mill said. "Did he say anything to you that might help? That could confirm … ?"

"Did he really have to when we were attacked by …" I bit off the word as another nurse walked by, her nose in her phone. "A bunch of them in the parking lot a few minutes ago?"

"Confirmation is nice," Iona said. "It keeps us from wasting time flying off in different directions, ones we don't need to be going in. What if he was attacked by a bunch of glittering fae?"

I blinked at her, unsure how I should respond to that. "You should have seen the look on his face …" I murmured. "He saw something. He told me he didn't, but he did. And it terrified him."

This felt like my parents getting kidnapped by Byron all over again. The reality was that there was nothing I could do to protect these people in my life. I had too many ties, too many connections. Too many people who were important to me had big, fat targets painted on their backs now. And I couldn't be in more than one place at a time. It would be easy, too easy, for Draven to start picking them off one by one. Heck, he'd almost gotten Uncle Mike purely by accident. Presumably, since he thought Elizabeth was a vampire, and Uncle Mike, a human, probably wouldn't be of any consequence to her.

Right?

My throat tightened. The hair on the back of my neck stood up. Fear bubbled inside of me, my stomach churning as if I had swallowed acid.

"Cassie?"

I blinked, finding Iona and Mill staring at me. "What?"

"What do you think?"

"About?"

Iona rolled her eyes. "We should head back to your house. Decide on our next moves."

"But shouldn't we walk the street?" I asked. "Try and find clues? Trace these vamps back to … ?"

"Bad idea," Mill said. "They could have had spies watching

in the parking lot. If they got wind of what happened …
we're to be hunted as much as we are hunting right now."
He started back toward the elevator bank, and Iona just went
along with him.

I followed. "How is that any different than how it was
when we got here?"

"We've lost the element of surprise," Mill said, as we got in
the elevator.

We stepped out into the lobby, Iona huffing with
frustration.

"But I don't want to waste any time," I said. "Other people
in my family could be in danger. This whole town is in
danger."

"I understand that this is all a lot to deal with right now,"
Mill said.

"That's for sure," Iona said. "I hope that you remember to
spare us in your reckless slaughter of every vampire in sight."

I glared at her. "Not helping."

"Well, you're just expecting everything to fall neatly into
line," Iona said. "Stuff like this doesn't just work out. We
need a plan of attack."

"She does have a point, Cassie," Mill said. "We've been
running so hard to get here … we haven't had a plan this
whole time."

"Then help me," I said as we walked out into the night.
"Help me figure out how to fix all of this."

"You're asking for a miracle. You know this is your fault,
right?" Iona asked. "If you hadn't been so cocky around
Draven, told him where you were from—"

"This is not helping right now, Iona," Mill said.

"Someone had to say it." Iona glared back at me. "Because
your lack-of-plan seems to consist of just running into the
enemy and hoping we win every fight."

"Why is that a bad non-plan? We took out three tonight," I
said. "How many more could there be?"

"Hundreds," she said coolly, voice crackling in the quiet
night. "Thousands. We don't know. Draven has resources
and connections that far exceed what your puny mind could
understand."

"My puny—why in the world would he expend so many of his resources on me?"

"Because you defied him," Iona said. "Insulted him. And you keep doing it. That scene out in front of his building? Killing Roxy? Nearly starting a war with the Lord of Miami?"

"That last one—technically, that was me," Mill said. "And Roxy … was actually you."

It didn't make me feel any better.

"To save Cassie," Iona said. "Neither of us would have spat in Draven's face like this … if not for her."

The parking lot was dark. I glared at the ground beneath my feet, walking ahead of Iona and Mill. I didn't want to hear it. I didn't want to hear any of it. It was all too much to deal with.

She was right. I was stuck.

"Maybe I just need to cut off the head of the snake," I muttered.

Iona scoffed, her heels clicking on the pavement behind me.

A gentle touch on my arm made me look up. Mill had fallen into step beside me. The sound of his footsteps disappeared beneath the sharp clicks of Iona's boot heels hitting the blacktop. He smiled sadly at me. "I know you're struggling under the weight of all this."

The sound of Iona's boot steps suddenly ceased. Mill must have noticed the same thing, because the two of us turned around to see where she had gone.

And there she was, standing utterly still, her silvery hair spilling over her shoulders, a shining knife jutting through her chest.

Standing behind her was the most vicious, smiling vampire that I had ever seen.

Chapter 18

Everything around me froze. The air. Time. The spinning of the earth itself.

Iona was sagging against the man behind her, dark blood dripping out of the corner of her mouth.

The man was a head shorter than Mill but built like a UFC fighting champion. Rippling muscles were clear underneath his dirty, stained white T-shirt. His jeans were torn at the knees. He had no hair, his pale head gleaming in the light from the lights around the parking lot.

He gripped one of Iona's shoulders with one of his thick, large hands.

The other twisted the knife in her back.

Iona gasped and sputtered, her face tight with pain. Her eyes stared at us pleadingly.

Mill was already hunched over, the beast that he was, his teeth bared and a deep, low growl emanating from his chest.

I reached out and grabbed Mill's biceps to stop him from launching himself at the attacker. He would give this guy a run for his money; the muscles beneath my fingers were taut and ready to strike.

I hated myself for noticing — and appreciating—it at a time like this.

"What do you want?" I asked, ashamed of how my voice cracked.

"What, no time for introductions?" the man replied. His voice was deep and gravelly, almost like a purr. When he grinned, I saw a few empty spaces where teeth were missing. One of his fangs was capped with gold. He twisted the knife visibly, the blade rotating in Iona's chest.

"I'm ... the head of the snake."

Iona squirmed, and then let out a pained moan when the vampire shoved the knife in farther.

"Don't move, beautiful. I've got this knife just beside your heart. I wouldn't bat an eye at cutting it out of your chest."

The calm with which he said that made my skin crawl. I clutched Mill tighter—for comfort or protection, I didn't know which.

"So, who do I have the pleasure of speaking with?" he growled, grinning as he pulled Iona closer to him. She gasped, spasmodic breaths coming in judders.

Her blood was just as acrid and sulfurous as every other vampire I'd come across.

"Oh, come on, now," the vamp cooed. His eyes shifted to me, and his grin darkened. "Fine. I didn't want to be rude, but I already know that you ... are Miss Elizabeth."

Horror swept over my face before I could stop it.

"Yes," he said, nodding at my inadvertent confirmation. "And that means that you two are guilty by association."

He pressed his face against the side of Iona's neck and inhaled deeply. "Pity. It is always such a delicious shame to kill my own kind. I so loathe it. And love it."

"What do you want?" Mill asked. His voice was more menacing than I had ever heard it.

"I thought that was obvious," the man replied. He looked over at me again. "I was hoping to have a private audience with the great Elizabeth, vampire slayer and enemy to the Lord Draven."

Iona trembled, a full-body spasm. Her teeth clenched. Her eyes seemed ready to pop out of her head. She slammed them shut, squeezing tight to keep them in.

"Sorry to disappoint you," I said. "But there's no one named Elizabeth here."

The vamp's smirk grew wider. "Don't play coy with me. Where are these violent tendencies I've heard tell of? The utter lack of mercy? The thirst for black blood on your hands?" He sniffed. "Here, I thought I might have found a kindred spirit … someone who knows the painful joy of killing our own kind." He twisted the knife again, and Iona gasped, a hiss of a breath that came through her teeth.

The first little whimper echoed from Iona's throat. I was going to be sick. The cavity in her chest was widening, so much sticky blackness pouring out of it. Everything south of it was stained dark, and it pooled around her feet, like God Himself had poured ink down her chest.

The vampire sneered. "I want to see this famous maliciousness. Show me. Why don't you finish off your friend here? Show me the depth of your hatred?"

He turned Iona toward me, knife still deep in her chest. She gasped again, staggering.

She'd lost so much blood already. Mill had said they could recover quickly—but this was unlike anything else I'd seen him endure. The blood slicked the ground like an oil spill, caused her feet to slip beneath her.

She teetered forward—and then the pain twisted into anger. She tilted as though she were about to careen face first into the parking lot then tossed back a mule kick, slamming her boot into the vampire's knee. He grunted, staggered backward—

Iona reached behind her. Fingers dark and sticky with her own blood, she caught the hilt of the knife in her wet grip, and pulled it free with a sickening squelch—

Then she crashed hard onto her knees.

We moved.

I lunged across the distance toward Iona as Mill leapt over me to land on the other vampire. Iona met me halfway as she crawled toward me, slowed to near human speed, every movement obviously agonizing.

Tires squealed in the night, and blaring lights came into view as a car whipped around the corner.

"Come on!" I said, wrapping my arms around Iona, moving out of the way so Lockwood could reach us.

He stopped the car between Iona and me, and Mill and the other vampire as they fought. They sounded like rabid cats, howling and lashing. My blood turned to ice as I heard the other vampire laughing low and dark.

"This is the great joy, isn't it?" the other vampire shouted, voice echoing in the night. "The true hunt? The only one of actual consequence?"

"Get in!" Lockwood yelled as he threw the door open.

I helped him to pull Iona into the car. She howled in pain, and I apologized and apologized—but we had to get moving, damn it. We got her in the back seat, and as I slid in beside her, Lockwood was piling blankets around her, trying to pack the wound and stem the flow of ebony blood as it gushed out onto the seat. The acidic smell of it filled the car and made me light-headed. Or maybe that was the fear.

I looked out of the window at Mill. It was hard to distinguish between the two warring vampires as they thrashed, slamming each other's limbs and heads into the pavement in a blur.

"We need to do something!" I said.

"Cassie, buckle up," Lockwood ordered with uncharacteristic force, wiping his inky, stained hands on the front of his clean, pressed suit.

I did as I was told.

He pressed a button somewhere, and then he slammed his foot on the gas, and we started off through the parking lot.

Mill suddenly detached himself from the other vampire and threw himself at the car. The car shuddered as he made contact, rolling effortlessly over the top and landing himself in the trunk that Lockwood had just opened. He slammed it shut behind him.

The vampire rose where Mill had just left him. He looked at us as we squealed past.

And he smiled. Lockwood gave him a wide margin—no point in hitting him; I'd seen that once with Roxy, and it had done more of a number on the car than her.

He watched us go.

The last I saw of him, before the car rounded the corner and banished him from sight, was him retrieving the knife that he'd run through Iona, black ichor still dripping from the blade.

He brought it to his lips, grinning—and ran his tongue along its edge as he watched us disappear into the night.

Chapter 19

"Lockwood, I need something to staunch Iona's bleeding!" I said.

Lockwood passed a stack of hand towels back to me, barely glancing back as he floored the gas pedal, taking full advantage of the empty streets to propel us swiftly back to my house.

I unfolded the towels and started to press them against Iona's chest, but they were soaked almost instantly with the inky wet blackness that poured from her wound.

"Damn it, Iona," I said, "you've lost so much blood."

She gritted her teeth. They were stained like she'd bitten into a pen, every tooth edge dark from blood. "Well, he knew what he was doing then. In order to incapacitate a vampire, you have to make sure they lose a lot of blood."

"But why did he grab you?" I asked. "He wanted me ..."

Iona closed her eyes, steeling herself with a breath that was no longer necessary.

"He must be one of Draven's best."

I didn't know how to reply to that.

"He knew exactly what he was doing ..." Iona said a little more weakly. She tried to readjust, but gave up when another fresh flow of black blood spilled out onto the towels in my hands.

"Just take it easy ..." I said.

I was grateful that Lockwood's driving was as smooth as it was, even with the increased speed. Last thing I needed was to fly through the windshield.

"Are you in a lot of pain?" I asked.

Iona just arched a brow at me.

"Right. Yes. Well…" I had no idea what to do.

There was a tap on the moonroof, and Lockwood opened it up without question. As soon as it was open wide enough, Mill squeezed in through it and into the passenger seat.

"How … how did you get out of the trunk?" I asked, still pressing the soaked rags to Iona's wound.

"They all have releases in them nowadays," Mill said. "To keep kids from getting stuck. Or gangsters from using them to kidnap people, probably. Thanks, Lockwood. Quick thinking."

Lockwood nodded, his eyes on the dark road.

Mill turned in his seat and looked at Iona. "How are you?"

"Peachy …" she said, her hands with mine on the soaked towels around her chest.

"She needs attention, Mr. Mill," Lockwood said.

"I'm fine," Iona said, but even as she spoke, she coughed, dark blood staining the back of her hand.

"We'll need blood for her …" Mill said, looking back over the seat at me.

My own blood turned cold. " … From me?"

Mill shook his head. "No. But if I had known that things were going to end like this …" He trailed off and exchanged a meaningful look at Lockwood. "I'll drop you off at the house and then go and take care of it."

There was an air of uncertainty in his voice, and he turned back around in his seat, staring out the front window. He was preoccupied about it, and the twisted part of me wondered how he was going to procure blood for her.

In all the time that I had known these vampires, they'd kept that part of their lives private. For my sanity, I hadn't asked, and they hadn't told me, which I was grateful for. Theoretically, of course, I knew that vampires drank blood, but it was sort of how you forget that a big, juicy steak comes from the brown-eyed cow in kid's picture books. I had been able to keep the two separate. What did they call that? Cognitive dissonance? Blissful ignorance?

Maybe I wouldn't have to be in the room when she drank.

"Can you make sure that it isn't a living being that you bring back?" I asked quietly.

Mill didn't look at me. "Don't worry about it, okay?" Easier said than done. I stifled it anyway. Better to just … ignore it, for now, avoid facing it until the last possible moment.

"So … what are we to do about the Butcher?" Lockwood asked, breaking the awkward silence.

"The who?" Mill asked.

"Well, we need a name for that fellow we just encountered, don't we? 'The Butcher' seemed appropriate, considering that monstrous knife he was wielding."

Iona ground her teeth.

"Works for me."

"I guess …" I said, the knife in his hands flashing across my memory. "But if he was hunting vampires, why was he carrying a knife that won't actually kill them?"

"That's the worst part of it, I think." Mill sighed. "He's just brutal."

"Do you think he uses that knife to hunt humans?" I asked.

Iona shook her head. "I doubt it. He wouldn't need that knife."

"Miss Iona is correct," Lockwood said. "I believe that he must delight in wanton destruction. He had no qualms with causing you pain just for the fun of it."

Iona grumbled. "Great. We found an enemy that thinks it's fun to hurt other vampires."

"Is that better or worse than your average vampire, who likes to hurt humans?" I asked.

"Worse, obviously," Iona said, and picked up a hand to gesture at her wound. "So much worse."

"He was probably just as sick and twisted in real life," I said.

"It's probably why Draven recruited him," Mill said. "Most vampires prefer to stalk … tenderer prey. This guy seems to revel in fighting us."

"That's true," I said. "He was glorying in it. The stuff he said to you while you were fighting … "

Mill nodded. "This sort is valuable to Draven. Not the kind you really want as your enemy."

"Why didn't he follow us?" I asked. "Because that kinda freaks me out more than if he would have followed. Blind spot and all that."

Lockwood seemed annoyed about this as well. "He strikes me as the sort who believes he will win, no matter what. He doesn't care if it takes him some time or effort. He perhaps even enjoys the hunt. He will wait it out, ensure his victory."

That was not very encouraging. I chewed on the inside of my cheek. Pain was becoming preferable to fear, which made me feel sick constantly.

"Have either of you ever heard of this sicko?" I asked, wanting more than anything to latch onto any hope that I could find. "Because if he comes after me with that knife, he's going to discover very quickly that I'm not a vampire."

"Don't worry, Miss Cassandra," Lockwood said. "We won't let anything happen to you. You have my word."

It brought me only the faintest trace of reassurance.

"Thanks, Lockwood …"

We pulled into the driveway of my house. The street was quiet, a nice contrast with the feeling in my head, like a bottled up scream. Adrenaline was still surging through my veins, and I studied every nearby shadow, half expecting the Butcher to come jumping out, knife in hand.

"Let's take her in through the garage," I said, "so we don't get blood all over the house."

"Glad to know where I rate in your priorities," Iona spat. "Barely above the carpet."

I hopped out and crossed over to the garage doors, opening them up. The headlights from the car flooded the concrete space with bright light as Lockwood pulled inside. He killed the engine, and slipped out, opening the back door. Mill crawled over the seat and met him on the other side of the door. As gently as I could, I guided Iona out, which was mostly achieved by pushing, while Mill and Lockwood pulled her out and each slung an arm around her. She howled again, grunting breaths of pain that came unrelentingly, racking her body with a renewed wave of shudders.

97

"Cassie, grab some towels," said Mill. "Where do you want us to put her?"

"I mean, a bed would be best ..."

"Couch is closer," Mill said.

"Okay." I snatched up a few blue tarps from a bin along the wall and hurried inside to the couch, throwing them over it, hoping that the blood wouldn't seep through it to the plush fabric underneath. If it did—well, I'd have to worry about the creative explanation for that later. Grabbing up every towel in the house next, I laid out a path from the inside of the garage to the sofa.

"Okay, should be good," I said, panting a little as I greeted them in the garage. I moved aside to let them through.

I watched them cross the kitchen, slightly more optimistic, as I turned to close the garage door.

And froze.

Genesee was standing there in the driveway. She stood there looking at us—Lockwood and Mill carrying the bloody and wounded Iona.

The casserole dish in her hands slipped from her limp fingers and landed with a world-shattering crash at her feet as she stared at us, her mouth gaping.

Chapter 20

"Gen …" I breathed.

She stared at the spot where Iona and Mill and Lockwood had been standing moments before.

I hurried through the garage to her, out into the driveway, my shoes scraping against the pavement.

"Gen …" I said again, reaching for her.

But she flinched away from me, out of my grasp. Her eyes snapped back to me. It was as if she was looking at a stranger.

I had to get her inside. If she had seen … if she knew … I had to keep her quiet.

I dropped my voice to a whisper. "Hey…why don't you come inside. We can talk—"

"What is going on?" Genesee said, clutching her hands over her face. "That woman, Cassie … she was covered in blood!"

I held out my hands to pacify her, trying to shush her without freaking her out more. Terror was written over her face. She stared at me, horrorstruck.

"Gen, I know you must have a lot of questions," I tried, voice carefully metered. "And I promise that I will answer them. But I need you to come inside with me. Please."

I couldn't quite tell if I was getting through to her or not. But I needed to. If she cried out, her father, who lived just down the hill, would probably hear and come running.

Her I could handle. Him, not so much. At least with

Genesee, I could probably get her to trust me. Or understand. All of those years of friendship and trust surely would amount to something, right?

"Why are you covered in blood?" Gen asked, her voice trembling. "Is that blood? Or oil?" She sniffed. "It doesn't smell like blood. Or oil. What *is* that?"

"I told you," I said. "Come inside. I'll answer your questions."

"Is that girl dying?"

"Gen. Please. Listen to me. If I have ever needed you to just trust me, this is the time."

Somehow, that must have been the right thing to say, for after a long moment she relented with a shaky nod. She followed—but only at a safe distance.

Did she think *I'd* done this to Iona?

I tried to clamp down on the sudden wave of unhappiness that swept over me at that thought. All our years of friendship, and now this?

So much longing for home—and yet things had changed so much, and so quickly.

When we were in, I closed the garage door. Gen watched it all go down with an air of panic. For the first time, I thought maybe I understood how vampires preyed on humans, because Gen had just walked into what could have easily been a vampire trap.

But it wasn't. And I hoped that she'd be able to understand.

The smell of the vampire blood hung in the air as we stepped inside the house, and I watched Gen's nose wrinkle. We walked silently through the kitchen as if through a processional at a funeral.

Maybe it was. The death of our friendship. Then she stepped into the lounge and gasped. Even I had to grab onto the wall to keep myself from stumbling.

Iona was stretched out on the couch as if she were already dead, black blood oozing from her side and down onto the couch, like a small, thin waterfall down the tarps. Mill was standing above her, trying to pack her wound with fresh towels. Lockwood was using other towels to mop up the blood from the floor.

But she wasn't dead. Her eyes were still open, and she glanced over at us as we entered.

They widened at the sight of Gen. "Cassie," she said. If she had a little more oomph, she might have shouted, but it was clear she was drained.

Mill and Lockwood looked up, their own expressions mirroring Iona's.

"What's she doing here?" Mill asked.

"Miss Cassandra, you really shouldn't have—"

"She was outside, she saw us come in," I said, trying to keep my voice level, not spook Gen with hysterics. "I couldn't just leave her out there."

Lockwood and Mill exchanged a look.

"Great. Just what we need right now," Iona said, voice still icy even in her weakness.

Gen stared. All the blood had drained from her face. I couldn't imagine how this all must look to her. These people she had never seen. Me, standing there looking like I did. All this blood.

"You aren't going to tell her," Mill said, giving me a very pointed look.

"Tell her what?" I asked. "She saw everything."

"That woman needs the hospital," Gen said quietly, pointing at Iona, her face as pale as a sheet.

"The hospital couldn't help her," I said.

"Then she's ... she's going to die?" Gen turned her tilted dark eyes on me, her braids swinging. "Cassie, what's going on?"

"Come here," I told her. I didn't think I could spill the beans with all their eyes on me. "I'm gonna try and get cleaned up."

She followed me back into the kitchen where I located the cottony scented dish soap, tossing a good amount into the sink before turning on the hot water.

How in the world was I going to start this conversation?

"Look, Genesee ... I'm sorry that you were drawn into this. I wish you would have called first."

"I was just trying to bring you and your family something to eat, especially after your uncle's accident." She was blinking. "Aw, man, my mom's casserole dish."

"That was very kind of you," I said. "Believe me, I'm really sad that I won't get to enjoy your mom's cooking tonight."

The hot water stung my fingers, but I was sure that part of that was because of the vampire blood. It never did nice things to my skin.

"What I am about to tell you is going to sound … well, crazy," I said. "But it's the truth. And it will explain everything you've seen tonight."

"… Okay?" she replied hesitantly.

This was it. I had made the decision. I was going to follow through.

I was going to look someone in the eye … and tell them about vampires.

Someone who knew I was a compulsive liar who'd basically had to leave town because of my web of lies.

Sigh. This was going to go well. "That woman on my couch, and one of the men helping her … they're … they're vampires, Gen."

Gen looked at me, first blankly—and then, perhaps realizing from the look on my face that I meant it—or, to her, intended to make her *believe* I meant it—she rolled her eyes.

"Same old Cassie," she said.

"That … is the truth," I said.

"You know, my dad used to tell me this old tribal saying," she said in a superior sort of voice. "'Listening to a liar is like drinking warm water. You'll get no satisfaction from it.'"

"I'm not lying this time," I said. "Look, vampires have come to Onondoga Springs. They are the reason that all of this trouble has been happening. The thefts, the attacks. The deaths. My uncle …"

Genesee crossed her arms, sighing. She leaned against the counter and gave me a pitiful sort of look.

Her sleeve shifted. A beaded bracelet hung about her wrist—a bracelet I recognized; there was a matching one in my jewelry box back in Florida. Tied with blue string, strung with tiny glass beads, ten years had frayed Gen's just as much as my own, dulled the turquoise …

Why had all this happened? Why had my life fallen apart like this?

Turning away, I scrubbed my fingers desperately under the water, wanting all of the blackness to be washed away. I wanted it to disappear.

My fingers trembled. My eyes stung.

"Cassie, why don't you tell me what's really going on here?" Genesee asked, dropping her voice. "No more lies. Who are these people?"

I continued with my frenzied scrubbing.

"We've been friends for a long time. Told each other some pretty crazy things. You can trust me."

"And that's exactly why I told you the truth," I whispered, squirting more dish soap onto my sore palms. The sink was covered in soapy, inky tar, the dish soap too—and my hands, so damned thick with it.

She looked hurt, as if I'd slapped her. "Look ..." she said, staring at the floor and intentionally not at me. "I know what happened ... was hard on you. And the move couldn't have been easy, given all that. But you seem ... different somehow." She glanced over her shoulder toward the living room. "I'm thinking you've fallen in with the wrong crowd down in Tampa ..."

"You can say that again." The water foamed in my hands. I wondered if I might need to pull out the bleach. Gen's eyes flashed in alarm and she looked toward the lounge.

"Not those guys in there," I said. "No, they're the good guys."

Gen's face hardened. "Then I'd hate to see what the bad guys look like."

"Yes." I shuddered lightly, remembering the Butcher's smile. "You really would."

"Cassie, are they trying to get you to do things that you don't want to?" she asked, dropping her voice. "Drugs? Drinking? Gang violence?" Her face went straitlaced. "Tide Pod challenge?"

"You think eating detergent does that to a person?" I pointed a dripping hand back toward where Iona lay, a couple walls blocking us from seeing her. Not for the first time, and I was certain not for the last, I lamented this stupidly huge hole I'd dug for myself by lying so much and so often for so long. One of my closest friends in New York was more willing to believe that I was some kind of drugged up crackhead—or detergent-chewing idiot—than that I was actually being honest about vampires.

"I know everything I've told you sounds absolutely insane," I said. "Trust me, I felt the same way when the first vampire came after me." I steeled my voice. "He nearly killed my parents to get at me."

Gen paused.

"Your parents were attacked? Like her?"

"Kidnapped," I said, "because I wouldn't give in to this one guy, Byron. He crushed pretty hard on me for some reason. I wasn't interested, so he got pissed. Tried to ... well, he tried a lot of things. Like taking my parents."

Gen remained silent, her eyes boring into the side of my face as I tried to dry my hands. My fingernails were still stained with the blood, but I had managed to get as much off as I could.

"It all worked out in the end, though. I managed to deal with him," I said. My voice was low, but steady.

"I ..." Genesee started, but she faltered. She shook her head slightly as if to clear it. "What do you mean ... dealt with him?"

I opened my mouth to answer—but she covered her face in her hands.

"You know what? Don't answer that. I don't want to know." She shook her head furiously. "I don't want to know what you're into. What you're actually into. Heroin, underage sex—Why does my brain keep going back to the Tide Pods?"

"It's ... in the zeitgeist," I said. "Genesee—"

But it was too late. She was already turning to walk away from me, braids swinging as she did.

"I can't believe anything you're saying, Cassie. And I don't want to. How could I, when the whole reason why you and your family left town was because of your lying in the first place?"

"Just give me a chance," I said, feeling the sudden surge of doubt that it'd do any good. This whole thing was a painful reminder of why my parents still had no idea they'd been kidnapped by a vampire. "I can prove I'm telling the truth."

"Save it, Cassie," Gen said, and I was stung with the memory of Jacquelyn's words to me just days before. How was it that all of these people that I had once trusted with the deepest parts of myself hated me so much?

"Gen …" My voice trembled. My heart sank.

She went to turn the knob of the door leading back to the garage, but there was a blurred image of silver and black from behind her. So fast I could barely even see it, until—

She crumpled to the floor, an unmoving heap—and over her, clutching a lamp—was Iona.

Chapter 21

It was the simple shock of the situation that kept me from throwing myself at Iona and separating her head from her shoulders. It was like a shield, blocking the rage that filled me as I stared at Genesee's unconscious form on the floor. Then—

"*What did you do?!*" I shrieked, hurtling across the kitchen.

I dropped to my knees on the cold tile beside Genesee, my shaking fingertips feeling for a pulse.

"She's not dead," Iona said, clutching at her sides. She held a wall of blackened towels to her chest with one hand as she stepped away from Genesee.

Genesee was not dead: I felt a steady *bu-bump* against my fingertips. Nevertheless, I glared up at Iona, my eyes wide and my face manic. "You could have killed her!"

Mill and Lockwood appeared in the kitchen, and I was certain that if either of them could have paled in fear, they would have. Their expressions demonstrated their distress enough.

"Madam Iona, you have certainly had a busy night," Lockwood said, deadpan.

"I know what I'm doing," Iona said. She sagged against the wall, what little strength she had waning. More dark blood appeared between her fingers, seeping out of the mound of towels. The choking, iron smell bloomed in the air in the kitchen. "I am a vampire, after all. I know how to knock a human out without killing them."

For the first time, it hit me that Iona was more closely related to my enemies than to my friends. In those few seconds, I hated her. And I hated everything that she represented in my life.

I snarled and went to leap at her, ready and wanting to feel her icy skin in my burning palms, but Mill had done his creepy speedy jump and was there to snatch me before I moved very far. He wrapped his arms around my shoulders, his hold as strong as steel. But gentle, too, surprisingly.

"Miss Iona ..." Lockwood said. His voice was calm but I could hear an unfamiliar strain in his words, and there was a twist at the corner of his mouth, as if he was restraining himself from saying more. "You really should be resting. I am certain there was something else that could have been done in this situation."

"Yeah, you didn't need to knock the kid out," Mill said.

"Seriously?" I asked, straining against Mill's iron grip. "She clocks my friend, and you two are like two Lords arguing about parliamentary procedure. 'Shall we issue her a stinging letter of reprimand for her terribly untoward behavior?' 'Yes, yes, I think we shall—care for tea?'"

Mill squeezed me more tightly. As if that would help me relax at all. I struggled against him harder, but he held firm.

"It's nothing personal," Iona said, sagging against the wall. "Something had to be done. Or would you prefer she call the police, and you try and explain your story about vampires to them?"

That ... was valid.

"But ... this?" I gestured to Genesee's limp form.

Iona shrugged. "It was the fastest way to get the job done. And if I had to hear you whine at her for the next half hour, I was going to end up drinking her out of sheer irritation."

"Are you serious?" I asked, but somehow I knew she was exaggerating. I hadn't even thought of the repercussions of Genesee leaving. "I just wanted her to stay so I could make her understand."

"Which was your first mistake," Iona said. She winced, sagging farther still. She was now halfway down the wall, and leaving stains. She'd overcome her pain for this brief excursion off the couch, but now it was mounting again.

Good. I was glad that she was suffering a little after what she had just done.

"If she told anyone—*anyone*—about this, it would raise all manner of questions. Which would be traced right back here. And who knows what a desperate police force might do if they found anything that looked like lead in their investigations?"

How was it possible that all of this had gone as horribly wrong as it had? Every time I got involved with vampires, my life spun out of control faster than I could even keep up with. People got hurt. I was constantly in danger. I lived in a constant state of fear.

Somebody let me off this train. It's going too fast, and I didn't buy a ticket for it.

"I did what I had to do in order to keep this from turning into a crime scene," Iona said. "Or a murder." She closed her eyes and leaned her head back against the wall, which was now dripping with fresh vampire blood. "Which would also turn this into a crime scene, I suppose."

Mill still gripped me tight. His icy touch, his presence, softened me somehow. His leather and bergamot smell brought me back to earth, slow.

I forced myself to think about what she was saying. I hated to admit it, but I could see truth in it. If Gen had left, she could have told her father. They might reach out to the local cops.

"Just because I can sort of see where you are coming from," I said, "doesn't give you the right to cold-cock my friend."

Iona once again shrugged, but the motion caused her pain again.

"What were you expecting from this?" she asked, a little trickle of blood running out of the corner of her mouth, black against her pale skin. Her normally perfect hair was tangled and matted with blood. "A little trip back home, down Memory Lane? You'd just waltz into town, see your uncle, and slay some vampires, barely breaking a sweat?"

"Iona, that isn't fair—" Mill said.

"What isn't fair? That she's thinking like the teenager she is? It isn't my fault that she wouldn't listen to a century of combined experience between the three of us. She's Pollyanna, Mill." Iona glared at him with a little more malice than usual, pain bleeding out into her words. She turned back to me. "Because when you're facing Draven's hunters, it doesn't go that way. It's not bloodless. It's not painless." She waved at the oozing towels around her midsection.

My cheeks burned. "I didn't think … it was going to be like this," I said. My blood rushed through my veins, pounding in my ears. I wanted to hide. Wanted to feel older and in control, and not like the kid Iona and Mill thought I was.

I had really hoped, deep down, that this time things were going to be easy. That we could come here, figured out the problem, and then leave. Go home. Move on with life.

Save the day.

It always worked in stories.

Iona snorted. "Of course you didn't. No plan. You challenged the hunters of a vampire Lord with no plan. Just a dream and a wish in your heart."

Throat burning, I hung my head, staring at a snag in Mill's sleeve. "I just thought …"

There was nothing I could say. She was right. This wasn't what I had wanted.

But it was what I got.

"It doesn't work like that," Iona went on.

"What doesn't?" I asked. "Fighting Draven? Or …" My stomach dropped. "Or coming home?"

For the first time that day, I saw a flicker of pity in her eyes. The sadness I had come to associate with her, the despair that she tried so hard to hide shone brightly for a moment before disappearing again. It was a strange sort of longing that I recognized, but couldn't put my finger on the origin of. She opened her mouth to answer, but then snapped it shut.

"It doesn't matter," she said. "What's done is done, and we have to deal with the situation as it is, not how we wish it was."

I swallowed, bile rising in my throat.

Lockwood knelt down beside her. "Come, Miss Iona," he said. "We need to tend to that wound. No more surprises. No more fighting."

She didn't argue as he swept her effortlessly up into his arms and carried her back out of the room. I watched them go, and decided that Lockwood was definitely more than human.

Mill exhaled as he stared at the dark smears on the pale, yellow wall of the kitchen that Iona had just left. "After everything we did to keep this place clean ..." His breath tickled the back of my neck, the cool brush of air against my skin causing goose bumps to appear. A slight chill ran down my back—and not an unpleasant one.

In that slow way he always spoke, Mill asked me, "If I let go, you promise you aren't going to race in there to strangle her?"

"Strangling her wouldn't do a damned thing," I breathed.

"Do you promise?" he asked. He wasn't being harsh, but it was firm enough I could tell he wasn't going to take any crap from me.

Ugh. Just when I'd gone a record twelve hours without being treated like a kid. "I promise."

"Are you telling me the truth?"

My anger flared again. "Seriously? This is how it is? Is everyone going to question everything that comes out of my mouth for the rest of my life now? I *am* capable of telling the truth, you know."

"Just checking," Mill said, and released his hold on me.

Gen lay crumpled at our feet, still unconscious. How long was she likely to be out? And wasn't there, like, an actual risk of brain damage if a person was out cold too long?

"We should get her off the floor," Mill said. "And Cassie? We might have to do one more thing that you aren't going to like."

"What's that?" I asked, then let my head sag forward. "You're not talking about taking her blood, are you?"

"No!" Mill looked as scandalized as I'd ever seen him, as though I'd accused him of something particularly vile. Which ... I guess I had. "We have to tie her up."

I gaped. "We can't—"

"We can't have her trying to flee when she comes around." He was firm.

Just great. Things already looked bad enough—and now this?

Our friendship was never, ever going to recover. Not once she woke up, and found herself tied up, unable to escape.

It was a high price to pay.

And yet, here I was. Ready and willing to pay it. "Okay," I said. "Dad used to keep rope in the garage. I'll see if … if he left some behind."

Mill nodded. Somehow he'd just convinced me that this— tying up my friend, keeping her prisoner in my house—was a good idea.

First I was liar.

Then I was a vampire slayer.

Now I was a kidnapper.

What the hell had happened to me?

Chapter 22

After some argument with Mill, we settled on putting Gen in the armchair instead of one of the dining room chairs. I said that if she had to be tied up, she might as well be as comfortable as possible.

Especially given the circumstances she would awaken to find herself in.

Iona had resumed her place on the couch, still bleeding. Lockwood was tending to her wounds. Mill had procured some bags of blood, the kind they use at blood banks, from ... somewhere. Hopefully a blood bank, and not some random person on the street who woke up wondering there was a needle injection site in their arm. I didn't really want to know, but I did watch as he pulled the bags from a cooler that he had stashed in the trunk.

A sticker that said *In Case of Emergencies* was stuck to the side of it in violent orange. I guess this was an emergency.

He was still clutching the bags in his hand when Genesee stirred in the chair. I watched as she blinked, her eyes out of focus.

"Where ... where am I?"

Her gaze sharpened as she saw me, sitting in the matching armchair in front of her.

"Don't scream," I said to her as she took in a sharp breath.

"Or I'll knock you out again," Iona said. Though she didn't look very threatening from the couch sprawled out like that. She put some force into her voice, though.

"What did you ... why am I tied up?" Gen said, struggling against the ropes at her wrist and ankles.

"I need you to trust me, Gen."

Gen threw back her head and laughed a high, panicked laugh. "Yeah, okay."

I bit my lip and looked around. Mill? Iona? Lockwood? Anyone want to help me out here?

No? Guess I'm by myself with this one.

"This ... was not supposed to happen," I said. "I really am sorry about ... uh ... everything. From the casserole dish to the ropes to ... you know. Your unconsciousness."

Gen looked at me as if I had grown another head.

"I'm sure that everything you've done here seems reasonable to you," Gen said, slowly. "But ... this is crazy, Cassie. And trusting you even under normal circumstances would be difficult given...what's happened." Her dark eyes burned.

"I understand that," I said, my patience starting to wear a little thinner. "I'm not expecting you to forgive me for everything that happened ... before. I just need you to find it in yourself to ... to just try and listen to me right here, right now ... and understand that whatever might have come before ... right now, I am telling you the truth."

Gen's brow furrowed. "You really expect me to believe anything that you say about vampires? Cassie, I'm still not sure that the explanation that you gave me for why you were moving to Florida was even the truth!"

I really did not want to have this conversation with her. Not again. I had hoped that she would have been able to move past it. See the good in me that I really hoped was in there somewhere. Deep inside. Beneath all the old lies.

"You are the biggest liar that I have ever known," Gen went on. "The whole town knows it. It was all they talked about at school after you left. Anything and everything you say is suspect, from the color of the sky to where you got those earrings. And if it pertains to anything that could involve you covering up for your terrible behavior? Pfft. Definitely a lie. Like this. This ..." She looked at Iona. "This ... *vampire* BS."

It was as if years of my inadequacies had found their way to the surface. Was it true that this was how she had felt about me all along?

Gen nodded to the group standing behind me, who were all irritatingly silent. "So … did you all know about her being a compulsive liar?

"I heard a little something about it," Mill said.

"Her lies are kind of the least of my problems right now," Iona muttered.

"I, for one, believe everything Lady Cassandra is saying," Lockwood said, gracing me with a smile of support.

"Congrats on hiring a gullible butler, Cassie," Gen said, rolling her eyes at Lockwood.

"He's not my—" I sighed. "Thank you, Lockwood." I shot a glare at Iona and Mill. "Thanks so much for your support, team."

"I took a knife to the chest for you," Iona said. "What else do you want from me? Hugs?" She raised an arm. "Bring it in. Right over here. Ignore the bloodstains, your clothes will be just fine." Amusement flickered on her face. "See? I can lie, too."

"Come on, what kind of idiot do you take me for, Cassie?" Gen asked. "You ran away from home with a biker gang—"

I loosed a hollow laugh. "A biker gang with a butler?"

"I'm not really a butler," Lockwood said.

"I look like a biker chick?" Iona asked.

"You look more goth to me," Mill said.

"So … like a vampire, then?" Lockwood asked. "Though you did look like a biker in front of Draven's building that one time."

Gen shook her head. "So … you guys got into a rumble or something with other gang members—"

"Like the Jets and the Sharks?" I asked. "Are you kidding?"

"I don't think I dress like a gang member," Lockwood said, looking down at his immaculate grey suit—a new, perfectly pressed one, which he had changed into as soon as we'd gotten Iona's bleeding under control.

Mill looked Lockwood up and down. "Maybe the Mafia? You could have stepped right out of *The Godfather* in that getup."

Gen was obviously getting angry at all of the crosstalk, but she pressed on. "Now you're here, trying to cover up your gang fight and hide from your parents."

I wiped my hands. "That's—"

"More believable than anything else you could say," she said. "Especially any stories about vampires."

"There's just one problem with the whole 'no vampires' thesis," Mill said. He knelt over Iona and pulled her shirt up, exposing the gaping wound in her ribcage.

"Hey!" Iona said. "A little respect, please? Treat my stomach like you would Taylor Swift's—oh, forget it. My mystique is gone."

"But your gaping chest wound is still present," Mill said, still holding up her shirt. He'd ripped the top of the tiny tube on the blood bag clean off, and thrust it into Iona's mouth as if it were a juice box. "But not for long."

I watched as Iona started sucking the blood from the bag, like a magnet was drawing it in, like a baby unable to stop herself. It was even more disgusting to see it in person than I had imagined.

I was sure that my own face reflected Genesee's; mouth gaping, eyes popping, horrorstruck. And as she drank, the wound—was it really shrinking? No ... my mind was just playing tricks with me. Vampires healed quickly, I knew—but like that? As the seconds passed, it became clear, though: it was definitely getting smaller. First it was the size of a fist; then a lime; then a half-dollar; a quarter.

"Ah ..." Iona sighed, pulling the bag from her lips after she had sucked out every last drop of blood she could pull. She laid her head back on the arm of the couch, grinning. Her fangs protruded, long and coated with a film of red.

"That hit the spot," she murmured, reaching up to snatch another bag out of Mill's hand.

"The ... the ..." Genesee stammered. "Her wound!"

"Maybe I do have some mystique left," Iona said, running her fingers over her flawless stomach.

The wound was completely gone. The only thing that showed Iona had been hurt at all was the dark, thick blood still shining on her shirt and around where the wound had been.

For as long as I had known about vampires, I had never witnessed that sort of power. It frightened me, reminding me in a very clear way just how unnatural Mill and Iona were. They weren't human, no matter how much they acted like it.

"Do you believe me now about vampires?" I asked quietly as I forced myself to look back at Genesee. I didn't want her to see the fear on my face. I did my best to hide it.

Well, maybe her seeing the fear was a good thing. Maybe it would really convince her that I wasn't messing around.

Genesee's stare moved back and forth between me, Mill, Iona, and Lockwood, as if trying to size us all up. I could almost see the gears turning in her head, fighting against herself as her eyes saw what they did not want to see, ears hearing what they didn't want to believe.

But there was no denying it now. Not even I would go to these elaborate lengths to pull the wool over someone's eyes, and I was supposedly the greatest liar in the universe from the way Genesee was talking.

Finally, Genesee looked back at me, her eyes like great shining chunks of ebony. And she nodded, stunned to silence.

Without wasting a second, I picked up the knife I had set aside for this very reason, and started to cut away at her bonds. There was no need for them anymore.

Iona grunted, her lips around another bag of blood, but I ignored her.

"She's not going anywhere now," I said.

And Genesee remained where she was even after I had undone the ropes, as if to prove my words true.

"Now ..." I said. "Let me start from the beginning." I glanced over my shoulder at Mill. "Could you get us some water? We're ... going to be here for a while."

Chapter 23

"Look … I was reluctant to believe that vampires were a real thing for a long time," I said, patiently to lay out the explanation for Genesee. She was watching me, hands twitching now that they were free of the ropes, like she didn't know what to do with them. "The only reason I finally came around to the idea was because one of them was chasing me, and I met Mill and Iona here," I said, gesturing to Iona's sprawled form on the couch.

She wiggled her fingers at us, still sucking away at the blood bag. My stomach twisted at that, and I did everything I could to pretend like it was one of those organic fruit squeeze things for kids.

"Think of all the stories about vampires you've heard," I said to Gen. "Most of them are true—super fast, super strong. Die with a stake through the heart. Need to be invited inside before they enter a home."

Gen's eyes narrowed as she stared at a place on the carpet. Then an eyebrow twitched, and her eyes grew wide. "Oh … Oh!" she said.

She looked back up at me. "Ohhhh!"

"Oh, look, you've blown her tiny mind," Iona said.

I glared at her over my shoulder. "Not. Helping."

"But …" Gen said, scratching her chin, staring at the floor again. "How? How can vampires be a real thing?"

"How are dogs a real thing?" Mill asked, leaning against the wall, arms folded. Iona shot him a fearsome scowl.

"Bad example," Mill said with a shrug.

"That is a fair question," I said, ignoring the other two. "One I still struggle with. They do a great job at hiding in plain sight. I mean, look at those two. If you didn't know they were vampires, you wouldn't think twice, would you?"

Gen looked skeptically at them.

"Ignoring the ... bag of blood in her hands," I said.

"I don't know ..." Gen said.

"Vampires are a real thing," I said. "They just are, and they have their own whole underground world. I've been there. I've seen it."

Gen stared at me, wide-eyed. "Like, in tunnels beneath our feet?"

"Not literally underground," I said. "I meant secret. Hidden from plain view."

"Tunnels are for filthy creatures," Iona said, irony-free, sucking on a bag of blood. "Like moles. And dwarves."

"Dwarves ... are real?" Gen asked.

I shot Iona a look. "When do you become helpful again?"

"I took a knife for you," she said, waving me off. "If that's not useful to you and your tender, non-regenerating organs, I don't know what is."

The gears were still grinding behind Gen's eyes. "So ... are they like Dracula or something?"

"Kinda-ish," I said. "But more like *MTV Cribz* with blood."

"*Lifestyles of the Rich and Famous*," Lockwood said, whatever that meant. "But paler."

Gen's skepticism didn't soften. She frowned at me, then lowered her head into her hands. "What am I doing here?"

I realized, again, that with my track record I wasn't exactly the best person to be delivering this news to her.

"Fine," I said. "I get it. I could sit here and tell you every last thing about what has happened to me over the last four or five months. But are you going to believe any of it?"

"I don't know," Gen said. There was a weariness hanging over her. It was late, after all.

"But you believe the vampire stuff?" I pointed at Mill. "I mean, you saw what just happened, right? I definitely didn't make that up."

"I'm willing to consider it," Gen said. She looked worn out. I knew the feeling. "Look, Cassie. This ... it's a lot to take in. To comprehend. To ... believe. Okay?"

I supposed that was an improvement, at least.

"My life has been insanity since I moved to Florida," I said.

"And it was so calm and peaceful before," Gen said.

I paused to look at her pointedly. "Do you want me to tell you? Or do you want to fill in the gaps with your own assumptions?"

I felt guilty about being snippy with her, but I was really getting tired of everyone acting like they knew everything that was going on. Gen definitely didn't, and if I wanted to gain another ally—or at least avoid her parents involving the police, I needed to get her to pay attention.

"I know ... I'm a compulsive liar," I said. "And I'm glad I got found out. At least, now I am. I was an idiot. I really was. What started off as something small and insignificant just ... got out of control. I was lying to cover up the stupid lies I'd already told, just adding webs and webs of lies on top of ..." I paused, took a breath. "I know what it looked like when it all blew up here. How much ... humiliation came down on my family. All those lies. About ... every damned thing. They cost me everything. Jacquelyn won't even talk to me now," I said, bowing my head. My thumbs chased each other nervously as I clasped my fingers together.

I sank back against the chair.

"I didn't mean to hurt her. Or you. Or anybody, really." I pursed my lips. "I know I did, though. And I'm sorry."

Gen's face was angry, her jaw working. She didn't say anything, though.

"You know what happened after that. My parents were so embarrassed and '*concerned*,'" I made quotes in the air with my fingers, "for my safety that we moved. We all know that wasn't it. They were embarrassed, and they wanted to leave town because everyone knew their daughter was the biggest liar on the planet, way worse than any boy who ever cried wolf or bear or—hell, vampire. They couldn't deal with that. And I don't blame them. Luckily, Dad had already been considering an offer from a hospital down there. He jumped all over it like the last pair of discounted Lululemon yoga pants."

My voice was quiet and even, but even I could hear the sadness in it.

"It cost me everything. Everyone. Everything that happened was because of *me*. I can't put the blame on anyone else. I started it. And I've had to carry it with me and own it this whole time. And let me tell you—it's enough to have to work through without having to completely uproot myself and move away ..."

Shame surged through me, making my limbs as weak as jelly. I couldn't look Gen in the eye anymore. All of this would have been way easier to say in a text. And not in front of Iona, who was definitely judging me hard. Or Mill, whom I was already confused enough about. And Lockwood ... pure, sweet, Lockwood. What would they all think of me?

"In Tampa, I was a nobody, with the opportunity to start a new life. Make new friends. No one knew me as a liar. I could start fresh. Not be a liar."

I took a slow breath. "Until I met Byron."

I told her about how he had singled me out for some strange reason, found me irresistible, and how I had made it worse by fighting back. I walked her through it all—every failure, every lie, every ... everything, through killing Theo, meeting Mill and Iona ...

And the end.

"My life is literally upside down. And now here we are," I said, looking around. "Back in New York because Draven is trying to smoke me out of hiding, trying to do everything in his power to scare me into appearing. Which is why all of these vampires have showed up here and started wreaking havoc." The memory of the Butcher's long knife twisting in Iona's chest flooded my mind. "The one we ran into at the hospital a little while ago said as much."

Gen's face suddenly changed. She looked down at her hands in her lap, seemingly lost in her own thoughts.

Then she looked back up at me and blinked a few times.

"What?" I asked. "Are you okay?"

She opened her mouth, a mystified expression taking hold. "I think …" she said. "These … people you're talking about …" She scratched the back of her head anxiously. "The vampires? They must be operating up near Old Bear Peak. That old nature lodge that's only open in the summer?"

Mill and Lockwood glanced at each other.

"Old Bear Peak?" I said. "Maybe. It's remote. Deserted. Probably easy to fortify."

"There's been some rumors that a pack of coyotes has been picking off animals around that area," Gen said, thinking about it as she spoke. "But … my dad said that coyotes wouldn't do as much damage as what's been reported."

"Vampires will eat wildlife," Mill said. "It's not what you want, but it'll get you by for a while."

"So … you believe me now?" I asked, turning back to Gen.

"About the vampires? …I guess," she said. Not exactly a ringing endorsement.

"And about everything else I just poured my heart out about?"

She gave me a non-committal look. "I dunno. I've seen you lie a lot. You've done better work."

My mouth fell open.

"I mean, how do I know that you didn't get these three on board with all of those ridiculous stories about these other vampires?"

"That's not …"

But why finish? What was the point? We'd hashed this out enough now.

I didn't want to go over what had happened here between us before I had left too. Maybe she didn't want to either. Maybe it was better to leave it in the past and just move on. Pretend I hadn't said everything that I had about it. About how I had felt. How I was feeling.

Still, I couldn't deny the dejection washing over me. She was the first person I'd really poured my heart out to about the whole thing. In front the vampires, too. And Lockwood.

That … stung.

"Where is this Old Bear Peak?" Lockwood asked.

"About fifteen miles north of here," Gen said.

"We should go take a look," Mill said, putting the remaining blood bags back the cooler. He kept a steady eye on Gen. "You should come with us."

I didn't say anything, but that raised an eyebrow. I got it a second later—Mill didn't want to chance her running back to her parents and spilling everything. They'd punch a bunch of holes in the story we'd just told her, and who knew what would happen from there?

Oh, actually, I did. Police. At my house. That's what would happen.

"Yes, and there are some more questions that I think we would be interested in asking as well, if you wouldn't mind," Lockwood said. I guess he got it, too.

"Sure," Gen said. "I'd like to see an end to all of this, if possible."

Some relief mingled with the crushing sadness that had settled over me. At least she didn't hate me so much that she wanted to flee as soon as she could.

"You could go home if you wanted," Iona said. "As long as you don't blab."

There was a pause. Silence. Trust Iona to just throw it all out there.

I closed my eyes, breath catching in my lungs.

"I wouldn't," Gen said, and I started breathing again. "But no, I ... I want to go."

Lockwood seemed pleased by her response. And I was too, even if it hurt to look at her directly. I didn't want to put her into danger, of course. But if she saw things first-hand, then maybe she'd eventually see I was telling the truth.

Maybe the rift between us could begin to close.

Maybe this would be the first step down a road that led back to how things were before.

Iona excused herself to change, and Mill disappeared to the garage. If I knew him, he was organizing supplies in case we were greeted by unwelcome visitors once we got to Old Bear Peak. Lockwood turned his attention to cleaning up the mess Iona had left behind on the couch ... and the floor, and the wall .... Butler indeed.

"Gen?" I asked, when everyone but Lockwood had gone.

I wanted so badly to see her smile at me in that easy way she used to. See the glint of excitement in her eyes at the secrets we shared together, our inside jokes. But there was this unbridgeable gap between us now, a valley that I wondered if I would ever be able to cross. She was guarded. Hesitant.

"All those things I said before ..." I said carefully. "That was all the truth."

She searched my face for a second, and I waited, hoping that she would feel this connection between us, see that I was still her friend, that there was good in me and we could go back to the way things were before, that I could be trusted—But a sad smile crept onto her lips. "Sure it was, Cassie," she said, patting me on the shoulder as she passed en route to the garage.

My heart sank.

"Sure it was."

Chapter 24

Iona, Gen, and I were all squeezed into the back of the Mercedes as we headed toward Old Bear Peak. Somehow, I ended up stuck in the middle.

Thankfully, Iona no longer stank of sulfur from all the blood she had lost. In fact, the blood bags had lit a fire in her. Some of her nastiness had been exchanged for sarcastic glee, and she was doing nothing to hide it.

"So …?" she asked, giving me an annoyingly curious stare.

"So what?" I asked, keeping my arms crossed firmly across my chest.

"So, tell me about what happened here before you came to Florida."

"Pass," I said, "I just went through all that."

Gen quivered a little at my other shoulder. Maybe the AC was up too high. Maybe the night was too cold. Whatever.

I turned to stare out the windshield. Part of me wanted to drink in all of the scenery that I had missed so much. The headlights played over the trees and hills, night like a veil over our surroundings.

"You left a lot out," Iona said. "'Oh, things blew up and bad stuff happened.' I want to know how, why. The details."

"Oh, yeah?" I asked. "You first. Why don't you tell me why you are such a—"

"Cassie …" Mill said.

I scowled at the back of his head.

"So the lying thing goes way back, huh?" Iona asked.

"Oh yeah," Genesee agreed easily. "She was a huge liar. For like … years and years. Since forever. We just didn't realize how huge until just before she left."

I gritted my teeth. Fantastic. Now I was literally *and* figuratively in the middle.

Gen went on, "She'd look you in the eyes after crashing your car and swear *you* were driving it, drunk, while *she* did it."

I scowled at her, my best impersonation of Iona's iciness. "I did not crash your car. And I have never been drunk, okay?"

Gen shrugged. "Just an example." But she sagged a little, withering under my glare.

"Which way do I turn here, ladies?" Lockwood asked, obviously attempting to defuse the situation.

"Left," Gen and I said together.

We drove past the park that Gen and I would play in every Saturday afternoon in the fall. We would practice ballet, have epic races, climb the trees beside the river that rushed through it.

Neither of us acknowledged it. Just a spot of green somewhere beyond the reach of the headlights.

"It's a long road winding up through the hills," I said, trying to shove the nostalgia mingled with sorrow out of mind. "It meanders through the woods for a half a mile or so before you even see the lodge. If we pull over soon enough, they won't even see us coming. We can scope it out from one of the hilltops nearby."

Gen nodded. "If that's where they are, you don't want to drive right up. Clear night like this, they'll hear you coming miles away."

We turned into the nature preserve when the sign came into view. Paint chipped, squeaking as it swung in the breeze, it was obvious that it had been there for a long time.

Lockwood pulled over before we had even crested the first hill. He turned off the engine, and then turned around to look at us.

"I will stay with the car," he said, his green eyes bright even in the dark, almost glowing. "I strongly suggest that you do nothing more than look. Any of you."

Mill nodded. "Iona, Cassie, you come with me. Gen, you should stay here with Lockwood."

"Uh, no," she said, shaking her head. "You guys owe me. You tied me up and knocked me out. I deserve to see what's going on here." She flicked an assessing glance toward me. She didn't say it, but I nevertheless knew what she really wanted: to see if Cassie lied about this, too.

"It's not safe," I said. "Seriously, we don't know what's down there."

Gen's face hardened. "Yeah, but I have a right to know, don't I? You guys were the ones who decided to involve me in this whole thing."

"No, you did when you showed up at my house—"

"To bring you some food!"

"Hey," Mill said, whispering with enough force to cut us both off. He pressed one of his large fingers against the small analog clock set into the dashboard. It was nearly five in the morning. "The sun will be up in about an hour. How far of a walk is it from here?"

"I'm going," Gen said, and she got out of the car and closed the door quietly behind her before I could protest.

"This girl was your best friend?" Iona asked, an eyebrow raised. "I can see why. I like her." That was my cue to leave the car too.

"This is just a scouting exercise," Mill said once he and Iona were out of the car. "We are *not* tangling with vampires with two humans along for the ride."

"Hey, I can handle myself," I said, pointing to the twin stakes in my hair.

Mill shook his head. "Not against someone like the Butcher. He's way out of our league."

"Speak for yourself," Iona said, whispering in the dark. Her voice carried, but not too far.

"Need I remind you who had a hole through her belly not even an hour ago?" Mill asked.

Iona's face flared with irritation. But perhaps recognizing that he had a point, she turned on her heel and marched off through the trees.

"Besides," Mill said. "We don't want to put Gen in any more danger. Got it?"

"Got it," I said, and stalked into the forest behind Iona.

Treated like a child yet a-freaking-gain. This whole experience was really souring me to damned near everyone. I walked a path I hadn't trod in a long time, following behind Iona at a reasonable distance. Gen and Mill trailed behind me even farther. Even though I had three people with me, between the lies and the conversations and the guilt and the blame … somehow I felt like I was walking all alone in the woods at night … into danger.

Chapter 25

The forest was dark, and I had never wandered along the paths of the nature reserve this far from the lodge. Except in the winter as a kid, with my dad. But then we had snowshoes, and it was the middle of a sunny day. We could see the whole forest from the hilltops, our breath hanging in the air around us like little clouds, cheeks stinging from the cold, crisp air.

Now it was dark, moonlight casting a dim light over every branch. Every crack of the twigs underfoot, every branch brushing against another sent a shiver down my spine. I wished that I had the vampiric night eyes. I wanted to be able to see the enemy before they struck.

On the other hand ... maybe it was better if I didn't.

After a few hundred yards, Iona fell into step beside me while Gen talked quietly, a dozen paces behind us, to Mill. I could barely hear their words, but the desire to know exactly what she was saying burned within me.

"I can see why you don't want to talk about your past with your friend," Iona said, the moonlight tangling with her perfect silvery blonde hair.

"Do you?" I asked. "Because if so, let's please drop it."

"I don't really know much about you," Iona said, apparently not taking my cue to shut up. "Your past seems ... colorful. Intriguing."

"Iona, seriously, I'm not going to tell you anything else." I shoved my hands into the pockets of my jacket. "Besides, why are you taking a sudden interest in my life? Why care now?"

Gen's voice carried to me—"So … do you drink blood, like, all the time?"—and I welcomed the sound if only to distract me from Iona.

"Every day, yes," Mill said. There was a touch of annoyance in his voice, but I was sure that she would have missed it. Mill sounded annoyed at the best of times.

But Iona didn't drop it. "We keep getting tangled up in these things. And you—you aren't quite the goody-two-shoes I thought you were when Byron first latched onto you."

I grimaced.

"For every meal?" Gen asked.

Iona rolled her eyes. "I haven't heard you ask any of these questions."

I ignored her.

"Yes," Mill said, as he might to a child who asked "why" too frequently.

"But, like, you throw in some other stuff, too, right?"

I saw Iona shake her head beside me.

"Like, lentils, maybe? I mean, a body like that, you definitely aren't on a totally liquid diet."

"No."

"No … dessert?"

"N—well, I do enjoy a fresh donut every once in a while."

"Wow, Mill," Iona said.

"Really?" asked Gen.

"No, I'm messing with you," Mill said. "I only drink blood, because when you become a vampire, your taste buds basically die with your body, and you're left with no desire to eat except to fulfill the craving."

The memory of him offering to take me for pizza floated to the top of my mind. Unexpected warmth filled my chest. He was a slave to his cravings, found no joy in food—and yet he'd been willing to do that for me?

"So … are you thinking about eating me right now?" Gen asked.

"Well, I wasn't when we started this conversation, but

yeah, I'm working my way to it."

The rustle of leaves told me that Gen had stepped away from him. "You don't have to be that way about it."

"Heh," Iona said. "She's been chattier with Mill in the last few minutes than she has been with you since she woke up."

I was really starting to wish that Iona would just walk away and scout ahead.

"So," Iona continued, apparently undeterred by my body language, which strongly indicated I wished she'd shove off, "if you aren't going to tell me what happened … will you at least tell me why you lie to the people you love?"

"I don't know," I said automatically. This felt like the interrogation from my parents, after it all came out, all over again. That had been a long night.

"What did you lie about?"

"Everything."

I was not going to give her the satisfaction of letting her push me into responding with any detail. I had no reason to tell her what had happened. I had come close enough to reliving it all when I was trying to plead with Gen to believe me. I had a feeling it would all resurface when I got here, but couldn't Iona see how much it was bothering me?

But maybe that was exactly why she was being so persistent about it.

"How did you get caught? It sounds like it ended pretty spectacularly."

"Not the word I'd choose for it," I said, sympathizing with Mill for his irritation with Genesee's incessant questions. We were kindred spirits in that regard.

"We're getting close," I said, hoping to cease conversations on both sides. "We should probably keep quiet now."

But though Iona dropped her voice, she didn't stop asking questions. "You really don't want to talk about this, do you?" she whispered. "It makes me even more curious about what you're hiding."

If I didn't still feel bad about the fact that she had been impaled just a few hours before, I wouldn't have hesitated to stake her in the arm right then and there. Iona certainly knew how to get under my skin.

We crested the top of the knoll, and even at this distance, I could see the lodge. It was nestled on a nearby hilltop, a few scarce lights shining from deep inside the building.

If this was where the vampires were hiding out, it was easy to see why no one had bothered them. Cops never came out this far. At least not at this time of year.

"Guess Gen's theory was right," Mill whispered as the four of us stood there, surveying the situation from under the cover of a large oak tree.

"But those could just be ordinary people," Gen said. "How do we know they're vampires?"

"Look," Iona said, pointing at some shadows I couldn't quite make out at this distance. "Guards."

Mill nodded. I guess he saw it. Vampire eyes.

"Didn't you say it was just a nature preserve?" Iona asked.

"Yeah," Gen said.

"They're walking a patrol. Those are definitely guards." Mill stood up, tensing, a hand against the tree. "This is it." He set his jaw. "This is the place."

Chapter 26

"Decent place for a hideout," Iona said as we stared out at the lodge across the nature preserve. "I can see why they picked it. Isolated. Defensible."

We were all hunched behind a wide oak tree, trying to make as little sound as possible. The air was chilly for late April just before dawn. The smell of pine trees was more familiar to me than the smell of the salty air in Florida, even though it had been months since I had been around it. It was a scent I knew I could never forget.

"We need to be careful," Mill said. "I'm just able to hear them. If we speak any louder …"

"Wait, is that the Butcher?" I asked, pointing to a figure standing just beneath one of the lamps along the path leading to the lodge. He was wearing all black, and his bald head was uncovered, the moonlight making it look like a glowing orb in the darkness. Something glinted at his belt as he turned. Impossible to make out from here, with my human eyes— but I was certain it was his knife.

"It is," Iona said, tensing against the tree. "I'd like to sink my teeth into him and pull his windpipe right out of his body."

"This place is impenetrable," Mill said. "At least it is for us, with what we've brought."

"There's got to be thirty of them wandering around over there," I said with a sinking feeling. Even looking at the way I'd ramped things up since Byron, dealing first with one vampire, then four, there was no way the three of us could take on nearly three dozen vampires.

"That's probably not even all of them," Mill said. He sighed heavily. "Too many vamps. Too many ways this can go wrong."

"Then the next logical thing is to take some more of them off the streets before we even think about fighting here," Iona said. "Because storming this place as is would be suicide."

"I can't even see a way that we could get in without being spotted," Mill said. "The entrances are covered."

"Not to mention that it's on the hill. So, they would be able to see us coming whichever way we tried to sneak up," Iona said.

I groaned. "Well, this is hopeless."

Gen craned, squinting at the forms moving around the building. "Wow—kinda hard to tell from here, but … vampires look like regular people."

Mill stared around at her in disbelief, holding his arms wide like, *y'think?!* Gen's cheeks colored. "Oh, sorry. I didn't mean to … um … suggest that *you* didn't look like regular people. Or that you were weird. For wearing all black. At night."

Iona stared blankly at her.

"You shouldn't go jogging like that, by the way. It's dangerous," Gen said.

"Thanks for the tip," Mill said.

"What about Lockwood?" I asked.

"He wore grey," Gen said. "Not black."

"I meant he could help us," I said. "He's strong. And … not human."

Mill and Iona exchanged a look. "It's not his fight," Mill said.

"He's a driver," Iona said. "You shouldn't involve him that way." She sniffed. "Actually, you shouldn't have involved me in that way, either, but … here I am. Again. In the thick of this mess. Having my already dead internal organs ripped to pieces, as though they haven't already experienced enough trauma by dying once—"

"Fine," I said. "It's the three of us against a small army sent by Draven. I don't like those odds."

"It's really just two of us," Mill said. "Iona and me."

"What?" I asked. "Come on. I've proven that I can handle myself—"

"What about me? What am I? Chopped liver?" Gen asked.

"More like warm neck steak," Mill said.

"Mill, you can't seriously expect me to sit this one out," I said.

"I never said you should," he said. "But keep your voice down. We don't need to draw any attention."

I lowered my tone, but pressed on. "I've never seen Lockwood fight."

"He can hold his own if he has to," Mill said. "But Iona's right—it's not his fight. And even if it were, this is too much—for all of us."

"Draven will have sent trained fighters," Iona said. "Not drama queen, club-going shmucks, love-drunk idiots like Byron, or some gang of vampires more interested in posting photos on social media than actually doing harm. These are killers, straight up. Worst of the worst."

I seethed. My first two outings with vampires had made me innately familiar with fear. The way she told it, Byron and Roxy were like child's play. Nothing compared to what was to come.

Why was everyone always so intent on treating me like some damned kid? The Butcher was scary and all, but … was he that much worse than Byron, my own personal stalker, determined to drink my very life's blood while quoting Shakespeare to me? Or Roxy, who was ready to feed me to Draven to save her own hide?

I didn't think so.

Gen, thankfully, was keeping her own opinions to herself.

"We should go," Mill said. "Daybreak is coming."

"Why does that matter?" Gen asked.

"Sunlight and vampires go together about as well as fire and explosives."

"Oh," she said blankly. "Right."

Turning tail, we made our way back the way we'd come. Our lonely footsteps rustled the leaves as we made our retreat. Gen's questions resumed, quietly, and Mill fielded them in his usual short, tight-lipped manner. I ignored them both.

Iona didn't start up again though, and I was glad of that; I had my own things to be thinking about—like how in the world we were going to deal with thirty vampires, for one.

Unfortunately, no answers came.

Chapter 27

The ride back to the house was a quiet one. Mill was staring out of the window. Iona was browsing through social media(!) on her phone. Gen's hands were folded in her lap, and she wouldn't meet my eyes though I felt her gaze on me several times.

We got home just before six, and that was a good thing, because as we pulled into the garage, the first red of dawn started to bleed over the horizon. Birds sang in the trees—familiar sounds that I realized with a pang that I hadn't heard for months. The ones in Florida were so different. How had I already forgotten their songs, when I'd heard them literally every day of my life?

I helped the vamps get down into the basement, leaving Lockwood upstairs with Gen. I wasn't looking forward to spending time alone with her, which was weird, because normally I would have given my left arm so we could catch up on life in general.

I wanted that back. But like everything on this trip—and my whole life, lately—it didn't seem poised to happen.

"What are you going to do today?" Mill asked as he lay down on his air mattress.

Iona had dragged hers to the far side of the room, as far away from Mill as she could get, and was lying with her back to us, the light from her cell phone casting a faint glow around her head like a halo.

"I'm not really sure," I said. "Maybe go see Uncle Mike

again? Maybe just go … look around the hometown."

Mill watched me patiently, resting on one elbow. I could see the concern in his eyes.

I tried to ignore the burning in my cheeks as he stared at me.

"I'm sorry all of this is happening," he said. And just like that, for the briefest of moments, somehow the weight on my shoulders seemed lighter—as if, with that simple statement, he had shouldered the burden with me.

I felt an immense gratitude at that, one I didn't have the faintest clue of how to put into words … and a great wave of bitter sadness.

"G'night, Iona," I said.

She didn't answer.

I climbed the stairs and shut the door with a resolute click, not feeling any better about anything. It was as if I had swallowed a large stone, and my entire body was protesting it. I was exhausted. Muscles were aching, my joints sore. The dings and bruises from last night's scuffle were starting to ache.

Lockwood was in the kitchen, and had somehow procured an apron from … who knew where. He was standing at the stove, a hissing pan in his hands.

"Breakfast, Lady Cassandra?"

As if I wasn't embarrassed enough in front of Gen right now.

"Yeah, sure," I said, sliding into one of the cold, wooden chairs at the small table in the middle of the kitchen. The chair felt wrong, the table felt wrong. Out of place, probably because the ones that had been here in the kitchen my whole life were in Florida now. These were interlopers, and didn't belong here anymore than I did anymore.

Gen was pushing some scrambled eggs and bacon around on her own plate, shifting around in the chair beside me. It didn't look as though she'd taken a single bite yet—worried Lockwood was poisoning her, I guessed.

"Do they sleep?" she asked.

I shook my head. "Sorta, I think. I don't really know."

Lockwood turned and placed a steaming plate of eggs and

bacon in front of me. My mouth watered as the salty, smoky smell met me. I dug in greedily.

"They do sleep," Lockwood said. "During the day, usually."

"So they can't go out in the daylight at all?" Gen asked.

I chased the food with a chilled glass of orange juice that had somehow appeared beside my plate, then said, "They can, but only if they have the right gear. Iona wore like a motorcycle helmet and spandex riding suit this one time. It let her walk in sunlight."

"Why not just dress like that all the time?" Gen asked. "Then they could go anywhere they wanted."

"It can be less than one hundred percent effective, on especially sunny days, in direct light," Lockwood said. "And a visor so dark that no UV rays can penetrate it is also dark enough that even a vampire can't see through it." He smiled. "Why swim against the tide when it gets you nothing in return? Most vampires choose not to brave the light when the night works better for their purposes."

"Safer, sure," Gen said. "That makes sense."

"So … now I have an entire day of doing whatever I want to while they rest up," I said, leaning back in my chair, nibbling on another piece of bacon. Food was definitely helping my mood. I hadn't realized that I had been moving from hungry to hangry.

"We will find productive things to do," Lockwood said. "We won't waste the day. I know that's what you are concerned about."

"Lockwood, you didn't have to do this," I said, stabbing some more eggs with my fork. "It's delicious, don't get me wrong."

He turned, drying the pan with a dishtowel he must have found in a drawer, smiling. "I'm glad you like it. Sometimes there's nothing better for the spirit than a meal."

The morning light was starting to flicker through the swaying tree branches. I watched as it sparkled, the leaves dancing in the breeze. I was glad to be back here, instead of Florida, where the humidity alone was suffocating.

And even though it meant no further progress with the

vampire problem here in New York, it was hard to deny that I was kind of grateful for twelve hours or so without vampires. Without grunting from Mill or prying questions from an increasingly salty Iona.

It meant I could pretend my life was almost normal … and also not get treated like a kid.

"Yikes," Gen said, glancing at her watch. "I gotta get home. Been out all night. School. You know."

I could still sense the tension between us as she rose from the table, walking her plate to the sink. Lockwood took it from her and began scrubbing it clean.

She gave me an impressed raise of her eyebrows.

A flicker of relief. Maybe things weren't totally ruined between us.

"I'll walk you to the door," I said, also getting up.

We stood there awkwardly, looking everywhere but at each other. I decided on my sneakers.

"I'm sorry about last night," I said. "Iona is a little … impulsive." What I had wanted to say was *Iona is insane, and if you haven't realized that by now, then you weren't paying attention*, but I didn't think that would be the best way to earn her friendship back.

Gen shrugged. "After everything I saw last night … I guess I can kind of get it."

"I never meant for you to get involved in any of this," I said, grateful she was actually listening to me. "And I'm sorry we kept you out all night. You'll fall asleep in Ms. Carpenter's class for sure."

"I would have anyway," Gen said, chuckling under her breath. "And I guess I'm going to have to explain where this goose egg on my head came from." She reached up to gingerly touch the swollen bump there. Another shrug. "Oh well. I'll come up with something." Her eyes flashed. "I'll channel my inner Cassie."

I didn't flinch, but that stung. "You aren't going to say anything to your folks, right? About what really happened here?"

"No." She shook her head. "I'll just tell them we got caught up talking about everything, and we passed out on the couch like we used to. That was the truth enough times, they'll believe me."

I nodded. "Yeah … okay."

"I'll see you later," she said, pulling the door open.

The cool morning air rushed in, mingled with the smell of pine and earth.

"Cassie?" she asked, after stepping onto the porch.

"Yeah?"

"Be careful, okay? Don't get yourself hurt."

I smiled. "I won't. I promise."

Gen's face fell. "And don't make promises that you can't keep. That's just another form of lying."

With that, she turned and started off back down the driveway.

Lockwood was waiting for me as I closed the door. Still wearing his apron, he had a hot cup of tea in his hands. He pressed it into mine.

"She'll come around, Miss Cassandra," he said. "Just give her some time to process it all."

"That probably would have been easier if Iona hadn't nearly killed her."

"The friendship you have with her is a strong one," Lockwood said with that same smile. "The sort of friendship that is unaffected by miles or years. Something like this, while incredibly difficult to accept and believe, is just going to make you stronger together."

"I hope you're right," I said.

He patted my shoulder. "You should take this opportunity to rest."

"Yeah," I said, but even as I did, I knew that even if I were to lie down, sleep would not come. "I'll try."

I took a hot shower and forced myself to think of nothing aside from getting my hair clean. Mill had packed mini shampoo bottles, the little ones they had in hotel rooms, in addition to the clothes and dental hygiene stuff. I scrubbed and scrubbed, my already raw hands suffering under the hot water.

Once I was done, I threw on the most comfortable clothes that Mill had packed for me and crawled into the bed in my room.

The blinds were closed, the curtains pulled shut, but it didn't matter. My body knew it was daytime, and my internal alarm was telling me it was time to get up for school. Gen was probably getting ready right now—or trying to. With six siblings, she usually had a fight on her hands to get into the bathroom in the mornings.

Xandra, all the way back in Florida, was probably getting ready, too. As happy as I was with having her as a friend, I suddenly realized how little I knew about her in comparison to Gen. Xandra and I might have bonded over vampires, but that wasn't the same as having been friends with Genesee for fifteen years.

When had everything become so complicated?

I had thought I'd never see this bedroom again—and despite my pining for home, I had been okay with it. The last few nights I had spent in this room before moving were some of the worst in my life. I had either been screaming at Mom and Dad, or they had been yelling at each other. No matter how many pillows I had piled over my head, no matter how loud the music was blaring out of my headphones, I couldn't drown out the sounds of their voices. But even worse were the long, uneasy periods of silence where no one dared speak at all.

Or the silence. Whichever was hanging in the air at the time. The silence was worse than the screaming.

I rolled over away from the window, clamping my eyes shut.

Sleep, Cassie, sleep. But all I could think about was how much pain I'd caused them, both Mom and Dad—in the lead-up to moving, and then again, with all this vampire business in Tampa. We'd moved, tried to turn over a new leaf—but I was still the same old Cassie. They were probably going out of their minds right this minute, in fact, working with police to figure out where I'd gone.

I punched the mattress. Things shouldn't be like this.

This was all Byron's fault.

This room that had once been my sanctuary had become my jail cell during the last days of my time here. And how was it any different now? I didn't want to leave it, didn't want to have to face my parents back then. Didn't think I could handle it. Didn't really *want* to handle it.

I couldn't run from the past. All of the lies that had come to the surface had just as strong of a grip on me now as they had back then. It didn't matter that Mom and Dad were so far away. Their presence still lingered here in the house, all of that unhappiness, that sorrow once it all blew up. It clung to the walls like a stain.

I sat up and yanked open the curtains. Dawn was breaking, bathing the world outside in a beauty that was just out of my reach.

There was nowhere I could go, nowhere I could hide. My life was spiraling out of control—again—and it was like I could only sit here and watch it happen.

I got to my feet, knowing that staying in bed was only going to make things worse for me. My mind was my own worst enemy, and in order to combat it, I needed to ignore it. It was just after seven. Visiting hours would be starting at the hospital soon. Maybe Lockwood would be willing to swing through my favorite coffee place on our way there. Uncle Mike loved Americanos. In spite of his worries about caffeine clashing with his meds, it might cheer him up if I brought him one.

I found Lockwood in the kitchen still, putting away all of our dishes from breakfast. Last night's clothes were washed, dried, and now sat in three neat, folded piles on the table: mine, Mill's, Iona's.

"Lockwood, you should really get some rest," I said.

He just smiled at me. "I don't really sleep all that much."

Strange. He had been the one to drive us the entire way up here, and now gone through another entire night without sleep?

Who was Lockwood? Really?

"Can't sleep either?" he asked, folding Mill's jacket on top of his clothes pile.

I shook my head. "No. But I was wondering—could you take me to the hospital? Unless you want to stay here with them. I could take the car. I'll be back before dinner."

Lockwood smiled in a way that reminded me of my dad. "That's quite all right. Master Mill and Miss Iona will be just fine here. Besides, it wouldn't be safe for you to go out alone."

Figures.

As we stepped out of the house and into the garage, I cast a look over my shoulder at the interior of the house before sliding into the front seat of the car.

So many memories.

All tainted by the last days here, when my lies blew up ... and ruined everything in my life.

They still were.

If I never came back to this house again, I would be the happiest person in the world.

Chapter 28

It was a little easier to walk in the front doors of the hospital when I knew that I wasn't going to be waylaid by some crazy vampire assassin. Still, the chemical, sanitized smell of it wasn't any more appealing than last night.

What an awful place for a person to spend their last hours or days.

And what a morbid thought that was.

Still, I had two cups of steaming hot coffee clutched in my hand; Uncle Mike's Americano, and my French vanilla latte. The warmth from the cups seemed to seep into my bones. For a second, it would have been easy to believe that things were sort of normal for a second.

Sunlight always made vampires less scary than they actually were.

I rapped on the door to his room with the back of my knuckles, careful not to slosh hot coffee all over my hand.

"I'm decent," Uncle Mike called. I let myself in to a room that seemed starkly different from less than twelve hours ago. Bright light spilled in through the window, shining across pale, cheery blue walls.

"Hey, kiddo," he said from the bed, with a smile—only it was much more reserved than the smile he'd given me last night.

Alarm bells rung.

I pushed them aside for now.

"I brought you some coffee," I said, passing him the cup.

"Americano, just how you like them."

"Thanks," he said, but he didn't move to drink it. He just held it between his hands for a few seconds before setting it on the food tray beside his bed. Something was definitely wrong—no denying it, and no ignoring it either. I had to face it head on. "Okay," I said. "What is it?"

His jaw clenched, and then he looked up at me, his hazel eyes guarded.

"Cass, there's something that we need to talk about."

My stomach plummeted to the floor.

"Is it something to do with the attack?" I asked, almost hopeful that it would be.

He shook his head. "No, no … I'm fine. I'll be able to go home in a day or so."

I exhaled sharply. Okay, good.

"Your mom called me last night, Cass. Right after you left."

Damn. Even braced as I was for bad news, my stomach dropped.

It was a no brainer that they would have figured out where I was eventually. My entire life, pre-Tampa, was here. All my friends, the rest of our family. Everyone. Everything. Of course she would check here.

"I covered for you," he said, quietly. "But it sucks that I had to lie to my sister." He just shook his head, not looking at me. "What were you thinking, Cass? And how did you get up here in the first place?"

"Some friends of mine got me here," I said.

"Friends, huh?" Uncle Mike asked. "Not school friends, I'm guessing, because your mom said your bestie down there was pleading ignorance." Now he stared me down, unblinking. It wasn't anger in his eyes; that would have been easy.

It was disappointment. Brutal, choking disappointment.

From Uncle Mike. The only person who … when everything blew up …

Hadn't treated me any differently.

"What if something had happened to you?" he asked softly. "What if you had gotten hurt?"

"I'm fine," I said, my cheeks burning.

"Cassie," he just shook his head, "I don't know what's going on with you. I figured after everything that happened maybe you could use one adult in your corner. That I … I didn't have to land on you like a bomb the way your parents did." He looked away again. "But maybe I should have. You cut out of school and came halfway across the country without even telling your parents where you went. But your mom knows now."

My breath hitched. She knew?

My coffee cup, forgotten in my hand, trembled.

"How?" I asked.

"They didn't activate the alarm at your house," Mike said, his gaze finding me again across the short distance between us, "but your mom gets an alert whenever someone opens the doors. She got one yesterday. Then another. And there were no showings scheduled with rental company, so …"

Oh.

Oh, no.

"I hoped they were right when they decided to move," Uncle Mike said, shaking his head. "That maybe you really just did need a fresh start. But … I guess it didn't take, huh?"

A wild impulse to just spill everything almost overtook me. But I clamped down on it. It would be just the same as with Gen last night; I'd look like my penchant for lying knew no bounds. And without Mill or Iona here to prove anything …

"Your mom isn't stupid, you know," Uncle Mike went on. "We were all kids once too. We did dumb things. Maybe not quite to the level of going cross country as runaways, but … I've made my fair share of rash decisions. Done dumb things as a kid. And an adult."

I let out a low, hollow laugh. Kids, huh? What I wouldn't give to be the teenager who snuck out to drink beer and make out with her boyfriend and then get caught for it. Oh, how much easier my life would be.

"I'm serious," he said, voice hard. "You can't keep doing whatever you want to, whenever you want to. Your choices affect other people, especially your parents. When are you going to realize that you have to start taking responsibility for your actions?"

I had heard these words a hundred times before, but never from Uncle Mike. From Mom, Dad, even Aunt Becky and Uncle Carl. But never Uncle Mike.

"Ugh," he said, making a face like he'd taken a bite of something terrible. "Did you hear what I just said? Me? I said that. Yuck. I'm supposed to be the cool uncle, and now I'm talking to you like …" He hung his head, the picture of revulsion.

"Uncle Mike, I came up here to see you," I said. "To make sure you were okay."

He rolled his eyes. He *actually* rolled his eyes at me!

"Don't bullshit a bullshitter, Cassie," he said, and there was that disappointment again.

"But I—"

"Just … stop," he said, and there was such sadness in his voice, in his eyes. "Please … stop lying to me."

His words stung.

Worse than getting physically assaulted by a vampire.

Worse than Mom's grounding.

Worse than running for my life from Byron that first night.

I tried to blink away the tears that were starting to pool in my eyes. I was not going to cry. None of them understood anything. They just assumed that I was this bad kid who was bent on being selfish and stupid.

I had heard condemnation so many times that I should have gotten the word LIAR tattooed on my forehead for the whole world to see. Wear it like a badge of shame.

But the crushing feeling that came over my heart, breaking it clean in two, was that his tone told me that all this time, while I thought he was the only one to see the best in me, he really had seen me for what I was—and had been too kind to call me on it.

I swallowed hard, unable to look at him.

There was nothing I could say—no words I could give that would make this better.

I got up from the bed, shuffled over to the door, and tossed my untouched latte straight into the trash can before walking out into the hall.

I kept my tears at bay until I was safely back in the parking lot.

Chapter 29

It wasn't until I was sitting in the car sobbing my eyes out that I realized how wonderful Lockwood really was.

He didn't ask me what had happened, didn't press me for information. He just passed me a box of aloe-scented tissues, along with bar of chocolate. I blubbered my thanks, and Lockwood patiently drove around town until I had calmed down.

Then he offered to take me out to lunch. I declined, at first, out of politeness. But he insisted, said eating might make me feel better—so eventually I directed us to a local diner called the Blue Oak Café.

Spending time with Lockwood alone was odd for just how *normal* it was. He ordered food like a normal person. Ate a cheeseburger like a normal person. And asked me just often enough if I was doing all right like a normal person. Never once did he ask about my uncle. And I was grateful for it.

We left the diner, and the next thing I remembered I was waking up in the back of the Mercedes, slumped against the window.

"What happened?" I asked, sitting up and staring at the clock. It was a little after two in the afternoon.

"You fell asleep as I was driving," Lockwood said, setting aside his newspaper. "I knew you were exhausted. I assumed it would be best to let you rest."

Geez. I hadn't done that since I was a kid.

"Well … thanks," I said.

I looked out of the window. We were parked at the library. I knew everything here far better than I did anything in Florida—as a matter of fact, where *was* the local library in Tampa? Onondoga Springs might be run down, the streets damaged by snow and covered in potholes, but it was hard to deny how homey it felt in the daylight. Yes, at night, when a vampire attack might lie just around the corner, it felt wrong … but with the sun shining, my life not endangered, this place was just *right*.

"Hey, I think I'm going to take a walk around the town," I said, unbuckling my seatbelt.

"Oh?"

"Yeah. I want to wander around. Clear my mind."

"As you wish," Lockwood said, and he turned the key in the ignition. The car rumbled to life. "If you aren't opposed to it, I shall follow you at a short distance. Just in case you grow tired of walking."

Or in case vampires decided to do their thing. He didn't need to say it. I got it anyway. And I wasn't going to argue with him about it. He'd do it whether I wanted him to or not.

When I lived in Onondoga Springs, I never walked around town just because. There was always a place to go, someone to see. I never wandered just to wander. But now that I was here, it felt like a shame to pass up the opportunity to refresh my memories of the little old town.

And yet, very quickly, that sense of having returned home left me. The farther I walked, the more changes I noticed, stark even in their smallness. The cool air on my face may have felt familiar, but it wasn't mine to enjoy anymore. The budding trees were a nice sight, but soon they would change right along with the seasons.

The low mountains scraped across the sky in the distance, hills that I had once taken for granted. Florida's sky seemed so big, so vast. It was as if you could walk right off the ground and be swallowed by its expanse. Here, the hills fought for control of the horizon.

How was it that everything felt so different in such a short period of time? We had only been gone a few months, and it was as if the entire town had forgotten about us. Everyone seemed to have moved on. Our absence changed nothing.

How insignificant was I? A green Camaro passed me by, one I knew by sight. Unlikely the driver recognized me though—and if he did, he didn't look. I was, after all, just background.

Maybe if things hadn't ended the way they had, then my homecoming would have been happier.

Maybe it wasn't the town that had changed, but me.

That made more sense, honestly. So many things had happened since moving to Florida.

And here I was, still wrapped up in the same nonsense as I was down there, intermingled with all of the nastiness I had left behind me back here in town.

I wondered if there ever would be a way out of this for me. Every time I reached a conclusion of some sort, another problem arose. Was facing Draven the true end to all of this? And if that was the case, then what hope did I have of living long enough to see it through?

I sighed.

I had never felt more alone, more isolated from everyone I cared about in my entire life.

Up ahead on the sidewalk, a tall, thin girl was making her way toward one of the local nail salons. Her dark, wavy hair fluttered behind her as she walked, her nose in her cell phone.

My heart skipped a beat. I recognized that hair!

"Jacquelyn!" I called before I could stop myself—her name already tumbling out as I remembered out last phone call. She turned, gaze settling on me. A beat—then recognition dawned.

Her jaw dropped. "Cassie?" She did not smile.

"What are you doing here?" she asked. So much for a warm welcome.

"I did used to live here, you know," I said.

"Yeah, but … you were in Florida still when we talked the other day, weren't you?"

"I was, yeah," I said. "I just got in yesterday."

Her eyes narrowed. "Is that why you called to ask me about

what was going on around town?"

"Caught me," I said, and then with a surge of horror, realized I shouldn't have. Stupid Cassie. Wrong thing to say to the girl who got mixed up in all of your lying.

She didn't seem pleased either.

I cleared my throat, looking around, trying to force conversation now I was committed to. "So … how was school today?"

"Wouldn't you like to know," she said, but then a nasty grin spread across her face. "Gary was wondering if I wanted to go to a little Italian place for dinner with him this weekend. He says it's very romantic."

It was like she'd slid a barb under my skin.

I pasted on a smile. "That's great, Jackie. I really am happy for you."

"Look, Cassie, it was great running into you. *Really.*"

And I was the liar here?

"But I have things I have to get done today. Maybe we can grab some coffee or something before you head back to Florida."

Wow. Two lies in one shot. Maybe I'd rubbed off on her. Maybe it was too strong calling that a lie. But she didn't mean it—that much was clear from her voice. It was just a way of extracting herself from the conversation as gracefully as possible. There was too much water under the bridge for us. The realization was like a smack across the face.

My actions had consequences—and too much had happened for forgiveness.

Shoving my hands in my pockets, I nodded and produced a lie of my own. "I'd like that, Jackie. I really would." At least a half a lie. Because in spite of her acidic attitude toward me— I meant it. I honestly did.

But … it was never going to happen.

There was a blur of motion beside me, a rush of wind as something flew toward Jacquelyn.

The stench of fresh blood followed right after it. A vampire, its hand wrapped around Jackie's neck.

Covered head to foot in the same black leather that Iona had worn to protect herself from the sun, the vampire's masked face stared right at me over Jacquelyn's shoulder. Not a sliver of his skin was showing.

We should have been safe.

How could this be happening?

And then there was another, standing behind the first on the sidewalk, slowly stalking up the sidewalk, not making a sound as it went.

Another appeared behind me, and a fourth on the other side of the street, a long, shining knife clutched in his hands.

The Butcher.

Jacquelyn tried to scream, but the vampire's other hand had already closed over her lips.

There was no doubt about it.

Surrounded by vampires on a city street.

My former best friend their hostage.

I was in way over my head.

Chapter 30

There was no time to react. No time to run. No time to fight back.

It was just me and Jacquelyn one moment, and then in the next second, they were there, cat-like and ready for battle. And unlike the parking lot fight at the hospital, this was a battle they would surely win.

My veins flooded with ice. My heart slammed against my chest. The vampire behind me closed in, a low chuckle in his throat. I forced myself to think of Mill's training. Focus. Remain calm.

But how can someone remain calm when they are already terrified out of their mind? Snatching a stake out of my hair, I wheeled about—thrust, banking on the element of surprise— The stake bounced harmlessly off the vampire's armor.

Oh. That made sense. Armor under the motorcycle gear. Double protection from the sun. I stared, eyes wide and wild. Jacquelyn struggled, legs thrashing. Muffled grunts came from behind the hand clamped over her mouth. The Butcher meandered over, almost casual.

His knife, cleaned of Iona's blood and shining once more, glinted in the afternoon sun.

I had nothing. No protection. No other weapons. Unless I was able to get them to take their armor off or find a weak point, there was nothing I could do.

That was it. Standing in the middle of my hometown. This

was where I was going to meet my end. Jacquelyn stared at me, bug-eyed.

Expecting—hoping for—me to help.

And I couldn't.

Then—the vampire in front of me crumpled with a sudden cry.

Lockwood stood behind him. A silver-tipped stake in his hands was dark with vampire blood.

Lockwood moved with the grace of a dancer past me, a look of grim determination that I had never seen etched on his face.

The vampire behind the one clutching Jacquelyn stepped in front of Lockwood, as dark and fluid as a shadow.

Lockwood moved in to strike, his movements so fast and accurate it was like a scorpion's tail striking its prey. The Butcher surged for him—

"Lockwood!" I gasped—

But it was too late. Lockwood had been so invested in the other vampire that the Butcher had an opening. The blade sliced through the air, whistling as it went.

I watched as it sank into Lockwood's shoulder, like a hatchet into a log.

"NO!"

He teetered forward—blood spilled—

My horror died in my throat.

His blood was ... *silver?*

... What?

Silver blood? Another scream, a yell of pain—and I realized it came from the Butcher. He doubled over, leg clutched tight, a thin stake jutting from between his fingers. I stared at it, utterly stupefied at this turn of events—

And then I was swept up into the air, my feet leaving the ground, my ribs colliding soundly with bone.

Lockwood had thrown me over his shoulder, and he was tearing down the street.

"Lockwood, no!" I shouted, reaching back toward the vampires.

"My friend! They have her!"

"I'm sorry, Miss Cassandra," he said, his breath coming in

painful gasps.

The Butcher was still struggling against the stake in his leg while the other two were holding onto Jacquelyn, who was doing everything she could to get away short of breaking her own back. She was still gagged by the one vampire's hand—and being dragged backward—away.

Her eyes were desperate, panicked—on me.

This couldn't be happening. Her eyebrows arched, as though she were about to cry something to me—

And then in a blur they had vanished.

Lockwood surged back to the car—opened the door—and set me inside, buckling me in.

I let him. My entire body was frozen.

Jacquelyn was gone. And once again—it was my fault.

Chapter 31

The drive to the house passed in a fog.

Mill was there at the door to the basement when we got home, asking Lockwood all sorts of questions that I only half comprehended. He bent down and scooped me out of Lockwood's arms. I didn't even protest.

Jacquelyn. My friend.

Stupid best friend cliché —we met the first day of kindergarten. Her hair was long even back then, tied up in two pigtails with pink bows. She was standing in the corner of our room, looking around nervously. I'd walked over and told her that I liked the rainbow pony on her shirt. Her eyes had widened and she smiled at me.

We played together every day after that.

In second grade when the boys were teasing her about her crush on one of their friends, I stepped in and told them all that they were acting like a bunch of babies. When one of them, a big one, tried to challenge me, I pretended to cry and scream (lying already). When a teacher found us, the boys got in trouble and never bothered us again.

My favorite memory was in eighth grade. We had been at the mall. Genesee was with us. We had gone to the candy store and purchased as much licorice and chocolate and sour candies as our little purses could hold before heading to the movie theater and watching the same movie three times in a row. It was all Jacquelyn had wanted for her birthday that year.

I buried my head in my hands; the tears hadn't stopped since I had realized what had happened.

I had let her down. Not only had I betrayed my friendship with her, but I had allowed her to get taken by my enemies.

"Cassie?"

I looked up through my fingers, my vision blurred with tears, and saw Mill and Iona standing over me on the couch, looking down at me.

Lockwood had found his way to one of the armchairs. He had draped it in one of the painting tarps we had used for Iona before sitting himself in it.

What a guy. Keeping his silver blood off the upholstery while gravely wounded. Wonderful Lockwood. Kind-hearted. Ever thoughtful about others.

He had a towel clamped to his injured shoulder, and though I couldn't see it, the image of his blood, silver and stark, came rushing back to me. My confusion caused some of the fog to retreat. Eyebrows knitting, I asked, "Lockwood … what are you?"

"Cassie, that isn't really important right now—" Mill began.

"Did you know he has silver blood?" I said, pointing over at him. "I mean, I figured that you weren't human. At least, I wasn't entirely sure—"

"Cassie." Iona had stepped over. "This *really* isn't important right now."

I gaped at the two of them.

"Why can't anyone here … just treat me like an adult?" I asked. "Why do you just assume 'oh, she's a kid, she doesn't need to know'?"

"Because it doesn't concern you," Iona said.

"It sort of does," I said. "He's been driving me all around kingdom come, and I'm just now confirming he isn't a human?"

"You haven't had an issue with either of us not being human," Mill said, gesturing between himself and Iona.

"That's not the same, nor is it the point," I said. "Neither of you are claiming to be human. It's a tacit lie, playing human when you're not. Trust me. I know lies."

"Obviously," Iona said. Lockwood flinched, as though I'd

hit him.

Shame filled my chest. "Oh…no, Lockwood, I'm sorry," I said quickly. "I didn't mean it like that. It's just—"

"I understand, Miss Cassandra…" he said. But I saw the hurt in his eyes. The damage had been done. He had done so much for me since I had met him. Taken me so many places. Protected me. Gave me advice.

Today, he'd saved my life.

And how did I repay him?

By calling him a liar and getting angry that he didn't tell me everything about himself from the very beginning. Tears burned my eyes. I closed my eyes on them, teeth gritted, face downturned.

"I'm sorry," I said again, but it came out as more of a croak than a whisper.

"Is someone going to tell us what actually happened?" Iona said, her voice cracking like a whip.

"If I may, Sir, Miss," Lockwood said. "I think Miss Cassandra needs a few moments to catch her breath."

Another kindness I didn't deserve.

Oh, Lockwood … He recounted the day briefly, including our visit to Uncle Mike, the visit to town.

When he explained the vampires arriving suddenly, surrounding me and Jacquelyn, Mill gritted his teeth, as if the news caused him real, physical pain.

It ratcheted up when Lockwood added, "Our new friend was there, too."

"The Butcher?" Mill asked, his voice sharp.

Lockwood nodded.

"What happened?"

"They surrounded the girls. One of them grabbed her friend, and I was only able to just grab Miss Cassandra away from them."

"At the expense of yourself," Iona said, sending another wave of guilt crashing through me.

Lockwood inclined his head.

"I tried," I said hotly. "My stake just bounced off their armor."

"Armor?" Mill asked.

"A motorcycle suit like Iona's—"

Iona's brow furrowed. "Couldn't have been the same," she said.

"I know," I said, shuddering. "It had plating beneath. Extra protection. And they were out at this time of day. Scary. Nowhere, and no time of the day is safe anymore."

Mill scratched his chin. "Draven must have some scientists on this," he said. "New York seems like a pretty decent place to test it. The sun isn't as strong or as high in the sky."

"But that's bad news for the world if it works," Iona said. "Like, really bad news."

"I understand," Mill said. "My guess is that they still can't stay out for very long. It was probably supposed to be more of a snatch and grab maneuver. They didn't expect Lockwood to show up. Or that he was anything more than a driver, most likely."

"I mean, that sort of fully protective armor really isn't possible, is it?" I asked nervously, hopefully.

"I don't know …" Mill said, shrugging.

"Miss Cassandra, I am sorry that we didn't help her. There was nothing I could do," Lockwood said.

"I know, Lockwood," I said. "It was only because of you that I got away at all."

"Silver-tipped stake?" Mill asked.

"Right into the Butcher's calf," Lockwood said. "Very fortunate that I had it. Ordinary wood couldn't pierce that armor, as Miss Cassandra said."

"Do you think we can rescue her?" I asked.

Mill and Iona exchanged a look that told me everything.

My heart, my everything … I just sank. "I'll take that as a no."

I sighed and sank back against the couch, feeling like the world was pressing in on me from all sides.

"It's all my fault," I said quietly.

Mill sat down on the couch beside me, putting his hand on my knee. My heart skipped a beat as I looked into his eyes.

I could never actually decide what color they were. Normally when I was seeing him, it was dark and it didn't matter. But under these brighter lights overhead that help trick your brain into thinking that you weren't actually underground, I could see little flecks of silver and green in their smoky blue depths.

"Cassie …" he said. "It is not your fault."

Iona clicked her tongue, looking away.

"It isn't," Mill said. "How could you have known that the Butcher and his squad were capable of going out in the daylight like that?"

"But if Jacquelyn hadn't been there, she would have been safe. Or if she had walked away just a minute before …" I shook my head. "It's because of me, and her connection to me that she was taken … so it *is* my fault."

"You don't know that," Iona said. "They're attacking people randomly, and this town has … what, five people in it? The law of averages says she would have been coming up soon."

I blinked at her. She'd managed to insult my hometown and not make me feel better all at once.

"Iona is sort of right," Mill said. "Though she could be a bit more tactful. And you and Lockwood did everything you could have."

"Except actually help her," I said sadly.

"You'd have died if Lockwood hadn't saved you," Iona said. "Four of them in armor, against you? The only hope you'd have had of freeing your friend would be throwing yourself at Draven's servants and hoping they got so overexcited about bagging the big prize—you—that they forgot all about your friend."

"Well, I should've done that, then," I said.

Iona snorted. "They would have taken her anyway. Just to be sure."

Mill cut across us before the argument could progress any further. "It doesn't matter what you might have done differently. Hindsight is always twenty-twenty, right?"

He was right, but it didn't make things any easier for me. Guilt roiled through me.

Why had I thought coming here would go any other way than this?

I should have known better. I should just leave everyone in

this town alone for their own protection.

It was me that Draven wanted, after all.

Anyone else he hurt was just collateral.

"Cassie, when was the last time you slept?" Mill asked.

I honestly didn't even know.

"She hasn't slept much since we've arrived," Lockwood said. "Though she did manage to squeeze in a small nap just before our confrontation with the Butcher."

My whole body sagged against the couch. It was as if I was made of lead.

"You're exhausted," Mill said.

"Bags under your eyes, dear," Iona said.

I glared at her.

"Come on, you need to go sleep," Mill said, taking my hand and pulling me reluctantly to my feet.

"We can't do anything until it gets dark anyways," Iona said. "You might as well use the time wisely."

I was reluctant to shut down for the afternoon when my friend was in danger, but ...

"You'll take care of Lockwood?" I asked.

"Of course," Mill said. I glanced to Lockwood. "I hope you know that I wasn't angry at you ..." I said, doing my best not to gaze at the silver-soaked towel pressed to his shoulder. "It's just ..."

"Everything," he said, nodding his head amiably. "I understand. No harm done, Miss Cassandra."

I nodded, then climbed the stairs wearily.

Mill and Iona moved to tend to Lockwood as I reached the landing. I closed the basement door behind me, and sagged against it.

Climbing the stairs to my bedroom, sinking down onto the mattress, all I could see was Jacquelyn's face. Her terror. Knowing that something terrible was happening.

My inability to do *anything* to save her.

I drew the curtains on the afternoon sun, hoping it would draw the curtains on my thoughts too.

It didn't. Yet somehow I slept.

My dreams were fitful. I chased Jacquelyn down long halls, and she was always out of reach. She called out to me, screaming, her cries muffled. I finally caught up, reached out—

But she was as pale as a ghost, and she burst into flames.

I shrieked, and sat up in bed, panting, gasping for breath—

And then coughing, my eyes stinging.

Smoke.

An alarm blared out in the hall.

It was dark out, but there was a bright orange glow from beneath my curtains that flickered as if it had a life of its own.

Burning.

The house was on fire, and I was inside of it.

Chapter 32

It's every kid's worst nightmare to be stuck inside their house as it burns. They never skimped on the details in school. They made you live out the experience by sticking you inside a fake house and then making you find your way out. Any time the alarm went off while mom cooked dinner, children shuddered in fear, anticipating that crawl.

But to actually experience it, to register somewhere deep in my brain that my house was actually on fire, that was on a whole other level.

A veil of thick smoke filled the air, choking in my throat. It heated my windpipe on the way down, tasting of hot ash—and my lungs burned with each breath that filled them, as if the fires burned inside me too.

I squinted into the murk. The orange glow of flames cut through it, but the smoke stained the air, painting a grey, grainy cloud of gloom between me and the window. It stung my eyes too, so even if I held my breath, I was still assailed—and I needed my eyes now more than ever.

"Cassie!"

The calls came through the blaring fire alarm.

"Cassie, are you okay?"

It was Mill. Muffled—a floor below.

"Yes!" I called, jumping out of bed, throwing open the blinds. Dark shapes milling around in the yard, and even from this distance I could tell they weren't animals.

The vampires had found us.

"Cassie, you need to get down here, now!" Mill shouted. "We don't have much time!"

I looked around, knowing full well that all of my childhood training told me to not waste time looking for material things, but I couldn't leave the house empty-handed.

A few stakes, and a vial of holy water were all I had in my bag. Shoving them in my jeans with trembling fingers, I prayed that Mill had more downstairs with him.

I gingerly touched the doorknob—a quick check to ensure it didn't scald me—and then yanked the door open and shrieked.

It was as if I had stepped into an oven. Heat like I had never experienced rushed at me. The smoke was worse here, coming in a grey-black deluge that blocked out everything more than two inches in front of my face. I coughed, pulling my shirt up over my nose for some protection.

Flames licked up the walls, spreading out from Mom and Dad's old room.

With a lurch of sadness, I headed for the stairs in the opposite direction.

I raced down them, seeing glowing, dancing light from the landing.

"Cassie, here!" Mill loomed out of the smoke at the bottom of the stairs, reaching up for me.

The last two steps danced with fire.

"You're going to have to jump!"

I didn't hesitate. I sucked in my breath and jumped off the step. Heat licked at my ankles—and then Mill caught me. But the heat didn't stop.

"Cassie—!"

I looked down to see—

My pants legs had caught.

I shrieked, batting at the flame. Mill squatted and swatted too, extinguishing it with sharp strikes that would've hurt if not for the fact I was already distracted by the pain of freaking *fire* eating my ankle.

My jeans were scorched. Tattered holes looked through to pink, blistered skin. At least, I figured they'd be pink; a layer of ash covered them at the moment.

"Can you walk?" Mill asked with furrowed eyebrows.

I tested my weight, and nodded. Painful, probably excruciating once my nerve endings started growing back. But at least I could walk.

"Let's go!" he said, and we raced toward the front door.

Iona and Lockwood were there. Iona was supporting Lockwood, and she carried a solitary bag in her hands.

"They have the entire place surrounded!" she shouted over the alarms and the roaring flames. Something overhead cracked and snapped. A wooden frame; perhaps a piece of furniture. "Every exit is blocked. We have no choice but to head out and fight."

"What happened?" I asked.

"Not really sure," Mill said. "We were in the basement when the alarms went off. We came up just in time to see some of them lobbing Molotov cocktails at the side of the house. I'm guessing they saturated the roof in gasoline before they lit the place."

"They must have followed you and Lockwood," Iona said, sounding slightly strained. She had a nasty burn through the sleeve of her jacket. "By the time we got up here, they had completely surrounded the place."

There was another crashing sound, followed by a groan of metal.

"Our time is running short," Lockwood said. "I suggest we leave and hope that facing whoever waits outside is better than being burned to death."

I pulled a stake from my pocket. Mill gripped my wrist, his palm cool and icy and so, so welcome in the scorching heat of my childhood home going up in flames all around us.

"Stay close to me, and behind me," he said. "This is not the time to play hero. Understood?"

I nodded. I didn't feel like this was the time to bicker with him for treating me like a kid.

Hell … my childhood home was burning down.

We were surrounded by vampires.

I really was a kid in all this.

"On three—" Mill said, grasping the door knob. "One … two…"

He yanked open the door and dashed out. I kept close at his heels.

It was a flurry of motion as soon as we stepped outside.

The cold night air hit me like a wall after the heat of the fire, but there were vampires on every side, closing in on Mill and me.

But Mill was ready. He grabbed and pushed and flung enemies out of his path. No killing blows, no launched holy water or stabbing out—he was clearing a path, buying us freedom rather than expunging Draven's minions.

A vampire appeared out of the shadows, lunging at me.

I ducked, let it sail over top of me—and, taking no guidance from Mill, staked it through the back. It yowled—and I moved on, hoping I would get out of here alive to savor the death cry later.

Iona had set Lockwood down just beside her. She was holding her own as well, though in an entirely different way than Mill. Where he was all charge and power, she was sleek, fluid, graceful even. One of her kicks passed flawlessly into a dodge, then into a pinpointed punch to the throat of her opponent.

Another vampire lunged for me—

Mill swept in. He stilled the attack with a ferocious uppercut that sent the vampire sprawling backward—then he shoved me firmly against the trunk of a tree. Bark dug into my back, jolting white-hot pain through me.

We were boxed in—yet it stopped vampires from attacking from behind, for now.

"Get ready to run when I say." Mill launched an opponent into the air. He hit a trunk with a loud crash; if he had been a human, his spine would have broken clean in half. Since he was a vampire, he got right to his feet and back into the fight.

"Ready?" Mill asked, snapping another vampire's neck, its body crumpling.

"I think so," I said, still pressed against the tree, wobbly, definitely not at all ready.

"Okay—run! Head for the driveway!" Mill shouted. I dove past Mill's hulking, V-shaped body—

And stumbled back with a gasp as the Butcher leered down at me, blocking my path. The dancing light of the fire threw his face into stark contrast. His eyes were dark, glinting. His fangs, protruding over his lips, were as white as snow. He sneered, his long butcher's knife held lazily at his side.

As a human, that knife scared me more than his teeth did.

My life felt like one long nightmare. Every time I thought it couldn't get worse … it got worse.

"Cassie Howell …" the Butcher started, and my heart fell to my feet. "Just the girl I was hoping to see."

"Cassie—" Mill cried—and then was snagged by the shoulder, pulled backward and around by two vampire fighters. "Let—go!"

They did not relent. Assaulting him with a flurry of blows from each side, Mill had to duck and jag frenetically to have any hope of dodging their attacks.

I was on my own. Other vampires moved in, flanking the Butcher, their faces flickering in and out of clarity in the blazing firelight.

"What do you want?" I said, buying time again, and hopelessly aware that I could not hope to fight my way out of this one.

And how did he know my name? Wasn't he still under the assumption that my name was Elizabeth?

A stray thought cracked through in a blinding flash.

They'd confronted me in daylight. In armor.

And I'd been wearing none.

They knew I wasn't a vampire now.

The Butcher knew.

His face split into a wicked grin.

"We're just finding out all sorts of interesting things about you on this trip, *Cassie*," he said, and my skin prickled in fear. This all felt far too familiar … Roxy's face flashed across my mind, the same sneer of victory on her own face. "I really thought you were a kindred spirit there, for a while. Someone who could appreciate the joy of killing our own kind." He laughed. "But then … you're not 'our own kind' at all, are you?" His eyes glowed. "I didn't think you looked like much, but I have to admit—I'm a little impressed. Because a

ROBERT J. CRANE

vampire who kills vampires? That's a rare breed."

He swelled, like a peacock flaunting its tail feathers. The other vampires around were watching after him in great admiration. An alpha wolf in the company of his pack. "But a human who does it ... ?" He waved the knife, glinting the fire light. "That ..." He nodded with satisfaction. "Well. Truly. My hat would be off to you—if I wore one."

The Butcher turned to a vampire beside him and jutted his chin into the night. "Bring her here," he said.

More vampires appeared out of the night, surrounding me, blocking me from Mill and Iona.

This ... was so very not good.

A circle formed, tight around me, blocking my flight. Fangs everywhere, glinting in the night, the cold air coming from one side and the heat of the fire from the other. Dark eyes flickered, reflecting the flames, and from beside the Butcher came another shadow, stepping past him into the impromptu circle.

Her long, black hair spilled over her shoulders, hiding her face as she stepped into the light. She wore nothing more than a white dress that was flecked with dark, smeared spots. She stood straight and tall, and when she tossed her hair out of her face, I hit the ground, knees giving out and slamming into the lawn.

"Jac ... Jacquelyn ..." I breathed.

She was a vampire.

The whole world swam around me. Suddenly, nothing mattered anymore. I had lost. Even if I somehow, some way survived this, I had lost. I had brought a *friend* to a fate worse than death.

I might as well have been the one who'd stopped her heart myself. Numbness swept over me. My ears rung.

Every thud of my heart in my chest was accusing.

Jacquelyn blinked at me. Her once pretty face was now grey and sallow, her irises tinged with red that had little to do with the fire.

"Jacquelyn ..." I said, my knees shaking. "Jackie, I am so, so sorry. I never meant—I never wanted ..."

Tears choked my words dead. She only stared blankly back.

168

The Butcher laughed. His cohorts joined in, a cacophony of howls in the night.

"She told me everything I'd ever want to know about you," the Butcher said. "About your friendship. All your lies. Your family."

"You leave my family out of this," I said, my throat searing in pain as if I had torn it.

I was *so done* with all of these vampires meddling in my life. I was fed up with their taunting, their tricks, their schemes. They were evil, all of them.

And all I wanted for every single one of them to *die*.

My childhood home burned behind me, an uncontrollable blaze that suddenly felt like a perfect symbol for my life. Worse: it marked another crossed line. Vampires had already seen to the ruination of my life in Tampa. Now they'd meddled in my past, hurt Uncle Mike—and destroyed what remained of a life I could only look back on wistfully, tainting that which had been untainted.

Bastards.

I was not going to take this lying down.

Draven's vampires had stolen too much from me, too much that I would never be able to get back. Now they had stolen one of my friends.

I pulled a stake from my waistband and stood facing the Butcher, tears still staining my cheeks, all fear gone, replaced by a low, burning rage and determination. I twirled it in the tips of my fingers.

The Butcher threw back his head and barked a laugh. "Oh, I like you." The others joined him, laughter echoing in the night. "You see this, Jackie? Your little friend has spunk. She thinks she can take us on."

The smile vanished from his face as quickly as it had appeared.

"Kill her."

Jacquelyn flung herself across the distance between us, her teeth bared. Firelight danced in her eyes.

I braced—

She steamrolled into me, her body cool but not quite cold, the last warmth of her human blood still fading in her veins.

But she was powerful, more than she ever had been in life, and the impact sent me reeling backward—

"You have no idea how long I have waited to get back at you for what you did to me," Jackie growled, her voice guttural, lower than it had been in life, as if her vocal cords had been mangled—

"I really am sorry," I told her—and I ducked her arms, sliding out of her embrace and sidestepping, achieved thanks to a combination of my training and her total inexperience as a vampire. "I hope that you can forgive me someday."

"Never!" Jackie shouted, and she lunged again.

I pulled the tiny, cool bottle of holy water out of my back pocket, uncorked it with my teeth, and to her surprise, threw my arms around her neck as she collided with me.

In the fraction of a second before she shoved me away, I flung the tiny, open vial past her—and toward the Butcher.

The vial struck the arm of his jacket, the arm that was holding his knife at his side. It splashed all over the sleeve— then rushed down to meet his skin.

Mill had told me that the pain from holy water on bare vampire skin was about as agonizing as concentrated acid on human flesh. It hissed, smoking where it struck him. He screamed and dropped his knife, clutching his injured hand with his other. Jacquelyn stared in horrified confusion at her new master's distress—

I shoved past her, surging for the Butcher himself.

As I leapt, I yanked the stakes free from my hair, ready to stab—But he had already recovered. Still agonized, his expression distraught, he lurched away from me—

Two other vampires leapt into the space between us, snarling.

I didn't have time to react. Carried through ash-filled air by momentum, I hurtled toward their clawed embrace, dragging my stakes up and hoping desperately that I could plunge them home—

Then something solid grappled me from behind. I was pulled backward. My hair whipped out in front of me—

"Lockwood!" I shouted.

He was carrying me underneath my arms and my knees like

a sleeping child, and we were hurtling away through the trees, through the woods behind the house, the vampires, the roaring fire and the destroyed house disappearing quickly behind us.

"Nice aim, Miss Cassandra," he said, smiling at me, his green eyes bright in the dark. "That little stunt surprised everyone. Even me."

"Where are Mill and Iona?" I asked.

"Distracting them," Lockwood said. "The other vampires were entirely too focused on what was happening between you and the Butcher. Lost interest in us rather quickly. Mill took your holy water trick as a chance to attack from the back. Iona followed. They should be here …"

And as he said it, Mill and Iona appeared as blurs beside us.

"I'll take Cassie," Mill said, and Lockwood passed me to him as we ran. "Iona will help you, Lockwood. Let's run."

The trees rushed passed at a blur, the wind making my eyes water. But it was better than the sting of smoke from my burning house. So, too, was the cool air, filled with the scent of damp wood.

Mill's arms were tight around me, more comforting than he would ever know.

I closed my eyes. The trees barreling toward me were too much.

"Where should we go?" Mill asked. "Where is a place we could lay low that's close?"

"Gen's house," I said, pointing through the trees to the east. "Just on the other side of the road."

He turned on a dime and dashed off.

I glanced over his shoulder. Bright, golden flames fanned out, lighting the night, consuming my past with unstoppable power.

I closed my eyes again. I couldn't bear to look at it for another second.

Chapter 33

We reached Genesee's family's property a few minutes later. It was downhill from my house, and as we stood out on their back porch, I could just see the smoke from the fire as it burned in the distance.

It still didn't seem real. I wasn't sure if it ever really would.

I knocked on the door, and to my immense relief, Genesee answered.

"What in the world are you doing here?" she asked in a whisper, slipping out onto the porch, closing the door behind her. "And why are you all such a mess?"

I pointed over my shoulder up at the house. Black, oily smoke was billowing up into the sky, visible against the twilight by the orange inferno lighting it from beneath.

Her eyes nearly popped out of her skull.

"Get in," she said. "Go up to my room. Go quietly."

I waved the others behind me as I stepped over the threshold.

Genesee's house had been more comforting than my own some days. Any time my parents and I were arguing, really. It smelled like burning wood from their stove—no longer quite the welcome scent it had once been—but it also smelled of warm spices; cinnamon and nutmeg.

Where my house was orderly and modern, Gen's house was colors and fabrics, a happy hodge-podge of all sorts of furniture. Handmade tables, knitted blankets, couches covered in slipcovers, and lamps straight out of the eighties.

I snuck Iona, Mill, and Lockwood through the kitchen to the stairs at the back of the house. The television was on in the living room; whoever was watching it was enjoying a baseball game. The cheers from the crowd carried through the house.

We made our way up the carpeted stairs to the room at the end of the hall.

Gen had the best room. Her large four-poster bed, covered in a green quilt her mother had made, stood against the back wall. Her window overlooked her front yard, which gradually sloped upward into the forest where my house lay.

Fire danced behind the trees through the glass. I looked away.

Lockwood closed the door behind us. His phone was pressed to his ear.

"Hello, fire department?" he asked. "Yes. I would like to report a fire on Forestview Avenue. Yes. I was driving by and saw the smoke. I think it's a house fire. Yes. Thank you very much."

I blinked at him. I hadn't even thought about that ...

"That will keep the vampires away for a while ..." he said, replacing his phone in his pocket. He located Gen's desk chair and sat down in it, and I realized with concern that he was looking rather pale. "Plus, it will help give you the chance of possibly salvaging ... something."

I sank onto Gen's bed, head in my hands. "My parents are literally going to kill me now."

Consequences, I realized. I was finally seeing the consequences to all of my actions. Everything was coming full circle. I messed up, people got hurt.

A vast, echoing emptiness filled my mind. The house wasn't the worst of my problems.

Mill and Iona hovered beside the window, gazing out into the darkening night. The moon hung near the horizon, just visible as a sliver through the trees. Stars were probably out. Outshone by the fire, though, I couldn't see any of those twinkling specks.

"Some place she has here," Iona said, looking around at all of the knick knacks and collectibles. She lingered on a porcelain doll in traditional Native American garb.

I couldn't tell if she was being nasty, pensive, or it was her form of a compliment.

Gen's door opened, and my stomach lurched painfully until I saw Gen squeeze inside, closing it behind her.

"Wow, I don't think I've ever had this many people in my room all at once," she said, looking around at us all.

"Are both of your parents home?" I asked. "I'm so sorry to just show up like this, but—" I pointed at the window again.

"No, just Dad. And he won't come up here. I told him that it wasn't anyone."

"Lying to them is easy like this, isn't it?" I said with a tight smile, mirthless.

Gen didn't reply immediately, but she cringed a little. "It's not lying to them that's the problem. It's—"

"When it's all you do," I cut in for her. "When it consumes you. When you don't even need to tell a lie to cover up for another lie, you just do it because ... it's habit. Yeah, I know. Compulsive, remember?" I pointed to myself.

Gen came to sit beside me on the bed, concern coloring her cheeks.

"What happened, Cassie?" she asked. She looked down at the bottoms of my pants. "Your legs ... you're been burned."

"Boy, have I." The lies. The consequences. Oh, and literally.

She frowned. "We need to get something on those. Hold on, I'll go get the first aid kit."

Just as quickly as she left, she was back with her arms full of bottles and a red tin box.

She knelt down in front of me.

"Listen, Gen, you don't have to do this. I'm fine. I can—"

"When are you going to stop refusing help from people, hmm?" she asked. She took a pair of scissors and started to trim away my jeans just below my knees.

I winced as she worked; now that I was out of imminent danger, the pain from the burns was becoming worse with every movement, every brush against something.

"So what happened?" she asked, slowly peeling away the

denim. It had stuck to some of the blistering burns that were oozing—and damn, did it hurt as it got unstuck. I bit back a gasp of breath, clenching my fingers, nails dug into Gen's bedcovers. "Sorry," she said. "This should help." She dabbed cool water on my skin to aid the separation. "Did those vampires do this?"

"Yes," Mill said.

"And Gen ..." I said. "They got Jacquelyn."

She froze in her cleaning and looked up at me. "What do you mean?"

"She's a vampire now," I said quietly. "... They turned her."

She sat back on her heels and stared at a loose stitch on her quilt that spilled over the side of the bed. She didn't say anything for a few moments, a bloody gauze pad in one hand.

"Is there anything that we can do to save her?" she asked quietly.

I shook my head.

"No way to change her back?"

"I'm sorry ..." Mill said. "But no."

Gen stared, lost in thought again for a long time. Then, at last, she creaked back into motion. Sighing a long exhalation, she leaned forward again and resumed cleaning my wounds.

"I'm sorry," I said, my eyes stinging. But no tears came. I didn't think I could cry anymore, even if I wanted to.

Gen shook her head. "Don't be. It isn't your fault."

"But it is."

"Cassie ..." Mill said gently. "Now is not the time for a pity party."

Lockwood moaned, and as we turned, Mill basically teleported across the room to catch him just before he fell out of the desk chair.

"Here," Gen said, getting to her feet and pulling back the covers on the other side of her bed. "Lay him down there. He looks exhausted ..."

"Is it his injury?" I asked as Mill laid him down.

My heart ached; Lockwood looked so frail, so vulnerable. Silvery blood had seeped to the surface of his bandage.

"That and his exertion to get you away from the fight ..." Mill said.

Guilt upon guilt.

"He used strength that he obviously didn't have," Iona said. "I'll re-dress his wounds."

Gen spared him another quick glance before kneeling back down on the floor beside my legs. She opened a small, glass jar and began to rub a soft, velvety sort of lotion all over. It smelled tropical, like a beach. The first touch caused pain to flare—but then the gel soothed, stifling the pain like a fire under a blanket.

"What is that?" I asked.

"Coconut oil," Gen replied, going back for some more. "Mom swears by it. And I'm mixing in some antibiotic cream, too. Gotta have something stronger for burns like these..."

I waited in subdued quiet, watching Iona fussing over Lockwood with an unsurprising lack of bedside manner. Though out cold, he did not look at peace for it: his features were taut, grim, and set into a line.

"I'm both amazed and glad that your burns aren't any worse," Gen said as she wrapped a bandage around my shins. "Because any sort of mess that I couldn't explain would make my parents mad."

I rubbed my hands over my face. "Ugh ... why does everything always go so badly?"

Iona snorted. "Because you decided to fight vampire hunters that Draven sent to your town. Which part of that did you think would be easy?"

I turned around as far as I could and glared flaming arrows at her. "What the hell is your problem?"

"You," she said. "You are my problem. The whole entirety of it. I tried to help you once, and now—what is this? I'm in rural New York, I was gutted a day or so ago, I keep having to go to sleep in the same room as this weirdo—" She pointed at Mill.

"Um, standing right here?" Mill said.

"*You* are my problem, Cassie," Iona said, ignoring him. "I thought I could just help you with Byron, but after that, and there was your Roxy problem ... and your Miami vampire Lord war problem ... and now this house-burning-down-best-friend-turned-to-vampire-and-Butcher-after-us-problem ..."

"That's a lot of problems," Gen whispered.

"I'm starting to think," Iona said, "*you're* the problem."

Well, at least we found some common ground to agree on. Not that I'd give her the satisfaction of knowing that right now.

"Because Byron was a totally normal guy who never stalked and killed anyone?" I asked.

"Because you're not a normal girl who could just let it go and be grateful she got out with her life once everything was over. Because you have some kind of defect where you have to keep throwing yourself into this—"

"I did not want to throw myself into anything—" I said.

"You could have left this alone. Draven's guys would've sniffed around for a while and when they found nothing, boom, you would have been fine. You could have lived a normal life. But that's not what you chose."

Gen's gaze darted anxiously back and forth. Clean-up forgotten, her face was pale.

"I couldn't leave it alone because people are getting hurt," I said.

"That's not your problem," Iona said, her body tense and taut.

"But it's my fault," I said. "So it *is* my problem."

"That's not normal!" Iona said, voice rising. "This is not what normal people do, looking for ways to get involved in vampire feuds when they could hide until they go away."

"Everything okay up there?"

It was Gen's dad; his voice carried up the stairs.

We all froze, even Iona.

"Oh, I, uh ..." Gen said, scrambling to her feet and yanking the door open. "Sorry! I had the Netflix on my phone turned up too loud!"

Her dad must have been satisfied, because he didn't say anything else or attempt to come upstairs.

Gen's face was murderous when she closed the door behind her. "Quiet the riot, will you?"

177

Iona and I were both seething, staring at each other as if we would like nothing better than to resume arguing, regardless of who would discover us. Iona, shaking with rage, growled low in her chest, and walked over to Gen's closet, shutting herself inside.

"That's ... not a walk-in," Gen said.

"You know ..." Mill said, "I don't think she cares at this point."

I turned away from Iona and her drama in the closet, facing out the window. Dark now, little sign of flames. Things were improving out there—the firefighters, probably. It was far too late to salvage the house ... but, I assumed, it had not totally been reduced to ash. And that was ... well, something, I guessed. Against the darkness, my reflection stared back at me.

My hair was a mess, sticking up at odd angles. My shirt was torn at the shoulder and there was soot all across my cheeks. Long trails of dried tears gave me a ghostly appearance. My cheeks were red, eyes puffy.

Mill stood behind me on the other side of the bed, checking Lockwood's wound. He kept snatching glimpses of me, worry contorting his features. A painful lump stuck in my throat. Everywhere I turned, something that I cherished was in jeopardy. Or destroyed. It was as if I was this cancerous disease. Everything I touched became tainted. Ruined. Dead.

Everything I did made things so much worse.

Maybe Iona was right.

Maybe it was time for me to just butt out ... forever.

Chapter 34

The only problem with choosing to duck out of this vampire war now was that there was something tying me here.

The Butcher knew that I was a human. That would have probably been the first thing that Jacquelyn would have told him.

The thought of her telling him everything about me as revenge for the pain I had caused her? It cut me like a dagger.

The bed sagged, and I looked over to see Mill had come to sit beside me.

"What are you thinking about?" he asked. "You've got this distant sort of look in your eyes."

I looked away.

"The Butcher is going to tell Draven that I'm human …" I said. "If he hasn't told him already."

Mill's expression was not encouraging.

I marshaled my thoughts. "These vamps … The Butcher and the others … they aren't just going to leave the town alone. They burned my house down. They're not going to stop there."

"They might," he said.

"Jacquelyn was just full of hate …" I went on. "She told me that fighting me was a way for her to get back at me for everything I had done to her."

Mill shook his head. "The Butcher probably poisoned her. Honed that sadness that she was feeling about you. Twisted it."

"No, it was already there," I said sadly. "Before we even came up here. Before I had seen her in town. She's hated me ... since before I left."

Something about that felt even more final than pronouncing her dead, and a vampire.

I paused, mulling it over, letting myself slip further into the black, melancholy waters of my regret.

"I just wish she hadn't been at the wrong place at the wrong time. If I'd had more sense, I wouldn't have approached her. When I did that, I painted a fat target right on her back. I should know that Draven will go to any length to get what he wants. He isn't above hurting humans. We're nothing but food to him, after all."

I sighed.

"And everything is my fault. If I hadn't fallen for Draven's trap and come up here, my house would still be standing. Jackie wouldn't be ..."

I couldn't bring myself to say it out loud.

"Cassie ... you know Iona didn't mean those things—"

"Sure she did," I said. "And she was right."

Mill shook his head. "Just because she wouldn't have done what you did doesn't mean you were wrong."

I paused for a second, mulling. "Do you think I should have jumped in head first? Flown up here at the first sign of trouble?"

Mill hesitated.

I let out a groan. "See? If all that was going to happen was my uncle getting hurt, then I should have been able to live with that. But out of fear of something worse happening, I came up here. And then it was like a self-fulfilling prophecy. Worse *has* happened. So much worse."

"You are being too hard on yourself," Mill said. "If we hadn't come here that first night ... Those vamps were going to finish off your uncle, remember?"

"I remember," I said. "They still could, because now they know he's my uncle. Before, he was just an inconvenient witness. But since Jackie ..." I shook my head. "They know who I am. She knows my family. All of them. This is ... it's so much worse now, Mill." I buried my face in my hands. "I don't even know what to do. Where to start."

"It's not your fault," Mill said. "You're not to blame."

"Aren't I, though?" I asked. "I *am* the problem, Mill. Everything that's gone wrong has one common denominator. Me."

"Not just you," he said. "Vampires too."

"Because of me," I said.

The door opened, and Gen, who had left a few minutes ago to talk to her dad, came in. She looked uneasy, glancing anxiously between me and Mill.

"Sorry," she said. "I didn't mean to interrupt your conversation."

The wind out of my sails, I deflated. "No, you didn't. It's fine."

She looked nervously around. "My dad just called your mom about the house. Apparently she just heard from the fire department right before he called ..."

I buried my head in my hands again.

"I guess she's already in town ... looking for you."

"See?" I mumbled, looking at Mill through the cracks between my fingers. "So much worse."

Gen kind of shuffled her feet, looking down. "She asked my dad if we'd seen you. He looked at me, I said no."

I knew it was only a matter of time before she found me, but it was a small relief. "Thank you for covering for me."

"That's what friends are for," she said, shrugging. "Besides, I know how she can be. Vampires versus your mom? ... Your mom is totally worse."

I looked at Mill, giving him a *told-you-so* sort of look.

He just shook his head.

"Ugh, why does this all suck so much?" I asked. "Literally everywhere I turn, something is just crumbling to pieces. My house, which is actually turning to ash as we speak ... my uncle who is recovering in hospital because of vampires attacking him ..." My voice caught in my throat. "My best friend ... who already hated me ... was taken and turned by vampires just to *spite* me ..."

"I already told you why," Iona said from the closet. "It's

you."

"Thanks for reminding me," I said.

Gen's face fell. "I thought I was your best friend…?"

And there was something else I'd screwed up. "No, Gen … you are. I didn't mean—"

Lockwood rolled over, a whimper of pain escaping his lips. My stomach somersaulted. But he did not wake—perhaps he never would, I thought, because of course I still didn't know the truth about him, about his mercury-colored blood. It was possible he was dying, the Butcher's knife attack killing him slowly even when we'd gotten away.

"Lockwood …" I said. "He's wounded because—"

"Of you, yes, we get the common, whiny theme," Iona said, still muffled by the closet door.

I glanced at the louvered closet door. "And Iona hates my guts …"

To this, there was no response.

"And…" I said, turning to look at Mill, the only person in the whole world who hadn't turned his back on me through this entire thing.

Since the beginning, Mill had been a rock, a constant presence that I had come to rely on.

Whether or not I wanted to admit it, I needed Mill.

My heartbeat quickened.

"I wouldn't blame you if you hated me, too," I said to him, looking into those dark eyes. "I dragged you away from home. I've gotten you injured more than once when you were trying to protect me … got your driver injured …" There was an uncomfortable stinging at the back of my throat. The words were difficult to say. "Your girlfriend is probably wondering where you are …"

"Oh, I broke up with her," Mill said.

I blinked at him, my heart skipping a beat as I was totally derailed from the pity party I was throwing myself.

"You … what?"

He shrugged. "I was only dating her to throw Draven's suspicion off of me. She was a soulless beast. I wasn't into her at all. I let it last as long as it needed to and I bailed." He laughed a little, staring at me incredulously. "Come on, she was the worst. You didn't seriously think I was interested in her, did you?"

I looked away, knowing immediately that my cheeks had turned pink. My eyes were fluttering, and suddenly I was struggling to speak to him. It was like he was whole new person.

A whole new *single* person.

"No—I mean, I didn't really think—didn't really *care* what you did with your life ... Umm ..."

Iona's voice suddenly rang out from inside the closet, muffled. "I thought you were supposed to be good at lying. No wonder you got caught and run out of town on a rail."

My cheeks burned even more. "I'm not lying!" I lowered my voice. "And I did not get run out of town on a rail. They don't even do that to people anymore. This isn't the 1700s, Iona."

I could just see Mill out of the corner of my eye, grinning. It was the sort of smile that made my heart pound in my ears. I looked away, out the window. "Thank you ..." I said, finally. "For everything you've done for me."

I chanced a glance up at him, inching my eyes up his form ... his strong, solid form—

Stop it, Cassie.

"Why have you done all this to help me, anyway?" I asked.

It was Mill's turn not to be able to make eye contact. "I don't know. I just like to ... help people." He scratched the back of his neck very intently. "And you killed Theo. He was a jerk. He never paid for his own drinks, kept sticking me with the blood bill whenever we went out ..."

"You're a worse liar than she is, Forehead," Iona said. The door slid open a few inches, enough that we could see Iona sitting against the wall just inside. "Just kiss her already."

And with that, she slid the closet door shut with a sharp *clap* of wood on wood.

"Why would he—"

But the rest of the words fizzled out like embers in the rain, because Mill had taken my face in his hand, gently tipped it up toward him, and pressed his cold lips against mine.

It was like an explosion went off in my head. Everything else in the entire world fell away. Nothing mattered except Mill and this moment.

He was gentle, patient. His lips were like cool water, soft and welcome. This close, the smell of his bergamot cologne was making my head spin.

It was an eternity. I had lived and died with him. It was like a million fireflies were dancing around us, lighting the way. It was like a Five Seconds of Summer song with all of its poetic lines and images.

He didn't push, didn't force any more than just a few small presses of his lips against mine.

And when he pulled away, his eyes were just as dazed and heavy as mine were.

"I'm … I'm gonna go get snacks," Gen said near the door, opening it a crack. "Would anyone like a snack? Maybe some cheese? A summer sausage?" She froze. "Not, uh—you know, forget that sausage thing. So sorry. Didn't mean it like …" She cleared her throat, stepped out in the hall, and poked her head back inside. "Just … cool off, you two."

And she closed the door with a soft *click*.

"What … what was that for?" I asked, wondering if there were actual stars shimmering over our heads or if my mind was playing tricks on me.

He kissed me. He had actually kissed me. Wanted to kiss me. I mean, he wanted to, right? That wasn't some kind of weird joke?

I wanted to touch my lips. I could still feel the echo of his kiss there. I was sure that I would never forget that feeling. Not in a million years.

"Uh … it just … felt right," Mill said. "I mean—"

"Oh, stop trying to explain your stupid feelings for each other," came Iona's voice from the closet depths.

I nearly jumped; how had forgotten she was there?

Oh, right. Something kinda big had happened a minute ago.

"You're an idiot self-hating vampire, and she's an idiot self-hating recovering liar. It's a match made in heaven."

I turned and glared at the closet door with an intensity that

YOU CAN'T GO HOME AGAIN

threatened to burn right through the wood. "I see why your romance advice blog never took off."

The closet door slid open, and Iona glared right back at me. "Are the kissy faces done?"

Mill arched an eyebrow. "For now."

"Great," she said, dragging herself back out into the room. "Can we get out of town before this whole thing gets worse?"

"I don't think that's possible …" I said, the real world crashing down around me again, pulling me away from the bliss was that Mill's kiss. Oh, why did that happy moment have to end? I would have given anything to stay there. "Things not getting worse, I mean … there's no way that this whole thing isn't going to get worse."

Mill sighed heavily, getting to his feet. He crossed to the window, peering out through the night. He must have been able to see something that I couldn't, because he squinted and stared intently.

"I think she's right," he said finally. "We're in too deep."

"The Butcher is still out there …" I said, gritting my teeth. "He's still hunting me. And now that we are here at Gen's family's house, we're putting them in danger."

Iona sighed, folding her arms across her chest. "Okay, I agree that we can't leave that maniac with the machete out there roaming the wilds. He needs to be put down for good."

"But their headquarters was locked down tight," Mill said. "The Butcher, if he's the one in charge, has a bigger team of bodyguards than Draven does. And that's saying something. Not to mention we have no idea how many are actually trained and skilled, or how many of them were just hired mercenaries."

"Vampires have mercenaries?" I asked, then I waved my hand before Mill could reply. "Don't bother. Don't know why I was surprised. Go on."

"All I'm saying is that we can't possibly break their hold on that place," he went on. "There are just way too many to fight, too many unknown factors that we can't know unless we got close."

"And we are not getting close," Iona said.

I was staring at Lockwood, watching him breathe steadily. All of this confused me, angered me. Not to mention Mill and the wrench, as wonderful as it was, that he had thrown into the mix …

Just over his shoulder, on the bedside table next to the bed, sat a collection of water bottles, all in various states of half-full-half-emptiness. I'd never understood Gen's water bottle habit, but as I looked at them now—

It hit me.

"Guys …" I said slowly. "We don't need to go in to the lodge." I hopped up from the bed, crossed to the water bottles, and picked one up. The plastic, out of shape through overuse, crinkled in my fingers. "And we don't need to fight them all … not really …"

I grinned, crinkling the bottle some more, the plastic giving easily under the pressure of my fingers.

"I think I have a plan."

Chapter 35

"… so that's the plan," I said.

I looked around at everyone in the room. Iona was glaring, Mill was studying me intently. Gen was somewhere between nervous and curious.

Iona snorted. "That's insane. And only half a plan. What do we do if it doesn't work?"

I hesitated. Hadn't thought that far ahead. "Um …"

Iona threw her hands in the air and started to pace. "Where are we going to get that much holy water?"

Gen, still cautious, looked at me. "From the baptismal font at St. Mary's Catholic Church. It's only two miles from here, and they leave their doors unlocked twenty-four hours a day so that anyone can come in and pray if they need to. The font is right there inside the doors."

Iona stopped and gave Gen a rare appraising look. "That … isn't a bad start. But still, twenty plus vampires is no small amount. How do you propose that we take out that many?"

"I don't know. There's got to be some way that we can get max range and target more than one of them at a time …" Gen said. "Give me a minute. I'll think of something."

Iona turned her attention back to me. "I get that you want revenge, but Cassie, this is stupid. Even for one of your plans. Do you know how easily this could backfire? Or get out of control? Not to mention the fact that you'd be breaking the law."

"The law is constraining us at this point," Mill said. "The

vampires are working outside it, and since we aren't humans, I think we can safely say that we can work above it this one time, too. It's not like they could successfully arrest us for it, right? We can outrun them."

"But your new girlfriend can't," Iona said.

"Their HQ is far out," Mill said. "We get things done fast, and we can get her out of there before any first responders even get a call."

"That could work," I said. "And then we're done. My family will be safe, the town will be safe."

Iona's eyes narrowed. "Are you sure you're willing to deal with the consequences here? Once you pull the trigger, there's no going back. Not to mention there's no bringing back what you're going to destroy."

"The vampires started this," I said. "They're a real danger to the people of this town. Can you think of a better way to get rid of them all?"

Iona opened her mouth to protest, and then snapped it shut. "Fine," she said. "I asked you for a plan, and you have delivered one. Hardly optimal, but ..." She shrugged. "Okay. Let's do it."

For the first time since arriving in New York, her anger softened. Just a little—but enough that some of the sadness I knew so well in her eyes was back, as though she were the most hopeless person in the world again, not some angsty teenager with a chip on her shoulder.

"All right, stocking up on some holy water is a good start," Mill said. "You said it was only a couple miles from here?"

Gen nodded. "And don't worry. I just got an idea for how we can use the holy water. But we will need some ... stuff." She turned around and snatched the half-empty water bottles off of the table, handing them to me. "Here. If we dump these out, we can fill them with water at the church."

"What are you thinking?" I asked. "Wait, are you coming with us?"

"Well, yeah, I was kind of planning on it," she said.

"No, Gen," I said, putting my hands on her shoulders. "You need to stay safe. I can't lose another friend today."

Gen's brow furrowed, her braids swinging as she shook her

head. "Cassie, I'm not arguing about it. I'm coming."

"If we need to walk all the way to the church," Mill said, "We're burning moonlight."

"'Burning moonlight,'" Gen snickered. "Look at you changing up colloquial phrases, making them all relatable. Hashtag."

I snorted.

"Here's another for you—let's war out," Iona said, picking her jacket back off the floor and throwing it on. "Don't need Mill to get his eyebrows in a knot. Though for him, it wouldn't change much." She looked at me. "Seriously, I don't know what you see in him …"

But I could have sworn a saw a smirk on her face as she stepped out into the hall.

"What about Lockwood?" I asked, glancing at his still form. He hadn't moved, nor made any further noise. "Will he be okay here?"

Gen bit her lip. "Flip the lights out. My dad will think I'm asleep. He shouldn't come in."

I glanced to Mill. "What do you think?"

He shrugged. "Best we can do. He's dead weight."

"Literally," Gen said before wilting under my gaze.

"Lockwood isn't a vampire," I said.

"Sorry." With an apologetic smile she slipped out of the room.

I really didn't want her to come. She was going to be in too much danger. She had no idea what we were up against. She hadn't seen how vicious the vampires truly were yet. Hadn't seen how easily they could snap necks. Break bones as easily as twigs. She hadn't seen the Butcher wield his insane knife, like he was some monster straight out of *The Purge*.

Mill watched me apprehensively from beside the door. "You okay?"

I shook my head. "I am scared for Genesee."

"You can't exactly force her to stay."

"I know …" I said. "But I wish I could."

Mill smirked. "Now you know how I feel."

"What?"

"About you."

189

I looked down. "Come on. We should go too."

With night fallen, and away from the fires that engorged my childhood home, the evening was much cooler. Gooseflesh rose on my arms and I rubbed my hands against them as we snuck through the back door.

"I forgot how chilly it can be here at night this time of year," I said.

My breath plumed. Gen's too.

None came from Mill's or Iona's mouths.

A physical weight settled over my shoulders and I looked up to see Mill walking beside me. The smell of bergamot hit me as he draped his jacket over my shoulders.

"Thanks ..." I said, immediately pushing my arms through the sleeves. It was not warm, though, I noted with some sadness. If this were a human man's jacket, it would've carried his warmth inside, heating me immediately. Instead, this was cold, just like Mill—just like his kiss—and would be until my own body heat filled it.

My heart sank just a little at that thought. How was anything ever going to work out between a human and a vampire?

"So, we're hoofing it, huh?" I asked, staring up at the hill we were going to have to climb to reach the church.

Mill nodded. "The car was in the garage at the house. It's unlikely that it made it."

"Guess we're flying back to Florida, huh?"

"You're probably going with your mom," he said.

I groaned. "Oh, please don't remind me about her right now. I need to pretend like she doesn't exist until all this is over. Thinking about her might summon her. I can't deal with that right now."

Mill smiled and took a few steps forward, his stride longer than Gen's and mine.

I heard more footsteps behind me and wheeled around, knowing Iona and Mill were already ahead of us.

And there was Lockwood, almost hobbling along behind us, one hand clamped over the bandage that Iona had cleaned for him just a short time before.

"Lockwood!" I said, stopping in my tracks.

Iona and Mill turned to see what was happening.

"When did you wake up?"

Lockwood smiled, his green eyes twinkling. "In the middle of your lip lock with Mr. Mill," he said. Thank goodness for the darkness, because I felt my face ratchet up to beet red in an instant.

"Way to keep quiet that whole time," Iona said, turning and resuming her trek up the hill. "Am I even going the right way?"

"Just head straight," Gen said. "We'll come up over a hill, and you should be able to see the church from there."

Iona turned and walked on, Mill following behind.

"I'm glad that you're with us," I told Gen as she fell into step beside me. "But ... also nervous."

"Why?" she asked.

"Because I don't want you to get hurt, obviously," I said. "Remember my formerly good friend Jacquelyn, now of the pointed teeth and forever paler-than-upstate-in-winter complexion?"

She shook her head. "I had to, Cass."

"Why, though? You don't have anything to prove," I said.

"Yes, I do."

"No, you don't."

"Cassie ..." she said. "Look. I didn't believe you before ... you know, when you ended up leaving town—"

"Because I was lying. About literally everything. I think I even lied about why I was leaving, I don't even remember at this point, I was so thick in the lies."

"Yeah, but I feel awful about it now," Gen said. "I mean, when it all came out...that you had told, like, a million lies, that your mom wasn't even going to be able to keep working at her law firm because everyone figured that being a liar must run in the family..."

I winced. "That's not necessarily a deal breaker for a lawyer. She didn't get forced out or anything, it was just ..." I shook my head. She didn't mean it to sting, but that didn't mean it didn't. "Anyway ... I don't blame you for not believing me at first on this."

Gen was quiet for a moment, our feet swishing along the

grass under our feet. "Nobody stood by you when it all hit the fan, did they?"

"I'd lied to everyone. Why would they?" I asked.

Gen was still looking down at her dew-drenched sneakers. "Well ... a real friend would have maybe said something like, 'I don't like what you've done, but I'm still your friend.'"

There was a prickling at the back of my throat, and my eyes stung with tears that came unannounced.

"That would have been asking a lot. Of any friend," I said, my voice cracking a little. "I kinda screwed over ... everyone."

"Well, that's kind of what friends are for, right?" Gen asked. "Standing by you when you get outed as a massive liar. Hanging with you when it turns out that you weren't lying about vampires invading the town."

"Yeah, but ... there's a reason for that cautionary tale about the boy who cried wolf," I said.

She stopped walking and looked up at me, her dark eyes reflecting the moonlight overhead.

A flicker of amusement lit her eyes. "Even if you weren't ... ya know ... do you really think anyone would have believed you on the vampire thing? Without seeing it?"

"Probably not," I said. "But ... being the girl who cried vampire ..." I shrugged. "I dunno. Maybe it's because I've been through the ringer of getting caught in big fat lies and seeing the reaction from others ... I haven't tried to tell people."

"Not even your parents?" Gen asked. She sounded sad about it.

I shook my head. "No-o-o. If I couldn't sell my mom on a little, believable lie at this point, how could I even come close to explaining a big, unbelievable truth like, 'there are vampires in the world and they're hunting me'?"

"I don't know," Gen said. "But I believe you. Now. Because I'm still your friend, and it's my job to back you up. No matter what."

"Also," I said dryly, "because you've seen vampires with your own eyes."

"That too," Gen said. And she smiled. "But still ... I am

your friend. And I do believe you."

Now the tears did come. I let them, throwing my arms around her neck and hugging her tight. It was a zero-to-one-hundred kind of emotional flip—but after everything I'd put myself and the people around me through, by lying through my teeth for so long, about so many things, to know that there was someone who still stood by me even when it was the last thing I deserved ...

Well, I couldn't help disintegrating into a blubbering mess.

"Yes, yes, everyone loves one another," came Iona's voice. "This is *so* great. And we're going to fight a bunch of vampires who want to kill us all. Such happy days ahead. Or short ones. One of those. Take your pick."

Iona's delivery still left something to be desired—but she was right: we had a battle ahead of us, one that threatened all of our lives. The time for tears was later. So I wiped my eyes as I stood, smiling at Gen.

Even in the dark, I saw her dry her own eyes with the back of her sleeve.

We fell into step again. Lockwood was doing better, seeming to gain strength with his every stride.

Iona stalked ahead, sullenly leading our pack.

"Is everything okay with her?" Gen asked quietly.

"I don't really know," I said. "She's usually pretty curt, but since we've been here, she's been acting funny. Maybe I should talk to her."

"Better you than me," Gen said, and pointed at her neck. "I like my blood right where it is, y'know."

"Then you should have stayed home." I jogged up the hill, catching Gen's smirk out of the corner of my eye, and regretting my exertion immediately as my legs strained against the incline, blistered ankles alight with needling pain. I caught up with Iona quickly.

"What?" she asked, arms clamped under her armpits as if she was cold.

"Do you need blood?" I asked, as mildly as I could. "A nap? Some handsome vampire to rub your shoulders or your feet?"

"Yes, no, and maybe," Iona said. "Not that it's any of your

business."

"This whole trip, something's been bothering you," I said. "What is it?"

Iona rolled her eyes. In that moment, I was reminded that she'd died a teenager, and was perpetually frozen as one. Most of the time I forgot that, seeing her 'old soul' rather than her youthful exterior. "Nothing," she said. "I just get touchy when I'm impaled, then nearly set on fire."

"I'm sorry," I said. And I really meant it. "For everything. Seriously. For dragging you in. For bouncing around without a plan. I wish I'd just left you alone, but … you keep helping me. And you're so *good* at it. I wish I was as good at all of this as you are."

Iona's face sobered. The angry lines around her eyes and in her forehead softened. That annoyance dissipated, it was easy to see what had lured Byron in all those years before: she was beautiful. But her blue eyes were sad once more.

"I … wish that I was more like you," she said, doing everything she could not to look at me.

That took me off guard.

"What, a liar?"

Iona laughed, but it was hollow. "Possessed of a pulse. In high school still. Doing normal things, not hanging out at parties with predators who just want to snuff out peoples' lives without regard for … anything."

Mill had shared similar things with me, things that he missed about being human.

It drew a sadness from deep within me. What must it be like to be in her shoes? To have had this sort of life thrust upon her with no regard to her desires or dreams?

"I know why Mill likes you," she went on quietly. There was no malice in her voice now. "You're the most human thing he encounters on a daily basis. When you live in the vampire world for a while you'll find it's all … appetite. Of every sort. Pure hunger. Viciousness. You lose connection with the human spark that we all—well, most of us who aren't named Harvey Weinstein—have within us. But being around you, Cassie … even doing these weird, non-normal, vampire-killing things that I hate …" she sighed. "It really is the closest I feel to being human anymore. And part of something ... normal."

I was blown away. Iona, brash, icy Iona had a tender heart deep down. I always suspected it, but to see it surface with nothing more than a touch showed me just how much she had been suffering.

"I sound so stupid," she said, shaking her head. "I miss all those things, though. Stupid things. Little things, like braiding my sister's hair..."

A distant look had passed over her face before she wiped at her eyes with her palms.

"I'm sorry. It's so dumb."

Part of me wanted to hug her, to try and take some of that burden she had been carrying around for so long, but I knew it wouldn't be received well. At least not now. She had made herself very vulnerable, had opened up enough to let me see this sliver of her soul. I would take that and be grateful, knowing that she would probably stitch it back up just as quickly and act like nothing ever happened.

"It's not dumb ..." I said. "It's ... human."

"But I'm not human. Not anymore," she said.

It wasn't dumb. Just terribly sad. I imagined a girl as pretty as Iona, just a little younger, sitting at a little vanity with the sunlight streaming in through the window, Iona laughing as she put her sister's perfectly straight hair into pretty braids.

Fear of death often occupied my attention when I thought about the possibility of being turned into a vampire, but I realized with a punch to the gut that it was the life I'd have to give up yet still watch from a distance that would be the hardest, most painful thing I'd have to go through.

And that terrified me even more.

I hesitated. I knew she was angry with me for all of this. I didn't blame her. I was angry with myself for it. Jacquelyn was only part of it, but easily the most painful.

"You know why I can't walk away ... right?" I said.

Iona spoke, but it was with a quiet dread. "Because seeing other people go through what you went through ... mentally unprepared to fight vampires ... to acknowledge that they even exist. It's like—"

"It's like watching myself being hunted by Byron all over again," I said.

"I know that feeling." She sighed. "I understand you better than anyone, Cassie. That's why I wanted to help you in the first place." She shrugged, her face sad. "But that's also what makes you and I different."

"What does?" I asked.

"You understood the cost without having to pay it the way I did. I only knew what it meant after I went through it."

Then, just as suddenly as she had slipped into it, she snapped out of her reverie, and picked up her pace. "Come on. I don't want to be maudlin anymore. Let's go kill some vampires."

"And then braid each other's hair?" I asked.

"Don't be a jerk, Cassie. I said I'm with you. No need to get out the sharp elbow for me."

And down the hill she went, the lights from the church shining in the distance.

The best, or worst part, was that I hadn't been kidding. I wondered who her sister had been. If she was even still alive.

While I didn't have siblings of my own, I couldn't imagine being frozen in time while Genesee grew up, grew old, and then died before my eyes.

With a heart-wrenching reminder, I thought of Jacquelyn, and the life that I had taken from her. It might not have been my hand that changed her, but it may as well have been.

I couldn't think about all of this. The sadness would paralyze me.

I had to ignore all of it, just like I was ignoring the fact that Mom was stalking around town, trying, probably desperately, to find me.

We had to get to the church. We had to get this done.

And later … once this was all over … maybe I'd open my heart again. And think about Jacquelyn, and everything I'd lost with the decisions I'd made.

Chapter 36

Eerie quiet hung over us as we finally pulled into the nature preserve. It was nearing midnight, and the streets had been all but empty. A heavy chill had descended. I realized, with a distant pang of regret, that I could hardly barely handle the cold. Six months ago, I'd have been fairly content—just another part of New York nights, New York life.

Lockwood had hotwired a car from a dealership near the church; a Lexus SUV with leather interiors, a backup camera, and heated seats. It was a low heat, the kind that crept up slowly.

"They won't miss this one during the night," Lockwood said as he hotwired the SUV. "It was parked in the back lot. With the trade-ins."

"Don't they have cameras in those lots?" I asked.

He winked at me. "I took care of it. Don't worry, Miss Cassandra. The only thing I did any damage to is the impeccably low mileage that this car had. They'll probably write our little jaunt off as a bookkeeping error."

We all sat there in the dark car, staring out into the night, knowing that just on the other side of the hills was the lodge where the vampires were prowling.

"Are we ready?" Mill asked.

"As ready as we'll ever be," Iona said.

He looked at me. "Should we go over the plan again?"

I shook my head. "Let's just do it. Otherwise I might lose my nerve."

Iona did one of her familiar snorts. "We could only hope you would lose your nerve. Then, just maybe, we'd stop getting into these messes." And out she went, first.

"Don't listen to her," Mill said. "I like your chutzpah."

"Bravery is admired attribute, Miss Cassandra," Lockwood said.

Gen kind of nodded her head. "You crazy, girl." We stared at each, and she finally shrugged. "What? You want me to compliment your bravery, too?"

I laughed. "Let's just go."

Kicking empty plastic water bottles around near our feet, the rest of us got out of the car and started up through the woods.

Lockwood and Mill were both touting large jerry cans that smelled strongly of gasoline. Lockwood had to keep the windows open as we drove so Gen and I didn't pass out from the fumes. Luckily the Lexus had a good heater.

Iona was carrying some thick sticks wrapped in cloth, also smelling of gasoline.

Gen and I, meanwhile, were both carrying large, plastic water guns, holy water sloshing around inside. Gen's was the size of a rocket launcher. Mine was red, and I carried a water tank on my back like ones that firefighters used. Water balloons, also filled with holy water, hung from our belts. In hindsight, not the best idea: they wobbled with our steps, threatening to pull my pants down. Also, water balloons were not the most secure containers; a stray branch had burst one of mine almost as soon as we stepped into the woods, soaking my whole right side. Since then, we'd had to drastically slow our pace and pick our path much more carefully.

Also? My leg was coooooold now. So cold. Truth was, we'd gone all-in on the water balloon idea. Gen's backpack was full of the things, plus more bottles of holy water—our ammo magazines, so to speak. I had one extra small bottle tucked away in my pants just in case she and I got separated. She needed the extra protection more than I did.

"You know, I always wanted one of these as a kid," Gen said as we stumbled through the trees, trying to avoid any and all dead leaves, gnarled roots, or fallen limbs. "They were so expensive though. And my brother was always more interested in the guns with the little foam darts instead of these."

"Just don't get any ideas about water fights," Mill said. "Your ammunition is limited."

Gen flashed a regretful smile at me. "Maybe when we're done here?"

I grinned back, but my stomach roiled. I knew what was coming.

"We're going to have to get closer than we did before," Mill said, as we reached the top of the rise and looked down on the lodge below. A million stars twinkled overhead, and lights burned in the lodge windows. "I see a few outside milling around. Lockwood, are you sure that you want to do this?"

Lockwood nodded. "Not a problem, sir. Leave it to me."

"Just be careful, okay?" I asked. "Don't do anything rash. Keeping them off Iona and Mill's scent should be enough."

He winked at me and then disappeared off into the night, leaving the gasoline canisters at Iona's feet.

"Okay … you know what to do," I said to others.

They nodded. Iona dropped her makeshift torches and picked up the canisters. A fresh waft of gasoline seeped into the air like an invisible mushroom cloud. I screwed up my nose and backed off, hoping that the vampires in the lodge could not detect the smell too. They would eventually—but too late to stop us, I hoped.

Mill hesitated before rushing back to me in the blink of an eye. He smiled down at me as my hair flew out from around my face as if in a gust of wind, and he kissed me again.

The same fireworks shot off behind my eyes, and the tips of my toes curled, a warm glow starting in my chest despite the coolness of his lips on mine …

He pulled away, planting another cold kiss on my forehead, and then resumed his trek away into the night. Iona rolled her eyes, and set off in another direction. The gasoline splashed in her jerry can—another thing that might alert the vampires too early. I crossed my fingers and toes that we were outside the range of their hearing.

"So ... do you really think this is going to work?" Gen asked as the shadows fell around us, leaving us alone with nothing but the lights inside the nature preserve's lodge for company.

"I hope so," I said, and steeled my nerves. "After what they've done to me, it's the least they deserve."

We fell silent, and I strained to hear the slightest thing out of place. But all I could hear was the occasional snapping twigs, the brush of the wind against the tree branches.

Still, that didn't mean that was all the vampires in the lodge heard. For all I knew, they could hear my breathing, my heartbeat, right at this moment.

Stop it, Cassie, I told myself. *Mill and Iona didn't stop you all here for nothing. They know the vampires' limits.*

Mil had also said it was necessary to get closer than before ... but I bit down on that thought, silencing it. My heart was beating fast enough as it was.

"I wonder what Lockwood is doing ..." I murmured. "I know that he'll get those vampires inside somehow but ... I don't know how."

Gen looked up at me. "So how did you meet these guys?"

I gave her a brief account of how all of them had sort of forced their way into my life.

"Florida seems to be treating you pretty well, then?" Gen asked.

I could hear the hesitation in her voice, the hope that it wasn't true. "It's nothing like here, that's for sure," I said. "I don't know. Part of me really hates it because it's *not* here, you know? It's hot and humid, and I've heard it just gets worse as we get closer to summer. Like, you know how it's so cold here in the winter that no one goes outside? It's the same in Florida, except it's literally too hot. I miss the trees, the forests. The grass. Is that weird? And I really miss the hills. It's so flat there."

"But you have beaches and palm trees and no snow."

"Those things are great," I agreed. "There's awesome food everywhere. And it always sort of feels like you're on vacation ... at least it did when we first moved there. Once the vampires appeared … well, that sort of killed it for me."

Gen nodded solemnly. "And school? Made some friends?"

I thought of Xandra for the first time in days, and Gregory's and Laura's faces swam across my mind as well.

"I guess," I said. "Though only because I had Byron chasing after me." I hung my head. "I don't know if any of them would have spoken to me otherwise."

I took a deep breath. The air smelled so much different than in Florida—like woods, damp earth, the subtle fragrance of a forest spread all around, instead of distant saltwater and exhaust. I wished I could bottle it and take it back with me.

There was the rustling of feet on the ground, and Iona and Mill stepped back into sight, Lockwood not far behind them.

"It's done," Iona said, dropping the empty can on the ground.

Mill was still bent over, pouring the gasoline in a line along the forest floor. He continued to pour it until he just about reached me, and then capped it.

Lockwood came to stand behind me, as did Mill and Iona.

I pulled a lighter out of my pocket, a cheap one I had picked up when we had bought gas and the cans from the store. It was red with a picture of an eagle on it.

Freedom. How I longed for it. How I would cherish it when this was all over. Freedom from these creatures and the claws that they'd sunk into my life and those around me. Freedom from the fear they caused, the sleepless nights, the feeling of helplessness.

I flipped it open and flicked it into life, the tiny flame casting dancing light over the ground.

"Here we go," I said—and tossed the lighter onto the trail of gasoline.

The effect was instant. Flames erupted in a flash of yellow-orange light. They tore across the gasoline circle in both direction, a roar of fire that filled the night, illuminating it as if the sun itself had been placed directly beneath the earth and its light released via troughs cut through to it.

The smell of forest was quenched. Burning gasoline replaced it, choking it out.

The flames cut through the forest with ferocious speed. I tracked them in both directions, as they circled toward the lodge—and then one curved right to the building's wall, rising, lapping hungrily.

"And now I'm arsonist," I said. "They weren't kidding; lying really is a kind of gateway drug."

I did genuinely feel bad. The lodge was a treasured landmark in the town. I didn't even want to think about how old the building itself was. But I also had known that the police would write the burning off as another crime in this sudden wave. Another lie, but the police were better off never finding out the truth. If this was a way that I could protect them along with everyone in town, then so be it. And now the smell of burning wood filled the air too, making my stomach turn. It had only been, what? Less than four hours since my childhood home was burned down? But I forced it down, watching, teeth clenched, as the flames ate up the entire side of the lodge—then found the roof, crawling across it as the wind blew it along.

I hoped that this wouldn't get out of control before the firefighters could get here. We didn't need a forest fire on our hands on top of the vampires.

It was like a beacon in the night, as bright as the sun, shadows dancing and flickering all around. A light in the darkness. Hope.

"It's kind of poetic, isn't it?" Gen said quietly, resolutely. "'Do unto others as you would have them do unto you.'"

"Not sure that's what the golden rule is really about," I said, "and I know revenge is a no-no, but aren't vampires damned anyways?"

"Watch it," Iona said. "Present company."

"Here they come," Mill said, obviously not hearing a word we were saying. He pulled a few small vials of holy water that I had filled for him—he and Iona wouldn't even step into the church when we were there—and moved to stand closer to me. "Get ready."

Sure enough, vampires were starting to stream out of the lodge and into the night, their snarls and howling filling the air. Some of them were half-dressed, definitely lacking armor.

"Nice work, Cassie," Iona said. She laughed wickedly. "See? How do you punks like it?"

I didn't want to say it out loud, but I was very pleased to hear her say that.

"Be on the lookout," Lockwood said, pulling a few silver-tipped stakes from the inside of his suit coat. Mill and I had talked about these before, during training. The silver gave them added piercing strength, in case of armor, something vampires occasionally employed. Lockwood handed two to me with a wink. "They will be on top of us any second."

I lifted the stakes and shoved them into my hair, feeling even more like myself with them there, and cocked the water gun, pointing it into the darkness.

"Let 'em come," I said, surprised at how steady my hands were. "I'm ready."

Chapter 37

The first vampire that burst out of the darkness almost elicited a panicked shriek from me, even though I knew it was coming. I could hear it stumbling through the woods, hear its angry snarling.

Almost. Because when it launched itself through the trees at us, even though a spear of terror ran through me, like it always did when I came face-to-face with these monsters—I acted on another instinct too: the instinct to stamp these abominations out.

I pulled the trigger of my water gun, hard.

A stream of clear water shot out of the end of the water gun, bathing the vampire's face. It stopped dead in its tracks, howling in pain as its face broke out in blisters and sores.

Another appeared, and Iona stepped in, shoving it out of the way as her shoulder collided with his side, sending him flying. She chased after him, nothing more than a blur. Something silver glinted near the house—the Butcher, his knife flashing with a reflection of the fire. He seemed to wait there for a moment, stalking back and forth like a hungry coyote, before taking off into the surrounding forest toward us.

"Not good," I said, squirting another vampire in the side as it lurched for Mill. "The Butcher! Guys, watch out! He's in the trees! Don't let him get behind us!" I called to Mill. I hoped Iona was close enough to hear, too.

"I'll find him," Mill snarled, and after shoving an open vial of holy water into the mouth of the vampire that he was fighting, he sped off through the trees in search of our main target. His last foe dissolved into black goo, shuddering and hissing under the effect of the holy water.

I didn't have time to watch Mill go. Another vampire launched itself through the trees, his fangs shining in the firelight.

With a squirt to the face, the vampire fell to his knees, screaming.

"Get behind me," I ordered Gen, who immediately obeyed.

I looked around, all of Mill's numerous, varying instructions whirling around in my brain.

Get to higher ground.

Find an advantage.

Run if you have to.

Anything can be used to help keep them at bay if you are clever enough. Glancing about in this brief respite, I noticed a tree with a series of low branches, easy enough to get up into without having to actually climb and let go of my weapon.

"Hop up there," I told Gen, pointing.

She clambered up, and as I followed, I had just enough time to pump the water gun before another vampire came hurtling out of the shadows toward us, a friend close behind.

Gen didn't even need me to tell her what to do. With a cry of fear, or adrenaline, or blood lust I didn't know, she shot the water through the air in an arch. The stream was a direct hit, on each of them in turn, hitting skin—an arm, the other's exposed chest. They recoiled, screaming as they blistered, skin hissing.

Their shrieks joined the cacophony already unfolding in the night, from vampires here, fighting us, and the ones who fled from the lodge in a panic, or perhaps caught alight unwittingly as it began its speedy collapse, dissolving from the trench the holy water had carved into its chest.

"Well done!" I shouted.

"Thanks!" Gen breathed, her cheeks flushed as I chanced a glance at her. "I'm glad that I've been going hunting with

Dad in the fall the last few years. It looks like it's coming in handy—" Then her words were cut off by a scream, and with horror, I wheeled around in the tree to see a pair of hands around Gen's throat.

Flashbacks of Jacquelyn sent me into a mad frenzy.

Without thinking about my arm scraping against the rough bark of the tree and ripping through my shirt, I raised my water gun to eye level and took aim at the vamp's hands.

The water splashed all over Gen's face—but the vampire let go, hissing. It lurched around the tree, hands burning and hissing.

A tall, thin male with stringy black hair, he gnashed his teeth at us—

A different girl might have frozen in terror, but Gen was very much the 'two' to the one-two punch I'd started. Loosing an enraged battle cry, she pumped her trigger, dousing him in holy water that sent him reeling back as though we'd turned a firefighters' hose on him—one spewing not water but hydrochloric acid.

But though he fell back, more pushed forward.

"Is there an end to these idiots?" I asked, leveling my gun and firing again. Unfortunately, the holy water did not totally incapacitate. Some of the first attackers were rising again, fighting back against the agony roaring through their bodies and preparing to launch a renewed assault on our position.

"Let's move," I told Gen, hopping down out of the tree. If any vampires were to grab her, I wasn't sure I could stop them, even if we had the height advantage.

A vampire with swinging dreadlocks appeared, running without a care for his comrades.

Both Gen and I took aim, but Dreadlocks dodged and weaved like a pro, avoiding our twin streams.

"Water balloons," I said, pulling one from a clip on my belt.

Gen readied hers. We threw.

More screams filled the air as they struck with a splash, our very own anti-vampire grenades. Dreadlocks fell down, missing half his head. He must have really gotten doused. Still more vampires appeared, taking his place.

"This is insane," I said, my heart thundering against my chest. My hands cramped as I pumped the lever on the gun again.

These were made for play. Not battle.

Another vamp stumbled as we hit it with a double bomb, its leg coming off.

But the one behind scrambled over her back and dove at us.

We kept moving back, away from the flaming lodge, the vampires pushing us farther and farther into the trees. The shadows were our enemy—and, I realized with a sickening lurch, as we moved away from the circle of fire they were growing in numbers.

"Cassie, I can't see anything," came Gen's voice behind me.

"We're going to have to make a run for the lodge."

"Balloon barrage on three?" Gen asked.

Clever girl. "On three."

Both of us pulled some balloons from our belts and tossed them back toward the lodge, into the seeping darkness—then—

"Run!" I screamed, grabbing her hand and sprinting through the trees parallel to the lodge, keeping it in sight all the while. Snarling came from behind us. No hands grabbed out, so I could only assume the temporary assault had given them pause.

But I didn't look back to be certain.

Gen's hand was slick with sweat, but I held onto it. I was not going to lose her as I ducked and dove between the trees back toward the lodge. I was going to keep her by my side if it was the very last thing I did.

I'd lost Jacquelyn already. Gen would not join her.

We had made it back around to where Mill had lit the trail of gasoline in the first place. A pile of Iona's makeshift torches were there.

"Here," I said, passing one to Gen. "When we get close, just hold it near the flames. We can use it as a defense."

"Got it," Gen said.

Almost the moment I'd said it, two vampires lurched out

of the darkness.

I raised my torch, Gen beside me doing the same—

But the gap they'd appeared from had been too close. If they'd taken a splash of holy water, they were well over it by now; they moved with insane speed, closing the gap between us—and sending the torches spinning out of our hands with sharp slaps that reverberated through the bones of my entire arm.

The torches landed, extinguishing.

Panic threatened to rise.

I swallowed hard, pushing it down.

This was the time I knew was coming. It was inevitable.

I was going to have to fight these losers.

"Stay behind me," I told Gen. "Whatever happens, stay behind me."

I looked at the vamps. "Who wants to dance?"

They surged for me—

Yanking one of the stakes out of my hair, I blocked one of the vamp's arms as she latched onto the front of my shirt in an iron grip. I plunged the stake into her cold flesh.

The vampire howled, black blood squirting out of the wound. Acrid and sulfurous, the smell fought for dominance against the gasoline and the fire.

But the other vampire was still coming, trying to scramble over the first as she fell to the ground, clutching her arm and wailing.

I reached up into the tree over my head, and latched onto the branch. Using my own body weight, I swung at the other with my feet. I caught her surging forward, sending her crashing back to the ground.

A water balloon sailed over my head and struck the vamp in the chest. She reared back with teeth bared, a faint sizzle rising over her snarls—but only the skin of her face was exposed, and the holy water had hardly touched it.

She repositioned her feet, lunged—

I threw myself forward to meet her. Stake raised, I stabbed out—right through her cheek and into her jaw.

The vampire screeched, a banshee wail, and I drew the stake free, tar-like blood coursing over my hands—

And then I plunged it into her chest, the silver tip cutting right through like a hot knife through butter.

The vampire collapsed backward. Body degrading, she fell into a heap, edges blurring and darkening as she seemed to collapse in on herself, turning to tar.

"Whoa," said Gen, eyes wide.

"'Whoa' is right," I said, clambering to my feet. "Thank you, Lockwood."

"You are quite welcome."

I jerked around, surprised. Lockwood stood with a pleasant smile on his face, backlit by the burning lodge, his suit utterly covered in black blood. He could have passed for a horror movie villain.

"There are more out here," said Lockwood, retrieving new stakes from his suit pockets and handing a pair to me. "We need to get back to the lodge, regroup with Miss Iona and Master Mill."

"That's where we were heading," I said.

"I'll lead the way," Lockwood said. "Stay close. I rather think Master Mill will never let me see the light of day again if I allow anything to happen to you or your friend, Miss Cassandra."

We followed him down through the trees and up toward the hill where the lodge was. It looked almost glorious, burning like a pyre, the flames licking high into the night sky, silhouetting the wrecked framework that it tore through with a crackling vengeance.

Three figures were silhouetted against it: the Butcher, long knife flashing, bald dome of a head shining; and Mill and Iona, blocking him in.

Lockwood said, "Miss Cassandra, I believe that I should stay back here with Miss Genesee. This fight ... might be a bit much."

I glanced over to Gen, expecting a fight. But her face had paled. The night's combat had caught up with her—as had the reality of the stakes (pun not intended), seeing me murder vampires in cold blood right in front of her to save our skin. I nodded. "All right. Take care of her, Lockwood."

"With my life, Miss Cassandra."

I jogged out toward Mill and Iona, ready to end this thing—

And then something slammed into me from the darkness. I cartwheeled over, a spinning firework of limbs. The forest spun, the flames too, and for a moment as I was airborne I realized how terrible this error had been, in forgetting Lockwood's warning, that other vampires were still out here—

I hit the trunk of a tree diagonally. My back bent around it, and I screamed with pain, sure it would break—

I fell forward, landed hard on my knees—

A sharp uppercut connected with my jaw, sending me reeling backward. I gasped—Then hands had me—cold, icy, concrete hands, gripping my shoulders from behind.

"Time for you to atone for your sins, *friend*," a voice hissed in my ear.

A very familiar voice.

Jacquelyn.

Locked in a furious embrace, we went tumbling back down the hill together into the shadow-drenched darkness.

Chapter 38

We hit the bottom of the hill with a thud, and the air was wrenched from my lungs.

I gasped for breath, but none would come.

A pair of wide, dark eyes leered down at me, their depths reflecting the firelight over our heads. Jacquelyn pinned me down, straddling my chest. I lifted my head, bracing to push—

Her hands shot out with lightning speed, fingers wrapping around my neck.

She squeezed—and the force of it dimmed my vision round the edges. I sucked hard for breath—

It wouldn't come. My throat was too tight. Had to—get her off me—

I struggled, bucking, my heels flailed as I tried to find purchase—

"No, Cassie. Not this time. Not after everything you've done to me!"

I closed my eyes. Teeth clenched, I forced every muscle in my body to obey me—to overpower her—

"No!" Jacquelyn screamed, and she lifted my head, then slammed it against the earth.

Stars exploded in the darkness.

"You did this to me! You turned me into this!"

She slammed my head down again—

"*Monster!*" And again—

"You made me the laughing stock of the school!" she

screamed. "You turned my own friends against me! You betrayed me!"

Again—

I couldn't open my eyes. The back of my head was warm and wet. Every limb was as heavy as lead. All I could do was lie there and wait for this to be over.

She was crying now, angry, hateful sobs filling the air. But she couldn't produce tears. Not anymore.

"You hear me, Cassie? I hate you! *I hate you!*"

She stopped, her grip around my throat weakening.

"Ca ... Cassie?" Her voice came from a great distance.

So much warmth, under my head ... Oh, but it hurt ...

"Oh, God ..." she said, and from a thousand miles away I felt the weight of her leave my torso and my legs. "She's...she can't be dead, right? No. I didn't kill her ..."

Scraping sounds—footsteps, on leaves, the detritus of winter, frozen for so long it still hadn't rotted.

"*WELL, GOOD!*" she roared, closer, only the words came warbled, as if through water. "I'm glad I did! It was what you deserved after everything that you did to me!"

Some instinctual part of me still lived, for at Jackie's shout, it tried to recoil. It could not: my body was frozen, a heavy, leaden thing I could not move.

But I was alive, I realized dimly—and at the moment I knew it, it was as if what bound me to the earth was lifted. I was still terrifically heavy ... but the invisible restraints on me were gone. My throat still ached, my head was pounding—but I could breathe, could fill my lungs with shallow puffs of forest air, filled with fire and wood and wetness and earth.

My toes—twitched.

My body would obey me.

I was alive.

It wasn't over yet.

I could still fight.

I cast my hands out mentally, groping to assess my position without opening my eyes. The pain was a heavy fog which was hard to penetrate, but I pushed through it, scrambling to ascertain my position, my surroundings, as I lay prone in the mist.

The remains of my water gun, or the tank at least, dug into my spine, the plastic sharp and fractured. Must've broken when I hit the ground. The actual gun, I couldn't feel; it was either somewhere nearby, or back on top of the hill, lost when Jacquelyn first assaulted me. I did have one last silver-tipped stake left, though. I felt it in my hair, somehow not dislodged by my flight, or Jackie's pounding of my skull against the earth.

I could kill her with it. Sink it into her chest, spill her new vampire blood down my hands—could watch her die.

No. I couldn't.

Jacquelyn and I might not have seen eye to eye before the vamps took her, but she had been my friend once. And though part of me thought I should free her from the life I had condemned her to …

I couldn't bring myself to do it. Not that.

So I had to escape some other way.

And that left …

The bottle in my jeans. Crumpled but not leaking, it rested against my aching hip.

Carefully, my eyes barely cracked—I could just about make out Jacquelyn's stalking through this little clearing, though she was a dark smear just like the rest of the forest—I slowly, slowly, began to reach down with tentative fingers.

"Of everything that you did to me, Cassie, abandoning me when these bastards snatched me from right in front of you was the worst," she said, hissing as she paced. "I didn't think you could sink any lower, but you just ran off. Never mind poor Jacquelyn. Leaving me holding the bag while you get away—again."

My fingertips grazed the bottlecap. It was no bigger than a kid-sized water bottle, really, because it was all that would fit in my pocket. So there wouldn't be much to work with. Didn't matter. I just needed to fend her off.

Slowly, my whole being focused on my slow movement, keeping it as close to silent as possible so she would not hear as she stalked and ranted at what she believed to be my dead body, I unscrewed the cap of the bottle just enough so that when I pulled it out I could just toss it.

There was a loud *CRASH* from back up the hill.

Jacquelyn twisted toward it. Smoke billowed high, I assume as another part of the lodge succumbed to the fire and collapsed entirely.

Now was my chance.

Swinging myself upright, I leapt up to my feet, opened the water bottle the rest of the way—

Jacquelyn pivoted back, confusion giving way to rage—

I lunged, and threw the contents of the bottle at the back of Jacquelyn's neck.

Her screams pierced the night as the holy water erupted over her. She fell to her knees, clutching at the back of her neck, scraping at it with her fingers as if she could get it off.

My eyes welled up with wet, hot tears.

"I'm so sorry," I said, holding my broken wrist to my stomach, elephant tears leaking down onto the forest floor, my lip trembling. Jacquelyn bared her fangs at me, an agonized grimace twisting her face into a horror movie monster. Smoke was hissing off the back of her neck, and her eyes were dark pools, watching me.

For all that, though, there was defeat in her eyes, and her voice, when it came, was quiet, filled with accusation.

"You're just never going to stop until you take everything from me, are you?" Jacquelyn asked. She wobbled to her feet, entirely too quickly. "Every last thing … down to my life." Her face twisted, anger cracking through where resentment had ruled a moment earlier. "Well … I'm stronger now … strong enough not to have to take your crap, Cassie—so let me show you—"

She threw herself at me again—

She still didn't know how to fight, but neither did I in this situation. Mill had only taught me how to fight to kill, not to disable. How could I find a way to hurt her enough to stop her attacks, but not kill her?

My stomach heaved; I wanted to throw up right then and there. No one, *no one* should have to think these thoughts about one of their own friends. Jacquelyn reached out for me, fingernails wedded to her new vampire strength, now claws that would rip me apart—

Then she jerked aside as Mill barreled into her.

She thudded into a nearby tree, the trunk cracking.

He grasped my shoulders with his hands, eyes wide and horrorstruck, staring into mine.

"Cassie, thank God …" he said, looking me up and down.

I could smell the blood on him, and could see a long scrape from his forehead to his chin, caused by some sort of blade. Inky blood dripped down his face like tears.

The Butcher.

"Are you all right?" he asked. "Hurt? Your wrist? What happened? You tumbled out of sight, and—"

"Where's the Butcher?" I asked. "Did you kill him?"

"I had to find you," he said, eyes wide. "You're bleeding. Cassie. We need to … we need to …"

I had never seen him look so frightened. Jacquelyn had already recovered. Pushing back to her feet, she gritted her teeth, surging at Mill from behind with a hateful grimace—

I opened my mouth to warn him, but as soon as I did, Mill's face fell, and shoved me out of the way.

I stumbled, twisting—

There stood the Butcher, his knife hanging lazily at his side, caked in drying vampire blood. He had gashes on either side of his face that looked unmistakably like gouges from fingernails. His bald head was nicked, oozing thick, dark blood. His eyes were fixed on me, glazed.

Blood lust. I could see it clear as day.

Jackie was behind me, diverted from Mill. She ran with lightning speed, too fast for my eyes to follow—

I braced, still falling where Mill had shoved me aside and my footing had gone out from under me, too late to stop either of them from converging on me. Searing, white hot pain sliced across my leg as I fell back to the forest floor. Pain bloomed on my thigh, and as I grasped at it, my fingers met hot, wet blood.

The Butcher lurched for me, a slave to his own desire—

And then Mill was there, roaring with a fury like none other. He snatched out for the Butcher's wrist with one hand, his shoulder with the other—and with a scream of pure anger, he *ripped* the Butcher's arm clear from his body.

Black blood gouted, spraying me, burning—

The Butcher could barely react. Mill lifted him, like a UFC wrestler—and then slammed him against the earth with a bone-shattering *BOOM.*

Jacquelyn's attack stalled, and she watched in horror. Her face would have paled if it could have, as she took in the crumpled form of the Butcher, barely moving on the forest floor—and Mill above him, chest heaving, face haggard.

"Do it, Cassie," Mill growled at me heavily. He nodded at the stake in my hair. "You deserve to, after all he's done."

With pleasure.

I rose—

Jacquelyn took a step toward me—

"Stop right there," Mill said, "or I swear to God you will be next."

Jacquelyn froze. Her gaze flitted between the two of us, weighing up whether she could enact her revenge before Mill acted, or if she were playing a fool's game by even considering it.

Dragging myself to the Butcher, swallowed by white stormclouds of pain, I removed the silver-tipped stake from my hair.

He looked up at me with glazed eyes, a wobbly smile sneaking onto his lips. "The … greatest hunter … "

"This is what you get for burning down my house," I said, my voice shaking—and I plunged the stake into his chest.

He grunted. His body tensed, jerked, as if trying to recoil, as black, oily darkness spurted—

"And this is for hurting my uncle," I said, pulling it free and sinking it back into his already desiccating flesh, relishing the feel of his body giving way, the scent of decay, the spasm of his muscles and the grunt in his throat as I killed him—

"And this is for hurting my friend—" And I sank it in, again and again, stabbing until long after the spasms had stopped, and the spurts were smaller, and my hands were covered up to my wrists with dark, burning blood—and still I stabbed, screaming as I went—

Hands gripped me under my arms, dragged me back. I panted,

struggling to free myself, fight my way back to the ruined, tar-like mess of decay that had once been the Butcher …

"He's gone, Miss Cassandra."

Lockwood. He and Iona stood above me, their eyes full of concern. Gen was hovering behind them, staring apprehensively at me.

I must have looked like absolute hell.

Also, I had just turned a champion vampire hunter into a pin cushion.

Dropping the stake, I tried to scoot away from the Butcher's body, now collapsing in on itself, oozing into the ground.

Jacquelyn just … stared.

I stared right back.

If I had been hoping for some sort of happy reunion, I would have been sorely disappointed.

With one last glance at the deteriorating corpse of her sire, she took one last look at me—

There was nothing of my old friend in there, I realized, staring into the darkness of her sockets, like a skull hanging there before me.

And she was off, through the trees, fear in her eyes obvious in the moment before she broke and ran.

My head throbbed. Threat dispelled, I collapsed backward, all the energy again leaving me, my body overtaken by pain once more. I didn't know which was way up.

The Butcher was dead.

The vampires were gone, scattered. The few who were left wouldn't stick around, I was sure of it.

Not with psychopath Mill to answer to. We had won. Cold earth embraced me as I drifted back, gaze cast up into the starry night.

It seemed to come closer. And then I realized—Mill had scooped me up in his arms.

"But I'm all bloody …" I said, my words slurring together.

He didn't answer. He just started back through the trees, the lodge burning behind him, swaying and dancing.

And everything went dark.

Chapter 39

The hospital in the next town didn't ask too many questions. After being carted into the ER by Iona and Lockwood, who had meticulously cleaned me up from all the thick, stinking vampire blood on our drive over and helped me into a change of clothes, the doctors plopped me into a room, gave me some stitches in my leg and head, and a sling for my wrist, shoved a tetanus shot in my leg for good measure, and then sent me on my way, telling me to rest.

Apparently, I did have a concussion, but they told me that I could go as long as I was careful and returned to the hospital if I experienced any sort of dizziness, nausea, or vomiting.

After the night I just had, I was sure to experience all three of those anyways.

Gen had somehow managed to avoid any sort of major damage, for which I was grateful. Iona and Mill had snuck into one of the blood banks in the hospital and were already healed completely.

Lockwood's injury was well hidden beneath his jacket. Looking at him, you'd never know he'd been hurt.

It was nearly four in the morning when I finally found myself in another hospital, back in my town, standing in front of Uncle Mike's room door. With the threat to him gone now, I wanted to check in on him again. I was on a limited time frame, though. The nurse didn't want to let me in; visiting hours were well past. But a look at my broken wrist, and the lie that I needed to leave for a flight soon, and she softened, told me that I could have five minutes, no more. He needed his rest still. Uncle Mike was awake when I stepped in, staring out of the window.

"You have a visitor," the nurse said.

"What—" he said, and then he saw me. "Cassie. What are you doing here at this hour? And what happened to your wrist?"

"Something stupid," I said. "The usual bad choices, that's all." I sat down on the end of his bed, lifting a faint smile.

He nodded, but except for that first glance, he wouldn't meet my eyes.

His expression was long and sad. I took a steeling breath of sterile, chemical haze. "There's something I wanted to say before I leave," I said, forcing my words past the lump in my throat.

He looked up at me curiously.

"I just wanted to thank you …" I started. "For not treating me different when I was outed as the biggest lying jerk on the planet. Everyone else bailed on me, and you could have distanced yourself … and you didn't, even though you had reason."

Gen's face flashed through my mind. *I don't like what you've done, but I'm still your friend.*

I smiled. "So … thank you for that."

The sadness left him—or at least lifted. A faint smile of his own crested his lips. "Cass … I'm sorry for getting so angry at you yesterday morning. I just …" He trailed off. "Look, kid, I care about you too much to sit back and watch you ruin your life."

Ruin my life? Pfffft. Vampires were hunting me here and in Tampa. What life?

"You know, your mom's looking for you," he said.

"I … needed some space," I told him truthfully.

He nodded. "I get that. But you still should go see her. You can't keep running from the consequences of your actions forever."

"Yeah," I said. Boy, was he ever right about that.

It was time to face the music.

219

"She's at the bed and breakfast in town."

"Then that's my next stop," I said. I stood and moved closer to hug him.

"I love you, kiddo," he said. "It means a lot that you came all the way up here for me."

"I did. I really did. And I'd do it again in a heartbeat."

He grinned, his cheeks flushing. "Take care of yourself, okay?"

"You too. Call me when you get sprung from this joint?" I made a little face. "Assuming Warden Mom will allow me to take a call."

"Will do," he said, chuckling.

With one last smile, I left the room.

I found the others downstairs in the lobby, waiting. I didn't have all the time in the world. Lockwood had to get the vamps somewhere safe before the sun came up.

And poor Genesee.

"You have to get home, get some rest …" I told her, playing with one of her braids. They were perfect again, shining ebony tresses.

"And you have to go face your mom, right?" she asked, a melancholy note in her voice. "I'm sad that we didn't get to spend much time together … Well, any time that didn't involve vampires."

I pulled her into a hug, savoring it in a way I never had before, relief and joy and sadness all spilling over me at once.

"Thank you, Gen. For literally everything. For believing me, for trusting me … for being my friend."

"Like I told you," Gen squeezed back, "it's what friends are for, Cassie."

We shared a tight smile.

"Hey, why don't we plan to have a video chat like, once a week or something? Pick a night that works for both of us," I suggested. "I could show you my room, our house. Take you around the town. Let you see some palm trees."

Gen's eyes lit up. "Oh my gosh. See something other than mountains and hills? I might not be able to handle that."

After another round of hugs, an increasingly emotional goodbye that I was struggling to keep under wraps—

"We've got to move, Cassie," said Iona.

My stomach sank. Of course. Dawn was coming. These guys needed to get someplace safe.

"We'll talk soon," I said to Gen, tears burning my eyes. "I promise."

She grinned. "You better." Extricating myself from her hug—the hardest thing I'd done tonight, by far—I turned to Lockwood. "She's all yours."

He smiled. "Thank you, Miss Cassandra." He stepped forward, placed a hand on my shoulder, and then extended his free hand to me. It was balled around something. He looked expectant.

"What's this?" I asked.

"Something I … procured. Off of your friend. When she and I got in a tussle. It fell off her wrist when she ran. I picked it up … thought you might like to have it."

Inside his hands was a simple silver bracelet. It had the letter *J* inscribed on the small silver heart dangling from it.

My fingers curled over it and I held it to my chest.

"Thank you, Lockwood."

I reached up and threw my arms around his neck.

He hugged me back.

"And thank you for taking Gen home. And getting me here. And saving my life, like, what … three times?"

He shook his head. "It was nothing."

"And I'm sorry …" I said. "I … don't care what you are, that you aren't human …"

"No offense taken, Miss Cassandra." His eyes sparkled.

I moved my attention onto Iona, who was standing beside the window, peering over her shoulder out into the waning night.

"Hey …" I said slowly.

"Hey," she said. She did not turn to face me.

"I just …" I started. Suddenly, words didn't seem sufficient enough. "Thank you," I said finally. "For everything."

"You're welcome." No emotion.

"When are you guys heading back to Florida?"

"Tonight," she said. A little flicker of irritation creased her eyebrow, for only a moment. It was a long drive, I supposed,

221

and she'd be spending trunk time with Mill again, which was hardly her favorite activity.

"Where are you going to stay?" I asked.

"Someplace dark, I hope," she said. "I think Lockwood booked an AirBnB for us. Some place with a spacious basement." She rolled her eyes. "I'm looking forward to not sleeping in a basement. Or a trunk." She shook her head. "My adventures with you really are the worst. Daylight and fire and trunks with lunkheads." She jerked her head toward Mill, who was a scowling only a little at her.

"I can totally understand that," I said. She'd been through a lot for me.

I glanced over at Mill again, and caught him staring at me.

"Oh, go talk to him," Iona said, tossing her silvery hair over her shoulder. "We don't need to sit here and make painful small talk. It's done, we won. Go ... play or whatever."

I looked her in the eyes, trying to really convey my thanks. "I am grateful for you, for your help. I hope you know that."

She rolled her eyes, but a small smile tugged at the corner of her lips. "Go."

Very aware of everyone trying to not look at Mill and me as I stepped over to him, I shrugged my shoulders. I don't know why.

"So ..." I said.

"So," he repeated.

And then I stood on my tiptoes, ignoring the pain in my legs as I stretched the muscles and burnt skin, and kissed him.

For a third kiss, I still felt every touch, every beat of my heart, every starburst in my mind.

"I'll see you soon ..." I told him in a low voice. "I promise. When you get back ..." My heart sank. "And I'm done being grounded. So ... two hundred years? That's 'soon' to vampires, right?"

He smirked and planted another kiss on my forehead. "I'll be waiting."

I turned to the others. "That goes for the rest of you. Once my grounding is done ..."

Gen laughed. "If your mom doesn't kill you."

She wasn't wrong.

I watched with growing sadness as they all clambered into the stolen Lexus … borrowed, as Lockwood kept reminding me; he intended to return it as soon as Mill and Iona were down for their rest.

My Uber driver showed up at the exact time that Lockwood had ordered. I handed the driver a twenty, telling her that she could keep the change.

I watched my little hometown out of the window of the car as Ariana Grande played on the radio. I missed this place, I really did.

But now … there was something else there. Pride? A protectiveness?

I had saved the town. *We* had saved it, really. These people, who had not known the true danger they were in, were all safe now. Soon they'd realize that those crazy Eurotrash people who were causing such havoc in town were gone.

Life could return to normal.

All those except the families of those who were lost.

My throat tightened.

We had avenged them, though. Damn it, but we had.

Their families would never know, of course … but it had to count for something. All of this did.

The bed and breakfast appeared all too quickly, nestled in some trees along a quieter part of town, overlooking the lake. It was a beautiful place, and I had walked by a thousand times but never stayed there.

I thanked my driver in a fog, and made my way inside. The receptionist gave me directions to the right room—13—and I climbed the stairs, my dread growing, turning me more and more leaden with every step … down the hall …

Then I stood before it, in a wood-paneled corridor with trodden-flat blue carpet—knocking—

The door was yanked open.

She stared at me, fire and fury written all over her expression.

"Hi, Mom."

Chapter 40

I liked to read. I always had, ever since I was a kid. But it was something that was a lot more fun to do when I had the choice to do it. Not when it was literally the only thing available to me.

I sighed, lying back on my bed, staring up at the ceiling.

The steady hum of the air conditioner running through the house was the only indication that time was actually moving.

Somehow, almost a week had passed since our return from New York. After the worst fight I had ever had with my mom in my life—perhaps even more epic in its horrificness than the confrontation on the night my lying came out—she'd ushered me to the airport and we got on a plane, where she ignored me the entire trip.

I got the same speeches from Dad when we got home. Everyone was mad. Everyone was disappointed.

But I had saved the day, yet again. I held onto that truth and took the brunt of their assaults with as much humility as I could.

A month's grounding without my phone seemed like a weak punishment, but it wasn't until that she told me I'd be confined to my room whenever I was home that I realized I was basically locked in jail. I was allowed to come out to use the bathroom and eat. Nothing else. I was just zoning out, ready to fall asleep out of sheer boredom rather than sleepiness, when—

Tap-tap.

The window.

I glanced at my clock. It was almost midnight.

Wow, more time had passed than I had thought. Iona's moonlight blonde hair swayed in the wind, waiting for me just outside the pane. I slid open the window and the warm night air rushed in.

"Good to see that you're still alive," she said, assessing me with sad, icy blue eyes.

"Yeah, it's been a bit of an interesting week…" I said, smiling. "No phone, no internet, no TV, no mercy. Glad to see you're home and well. Staying out of trunks and basements."

Her eyes glimmered. "It's good to be back."

I heard that. As much as I had hated Florida, as close as it brought me to Draven, it had been comforting to be back. "Sooo … what brings you to my window tonight?"

Iona stiffened. "I hadn't heard from you."

"Haven't had a phone. Except during school hours."

"Ah," she said, looking past me to the bed. "What are you reading?"

I followed her gaze to my book resting there. "*Little Women*." Her eyes kind of lit up. "You read it?"

"A long time ago," Iona said, in a misty, far-off sort of voice. When she was alive, I took that to mean. "Do you like it?"

"It's all right," I said. "Not quite in the modern style."

She nodded, once, a little sadly. "Well. I suppose I should go." Her cool gaze flicked up to me. "I just wanted to check in on you. Make sure you were … all right."

"Mom didn't kill me," I said, "though I'm pretty sure she thought about it, because her eyes? Way scarier than any of the vampires we fought in New York."

Iona didn't even crack a smile. "I should go," she said again.

And I realized …

"Hey, Iona?"

She stopped, halfway to turning to leave.

"…Would you like to come in?" I asked, tentative.

She looked at me, utterly stiff, not a hint of emotion anywhere on her pale face.

225

"Maybe … braid my hair?" I asked, feeling like I was just throwing things out there in hopes she didn't slap them back in my face. "Or … or…talk about boys?"

She just stared back, unspeaking. I worried she was going to just say, "No," and turn and drop off the rooftop into the night, because she was Iona and of course she wouldn't be interested in doing any of those stupid, little girly things I'd just suggested—

But then she *smiled*.

"Yes," she said. "Yes, I would."

And I stepped back from the sill to let her in.

Cassie Howell will return in

LIES IN
THE DARK
Liars and Vampires
Book 4

Coming July 17, 2018!

Author's Note

Thanks for reading! If you want to know immediately when future books become available, take sixty seconds and sign up for my NEW RELEASE EMAIL ALERTS by visiting my website. I don't sell your information and I only send out emails when I have a new book out. The reason you should sign up for this is because I don't always set release dates, and even if you're following me on Facebook (robertJcrane (Author)) or Twitter (@robertJcrane), it's easy to miss my book announcements because...well, because social media is an imprecise thing.

Come join the discussion on my website:
http://www.robertjcrane.com!

Cheers,
Robert J. Crane

ACKNOWLEDGMENTS

Editing and formatting was handled expertly by Nick Bowman of nickbowman-editing.com. Sarah Barbour did another heavy editing run through, with a final proofing pass by Lillie of lilliesls.wordpress.com. Many thanks to all of them.

Once again, the illustrious illustrator Karri Klawiter produced the cover. artbykarri.com is where you can find her amazing works.

Thanks to the great Kate Hasbrouck, my co-author (yeah, her name's not Lauren – there are reasons, we'll talk about it someday), who has been a wonderful collaborator.

And thanks as always to my family—wife, parents, in-laws and occasionally my kids—for keeping a lid on the craziness so I can do this job.

Other Works by Robert J. Crane

The Girl in the Box *and* Out of the Box
Contemporary Urban Fantasy

Alone: The Girl in the Box, Book 1
Untouched: The Girl in the Box, Book 2
Soulless: The Girl in the Box, Book 3
Family: The Girl in the Box, Book 4
Omega: The Girl in the Box, Book 5
Broken: The Girl in the Box, Book 6
Enemies: The Girl in the Box, Book 7
Legacy: The Girl in the Box, Book 8
Destiny: The Girl in the Box, Book 9
Power: The Girl in the Box, Book 10

Limitless: Out of the Box, Book 1
In the Wind: Out of the Box, Book 2
Ruthless: Out of the Box, Book 3
Grounded: Out of the Box, Book 4
Tormented: Out of the Box, Book 5
Vengeful: Out of the Box, Book 6
Sea Change: Out of the Box, Book 7
Painkiller: Out of the Box, Book 8
Masks: Out of the Box, Book 9
Prisoners: Out of the Box, Book 10
Unyielding: Out of the Box, Book 11
Hollow: Out of the Box, Book 12
Toxicity: Out of the Box, Book 13
Small Things: Out of the Box, Book 14
Hunters: Out of the Box, Book 15
Badder: Out of the Box, Book 16
Apex: Out of the Box, Book 18
Time: Out of the Box, Book 19
Driven: Out of the Box, Book 20
Remember: Out of the Box, Book 21* *(Coming August 3, 2018!)*
Hero: Out of the Box, Book 22* *(Coming October 2018!)*
Flashback: Out of the Box, Book 23* *(Coming December 2018!)*
Walk Through Fire: Out of the Box, Book 24* *(Coming in 2019!)*

World of Sanctuary
Epic Fantasy

Defender: The Sanctuary Series, Volume One
Avenger: The Sanctuary Series, Volume Two
Champion: The Sanctuary Series, Volume Three
Crusader: The Sanctuary Series, Volume Four
Sanctuary Tales, Volume One - A Short Story Collection
Thy Father's Shadow: The Sanctuary Series, Volume 4.5
Master: The Sanctuary Series, Volume Five
Fated in Darkness: The Sanctuary Series, Volume 5.5
Warlord: The Sanctuary Series, Volume Six
Heretic: The Sanctuary Series, Volume Seven
Legend: The Sanctuary Series, Volume Eight
Ghosts of Sanctuary: The Sanctuary Series, Volume Nine
Call of the Hero: The Sanctuary Series, Volume Ten* *(Coming Late 2018!)*

A Haven in Ash: Ashes of Luukessia, Volume One *(with Michael Winstone)*
A Respite From Storms: Ashes of Luukessia, Volume Two *(with Michael Winstone)*
A Home in the Hills: Ashes of Luukessia, Volume Three* *(with Michael Winstone—Coming Mid to Late 2018!)*

Southern Watch
Contemporary Urban Fantasy

Called: Southern Watch, Book 1
Depths: Southern Watch, Book 2
Corrupted: Southern Watch, Book 3
Unearthed: Southern Watch, Book 4
Legion: Southern Watch, Book 5
Starling: Southern Watch, Book 6
Forsaken: Southern Watch, Book 7* *(Coming August 7, 2018!)*
Hallowed: Southern Watch, Book 8* *(Coming Late 2018/Early 2019!)*

The Shattered Dome Series
(with Nicholas J. Ambrose)
Sci-Fi

Voiceless: The Shattered Dome, Book 1
Unspeakable: The Shattered Dome, Book 2* *(Coming 2018!)*

The Mira Brand Adventures
Contemporary Urban Fantasy

The World Beneath: The Mira Brand Adventures, Book 1
The Tide of Ages: The Mira Brand Adventures, Book 2
The City of Lies: The Mira Brand Adventures, Book 3
The King of the Skies: The Mira Brand Adventures, Book 4
The Best of Us: The Mira Brand Adventures, Book 5
We Aimless Few: The Mira Brand Adventures, Book 6* *(Coming 2018!)*

Liars and Vampires
(with Lauren Harper)
Contemporary Urban Fantasy

No One Will Believe You: Liars and Vampires, Book 1
Someone Should Save Her: Liars and Vampires, Book 2
You Can't Go Home Again: Liars and Vampires, Book 3
In The Dark: Liars and Vampires, Book 4* *(Coming July 17, 2018!)*
Her Lying Days Are Done: Liars and Vampires, Book 5* *(Coming August 2018!)*
Heir of the Dog: Liars and Vampires, Book 6* *(Coming September 2018!)*
Hit You Where You Live: Liars and Vampires, Book 7* *(Coming October 2018!)*

* Forthcoming, Subject to Change